THE BE-BOP BARBARIANS

GARY PHILLIPS
STORY

DALE BERRY
LAYOUT/PENCILS

J. BROWN
INK & PAINT

JUSTIN BIRCH
LETTERING

THE BE-BOP BARBARIANS

COMIC BOOK BOHEMIANS TO A 1950s JAZZ BEAT

GARY PHILLIPS   DALE BERRY

PEGASUS BOOKS

NEW YORK LONDON

THE BE-BOP BARBARIANS

Pegasus Books, Ltd.
148 West 37th Street, 13th Floor
New York, NY 10018

Copyright © 2019 by Gary Phillips and Dale W. Berry

First Pegasus Books hardcover edition February 2019

Page layout by Sabrina Plomitallo-González, Pegasus Books

ISBN: 978-1-68177-776-4

10 9 8 7 6 5 4 3 2 1

Printed in the United States of America
Distributed by W. W. Norton & Company, Inc.

DIG THAT BEAT

"These are facts, historical facts, not schoolbook history, not Mr. Wells's history, but history nonetheless."
—Casper Gutman to Sam Spade in *The Maltese Falcon* by Dashiell Hammett

The three real-life comics pioneers who inspired the characters in this story were unknown to me coming up as a kid who voraciously read comic strips and comic books back when we still called that part of L.A. South Central. Back when there was no internet, no robot cars except for those drawn by Jack Kirby populating the pages of the *Fantastic Four* and *Nick Fury, Agent of S.H.I.E.L.D.*, and four local TV channels and three national ones. What else was there to do once your homework was done and you had to be in from outside playing when the sun went down but read through a stack of four-color adventures of flying men and women, and an angst-ridden high school nerd who could cling to walls?

When Black "Wakanda Forever" Panther made the scene in that fateful issue of FF #52, a year or so after the pivotal Watts riots of August '65, us youngsters in the 'hood couldn't help but feel that, finally, we were getting some representation in the medium we most adored—even if there were no black writers or artists working at the Big Two, Marvel and DC. But there had been a history of those who plied their trade in the comics business before T'Challa ascended the Panther throne.

Turns out that in the 1940s, there were comic strip syndicators specializing in black comic strips: the black-owned Continental Features and Stanton Features, and the white owned Smith-Mann. They sold produced inserts featuring adventurers, cowboys, soldiers of fortunes, and resourceful women that appeared in black newspapers like the *Pittsburgh Courier* and the *Chicago Defender*. These strips often employed African American fine artists who did the work to pay the bills. There were also those who were cartoonists by vocation such as Jackie Ormes and Oliver Harrington.

Indeed Ms. Ormes, born Zelda Mavin Jackson, a staff reporter for the *Courier*, originated her strip in those pages, *Torchy Brown in Dixie to Harlem*, in 1938. She was the first African American woman cartoonist to have her own strip and is in the Will Eisner Comics Hall of Fame. Harrington produced an observational humor strip featuring a character called Bootsie, covered WWII in Europe and North Africa in words and pictures for the black press, wrote and drew the aviation-themed adventure strip *Jive Grey*, and produced hard-hitting editorial cartoons that ran in the likes of the communist *Daily Worker* newspaper. Langston Hughes called him America's most popular black cartoonist and a first-rate social satirist.

And then there was Clarence Matthew "Matt" Baker, who is often billed as the first black comic book artist, though that is not the case. He began his comics career in 1944 doing background art for the S.M. Iger Studio that supplied complete comics stories to publishers. This was where Elmer "E.C." Stoner, the actual first black comic book artist, had worked several years before Baker. As Iger recalled in an interview years afterward, "[Baker] came to my studio in the early '40s; handsome and nattily dressed." Baker would soon go on to producing his own sequentials and is credited as the first artist to illo a graphic novel, the noirish "picture novel" *It Rhymes with Lust,* and also did a syndicated comic strip *Flamingo* for Phoenix Features.

Once I knew these facts, the three wouldn't leave me alone. Now far as I know, they didn't know each other in real life, but that's where fiction came in. I set out not to do their biographies but tell a truth of a time and make it resonate with a trio inspired by these three. *The Be-Bop Barbarians* is set in the turbulent cauldron of late '50s New York City, with jazz, the burgeoning Civil Rights Movement, and the Red Scare as the volatile ingredients, where three groundbreaking black cartoonists defy convention and pay the price.

Our main players are Clifford "Cliff" Murphy, who is matinee handsome, a light-skinned, straight-haired black man who is a comics artist and writer known for his glamor-girl art. He's black uptown and white downtown. Stephaney "Stef" Rawls has her own romance-adventure strip for the largest black newspaper, but she must still work jobs as a domestic to make ends meet. But when she gets a lucrative offer to write and draw a "Negroes must reject agitation" insert for the FBI, can she pass up the opportunity?

Lastly there is Oliver "Ollie" Jefferson, a decorated Korean War vet who writes and draws editorial cartoons under the pseudonym Attucks for the daily lefty newspaper, *The Daily Struggle.* But when a cop beats him down when he's walking his pregnant Korean wife-to-be home one night, Ollie becomes a symbol of oppression as the streets threaten to explode with righteous rage.

Having developed the characters and hammered out an outline, I knew there was only a handful of artists I might call on to tell the tale. How happy I was that my friend the talented writer-artist Dale Berry said yes. It had to be somebody who not only dug that time period, but could get inside the characters' heads to portray by pencil and brushstroke their reactions, body poses, and quiet moments in artful panel-to-panel depictions as the story and its sub-plots unfolded. Dale is joined by colorist James Brown, who added depth and subtle dimension to the illustrations, and the skillful lettering of Justin Birch.

Have at it.

—Gary Phillips
Los Angeles

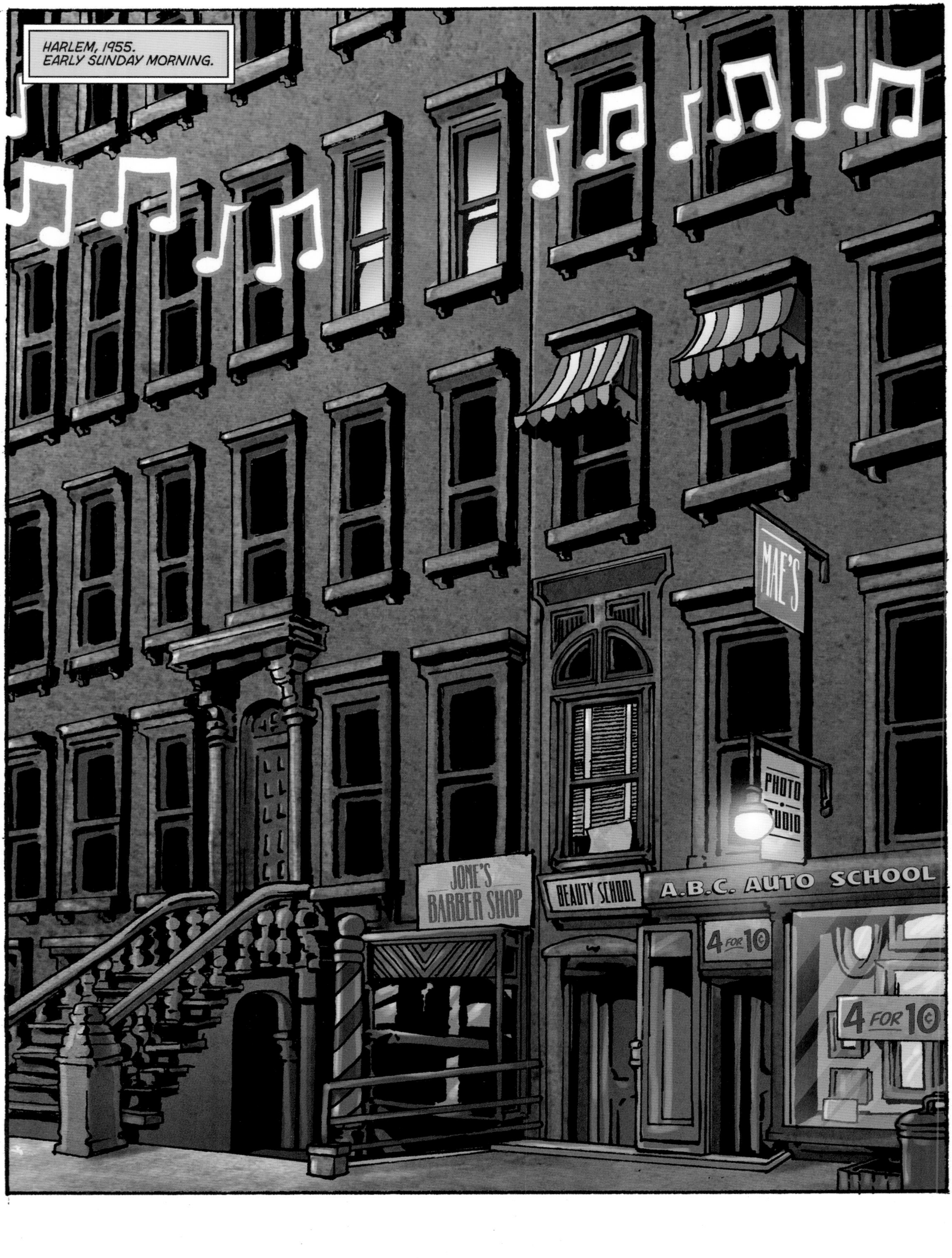
HARLEM, 1955.
EARLY SUNDAY MORNING.
MAE'S
PHOTO STUDIO
JONE'S BARBER SHOP
BEAUTY SCHOOL
A.B.C. AUTO SCHOOL
4 FOR 10¢
4 FOR 10¢

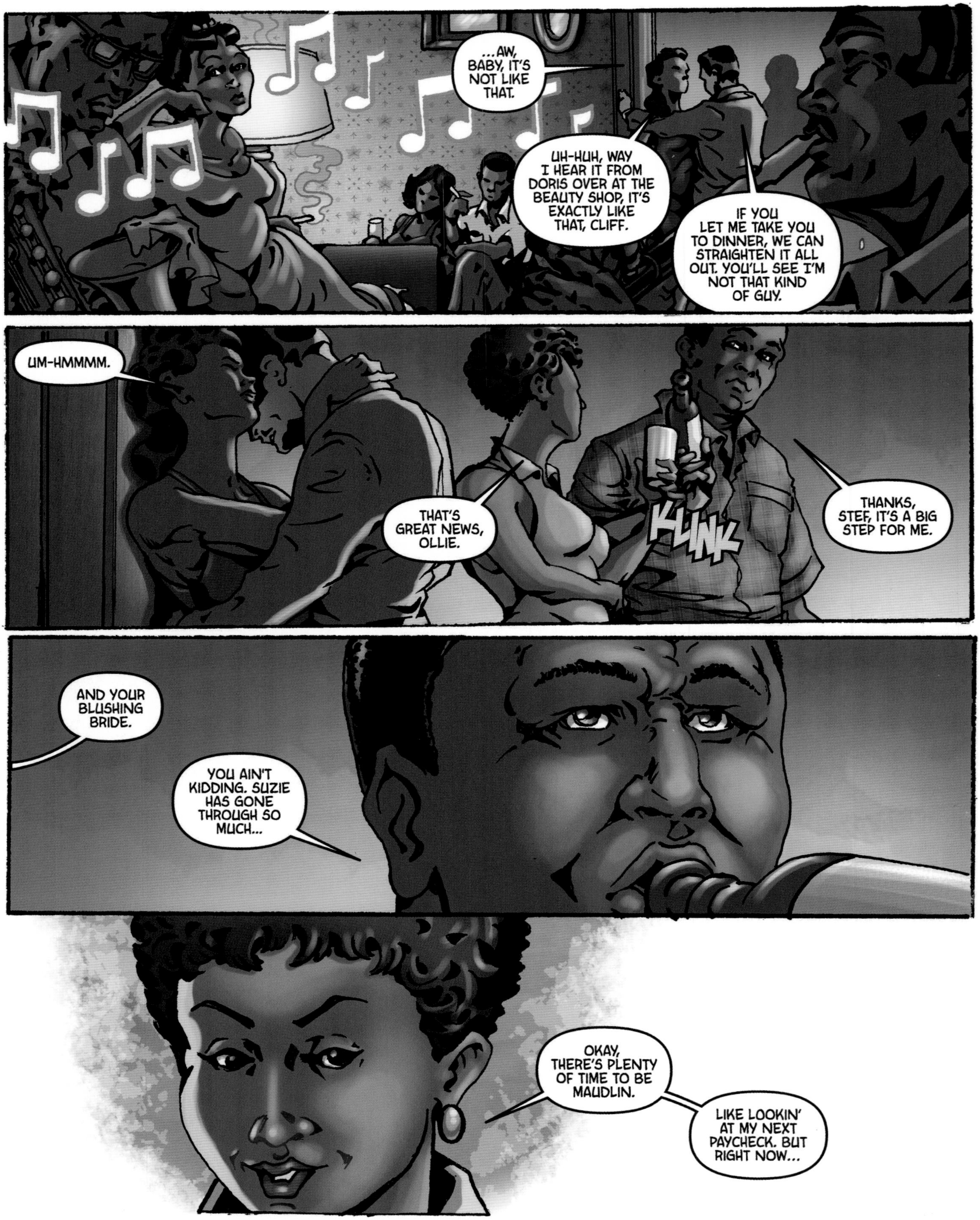
...AW, BABY, IT'S NOT LIKE THAT.
UH-HUH, WAY I HEAR IT FROM DORIS OVER AT THE BEAUTY SHOP, IT'S EXACTLY LIKE THAT, CLIFF.
IF YOU LET ME TAKE YOU TO DINNER, WE CAN STRAIGHTEN IT ALL OUT. YOU'LL SEE I'M NOT THAT KIND OF GUY.
UM-HMMMM.
THAT'S GREAT NEWS, OLLIE.
KLINK
THANKS, STEF, IT'S A BIG STEP FOR ME.
AND YOUR BLUSHING BRIDE.
YOU AIN'T KIDDING. SUZIE HAS GONE THROUGH SO MUCH...
OKAY, THERE'S PLENTY OF TIME TO BE MAUDLIN.
LIKE LOOKIN' AT MY NEXT PAYCHECK. BUT RIGHT NOW...

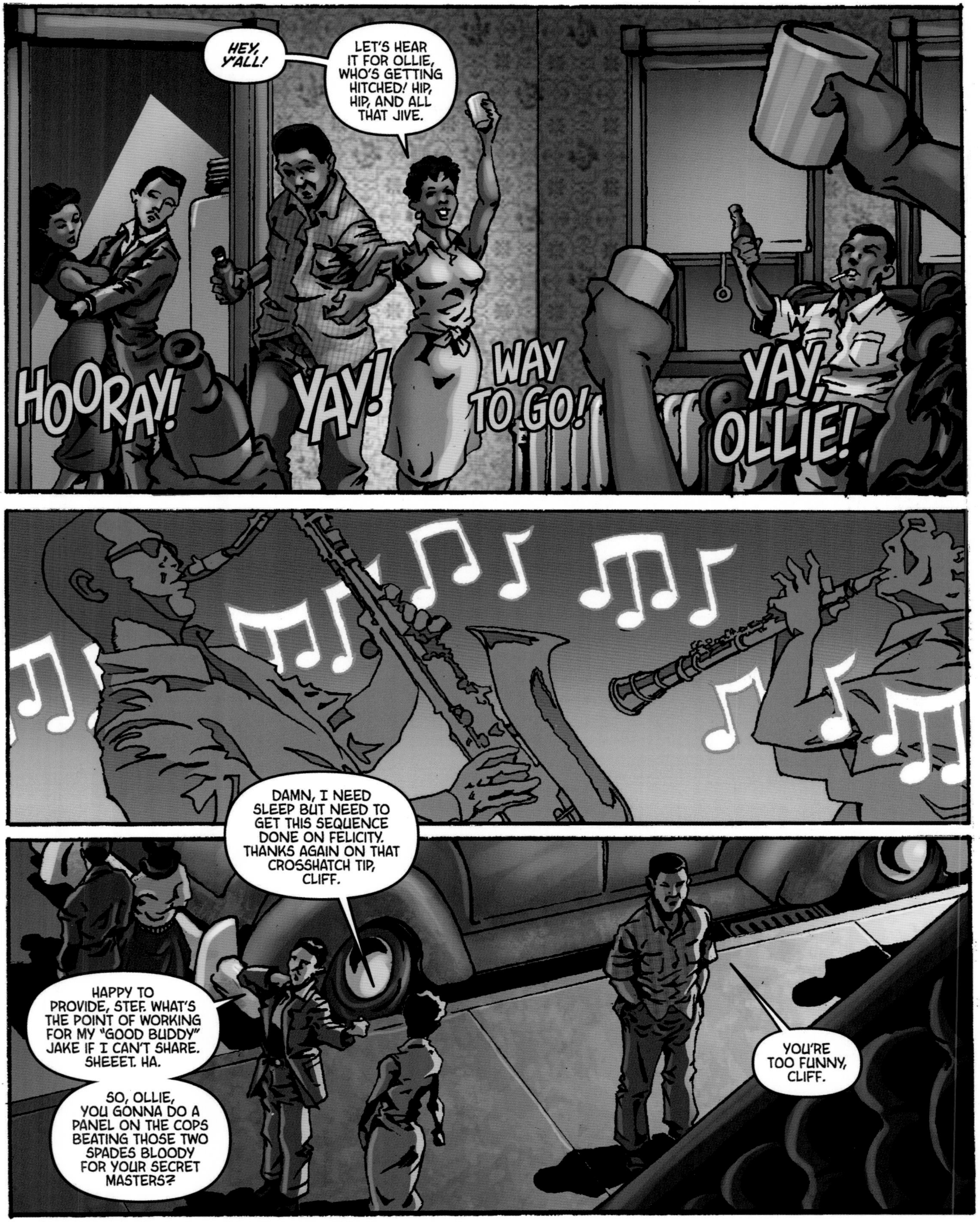
HEY, Y'ALL!
LET'S HEAR IT FOR OLLIE, WHO'S GETTING HITCHED! HIP, HIP, AND ALL THAT JIVE.
HOORAY!
YAY!
WAY TO GO!
YAY, OLLIE!
DAMN, I NEED SLEEP BUT NEED TO GET THIS SEQUENCE DONE ON FELICITY. THANKS AGAIN ON THAT CROSSHATCH TIP, CLIFF.
HAPPY TO PROVIDE, STEF. WHAT'S THE POINT OF WORKING FOR MY "GOOD BUDDY" JAKE IF I CAN'T SHARE. SHEEET. HA.
SO, OLLIE, YOU GONNA DO A PANEL ON THE COPS BEATING THOSE TWO SPADES BLOODY FOR YOUR SECRET MASTERS?
YOU'RE TOO FUNNY, CLIFF.

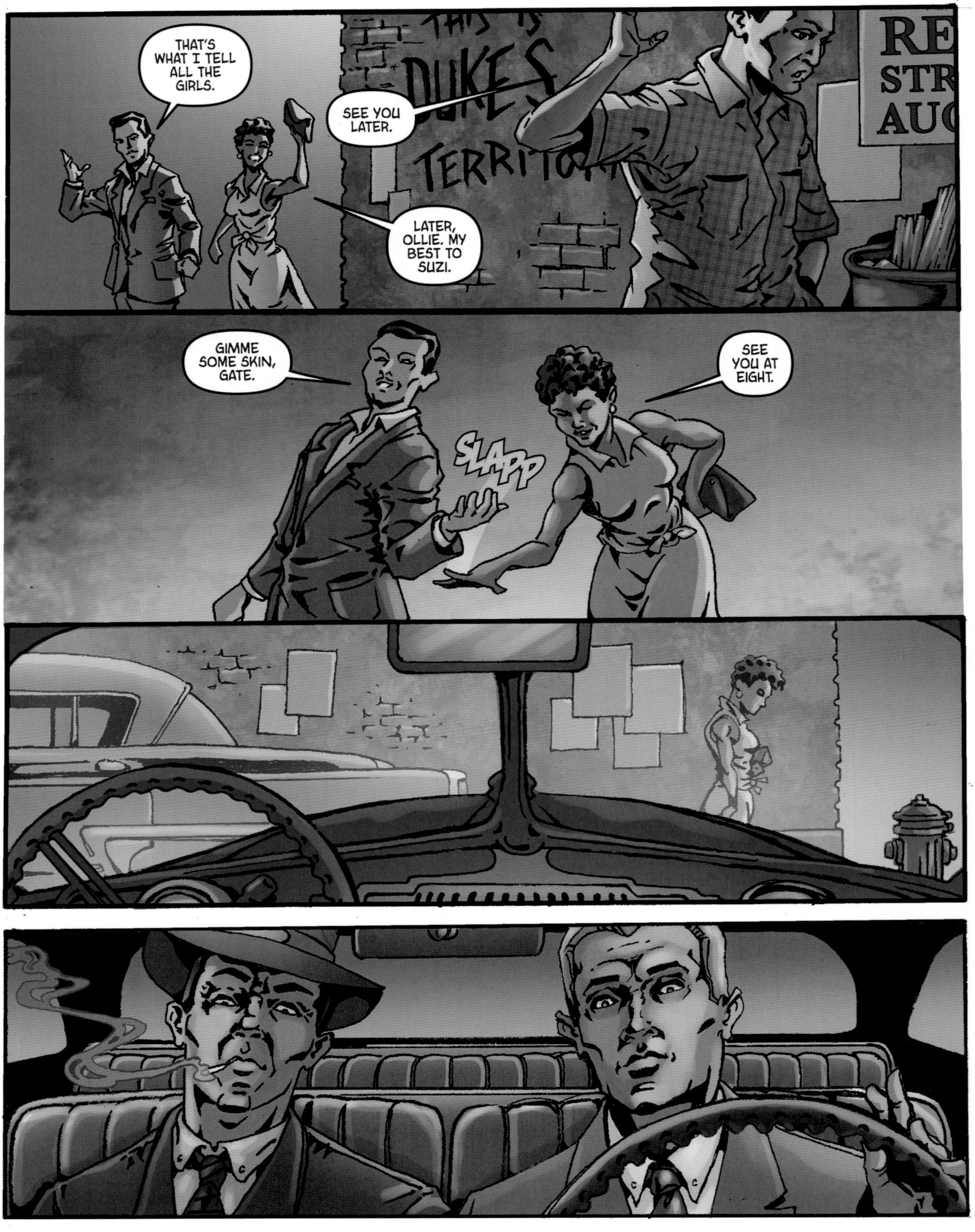
THAT'S WHAT I TELL ALL THE GIRLS.
SEE YOU LATER.
LATER, OLLIE. MY BEST TO SUZI.
GIMME SOME SKIN, GATE.
SLAPP
SEE YOU AT EIGHT.

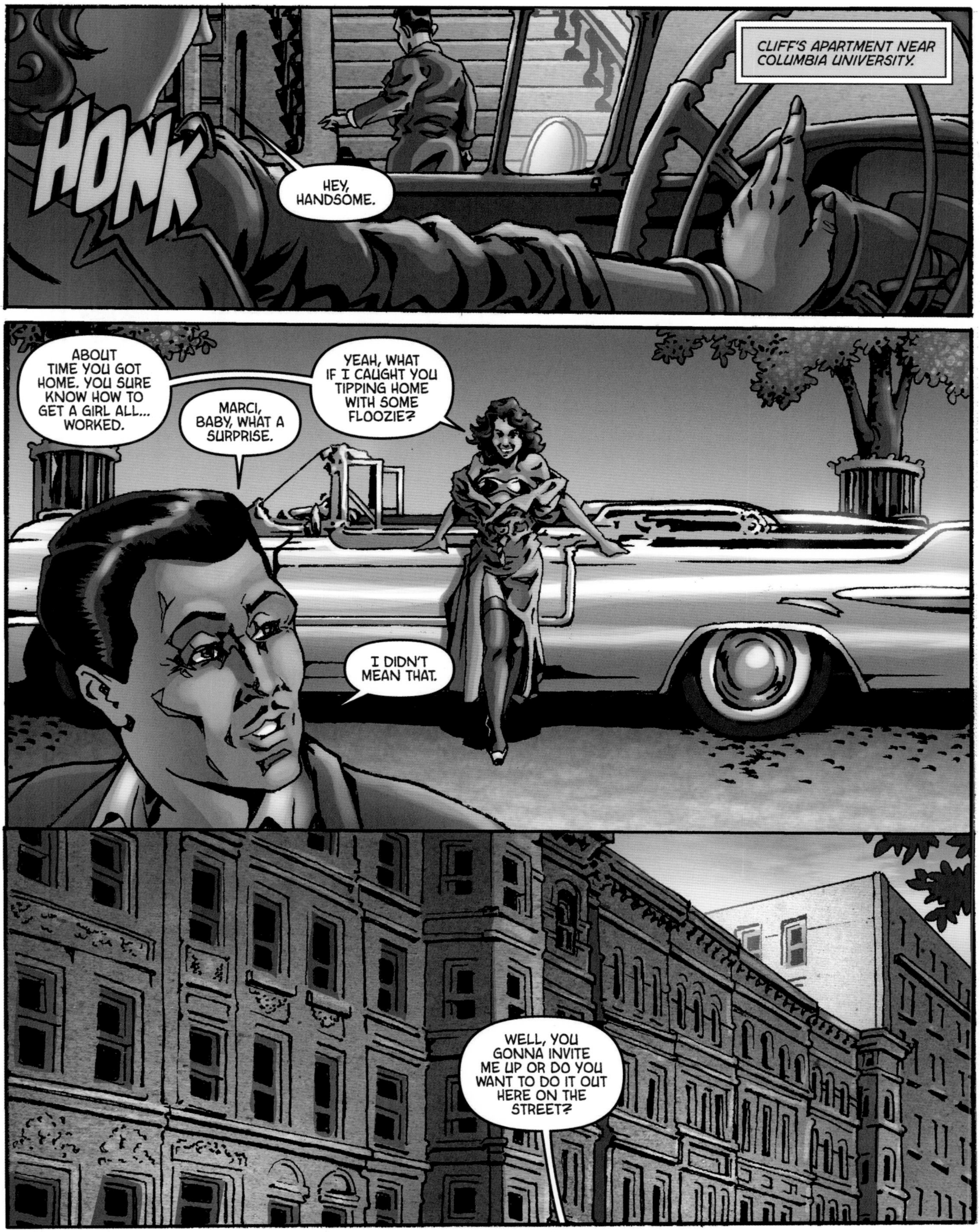
CLIFF'S APARTMENT NEAR COLUMBIA UNIVERSITY.
HONK
HEY, HANDSOME.
ABOUT TIME YOU GOT HOME. YOU SURE KNOW HOW TO GET A GIRL ALL... WORKED.
MARCI, BABY, WHAT A SURPRISE.
YEAH, WHAT IF I CAUGHT YOU TIPPING HOME WITH SOME FLOOZIE?
I DIDN'T MEAN THAT.
WELL, YOU GONNA INVITE ME UP OR DO YOU WANT TO DO IT OUT HERE ON THE STREET?

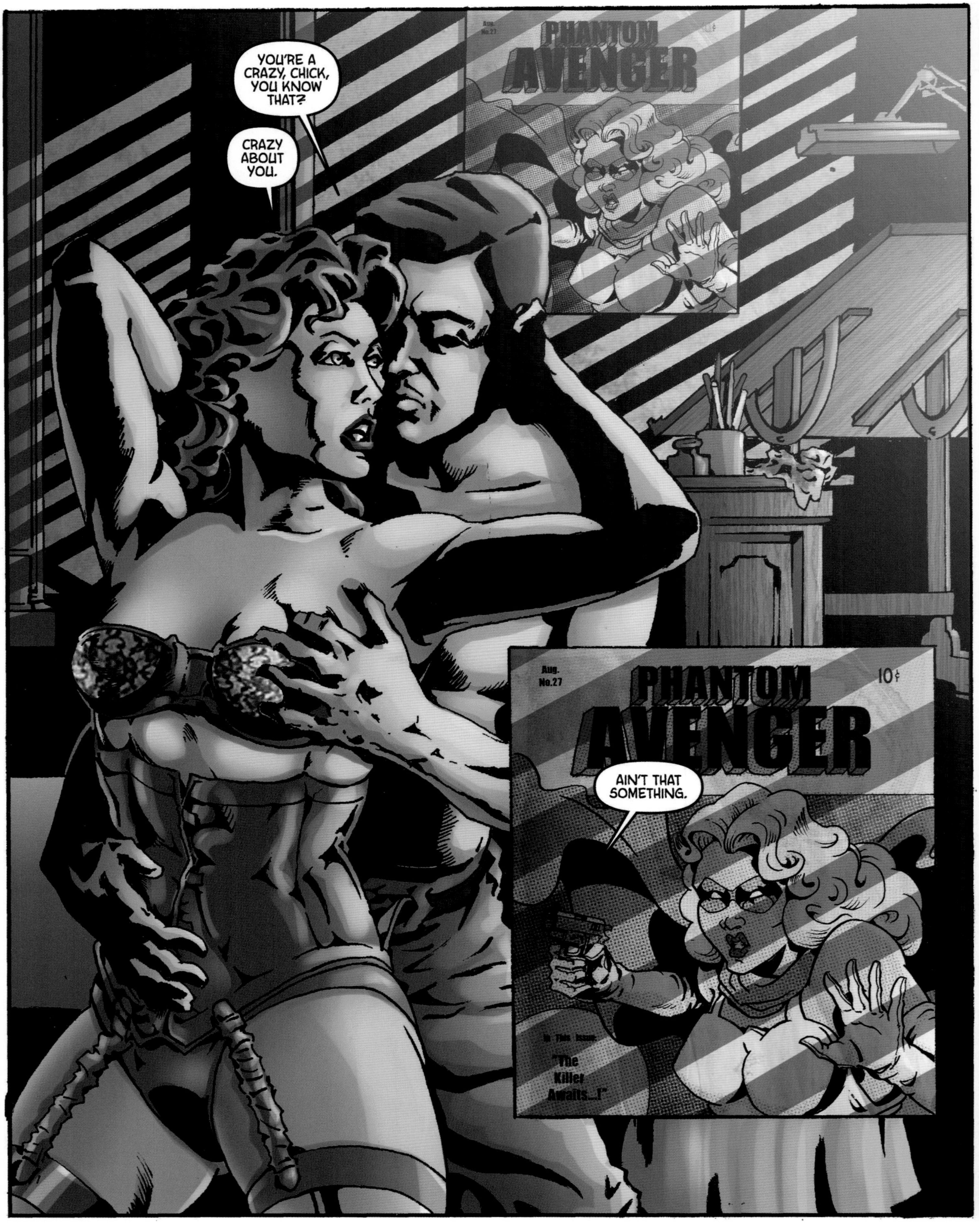
YOU'RE A CRAZY, CHICK, YOU KNOW THAT?
CRAZY ABOUT YOU.
PHANTOM AVENGER
Aug. No.27
PHANTOM AVENGER
10¢
AIN'T THAT SOMETHING.
In This Issue:
"The Killer Awaits...!"

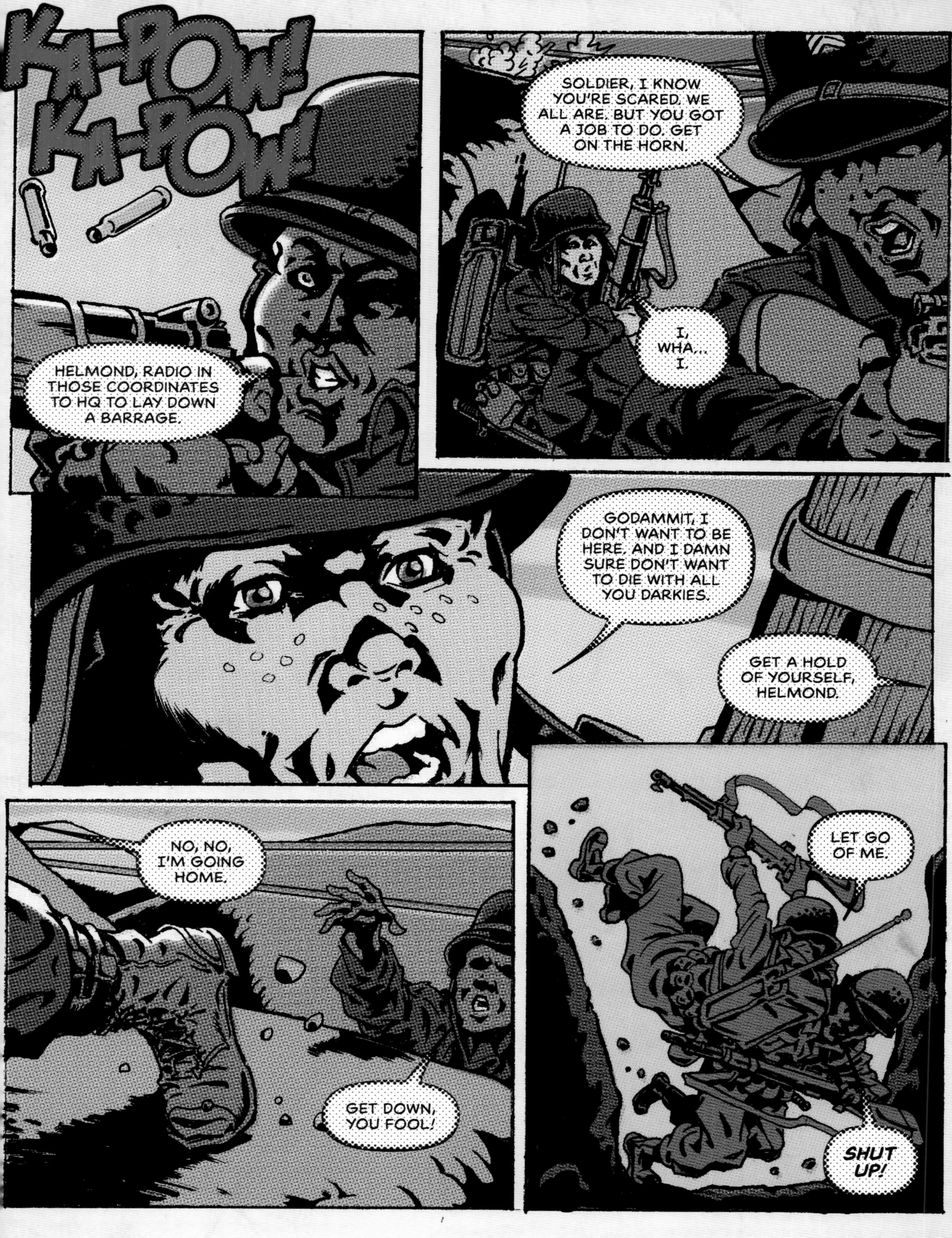
KA-POW! KA-POW!
HELMOND, RADIO IN THOSE COORDINATES TO HQ TO LAY DOWN A BARRAGE.
SOLDIER, I KNOW YOU'RE SCARED. WE ALL ARE. BUT YOU GOT A JOB TO DO. GET ON THE HORN.
I, WHA... I.
GODAMMIT, I DON'T WANT TO BE HERE. AND I DAMN SURE DON'T WANT TO DIE WITH ALL YOU DARKIES.
GET A HOLD OF YOURSELF, HELMOND.
NO, NO, I'M GOING HOME.
GET DOWN, YOU FOOL!
LET GO OF ME.
SHUT UP!

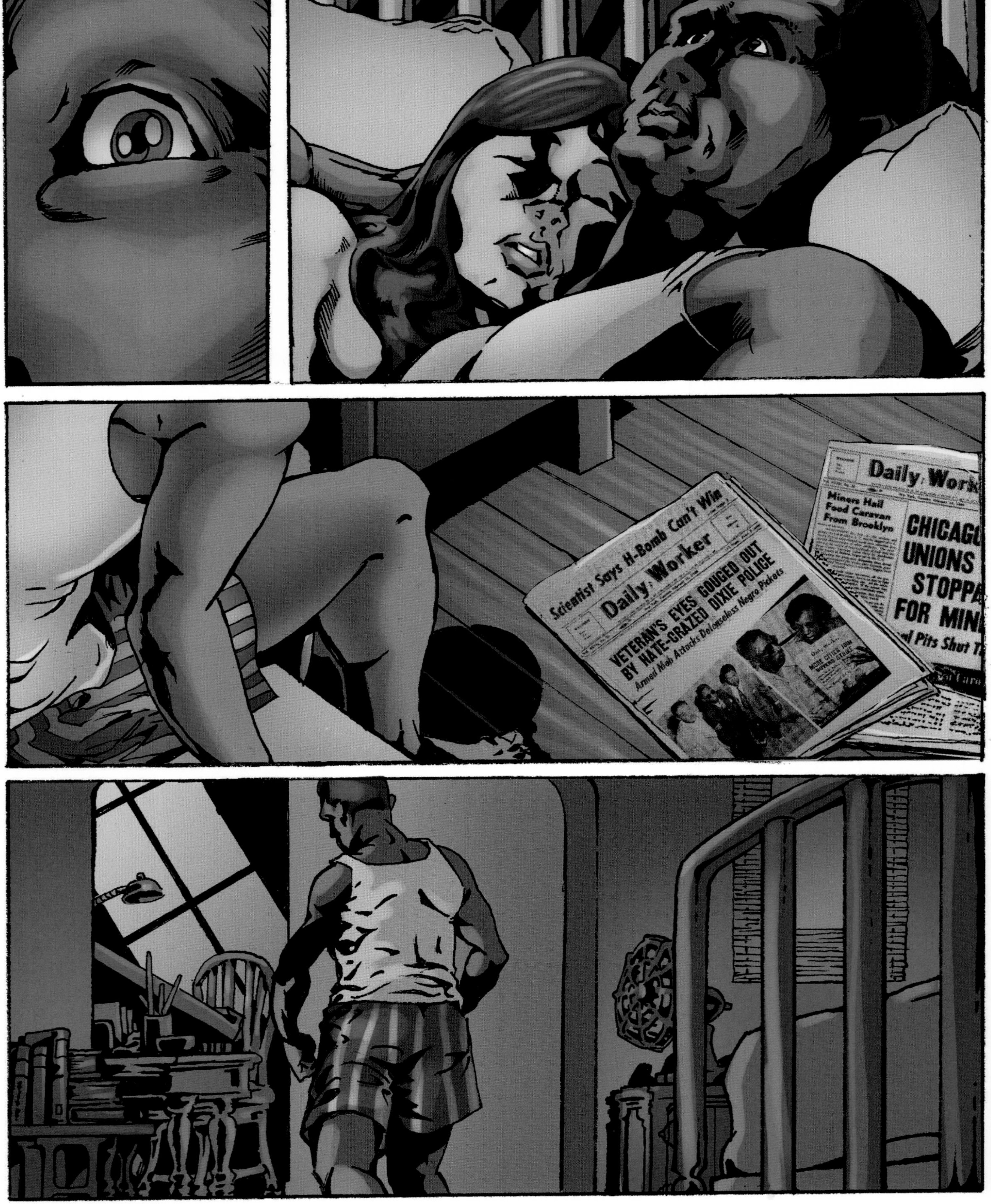
Scientist Says H-Bomb Can't Win
Daily Worker
VETERAN'S EYES GOUGED OUT BY HATE-CRAZED DIXIE POLICE
Armed Mob Attacks Defenseless Negro Pickets
Daily Worker
Miners Hail Food Caravan From Brooklyn
CHICAGO
UNIONS
STOPPA
FOR MIN

CLICK
CLICK
...THE REVEREND WILMORE HICKS HAS CALLED ON POLICE COMMISSIONER KENNEDY TO ATTEND A COMMUNITY MEETING IN HARLEM TO ADDRESS POLICE AND NEGRO RELATIONS.
AND IN OTHER NEWS, PRESIDENT EISENHOWER HAS ANNOUNCED A TWO-YEAR BAN ON NUCLEAR TESTING.

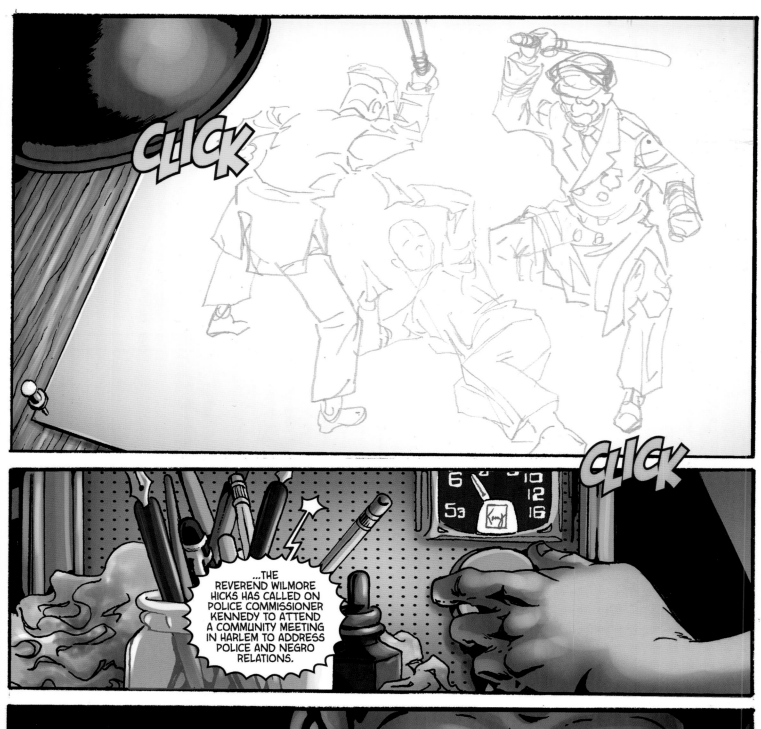

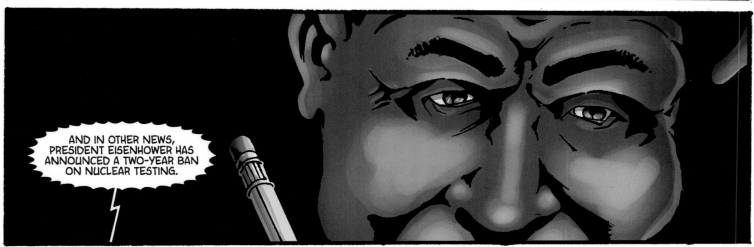

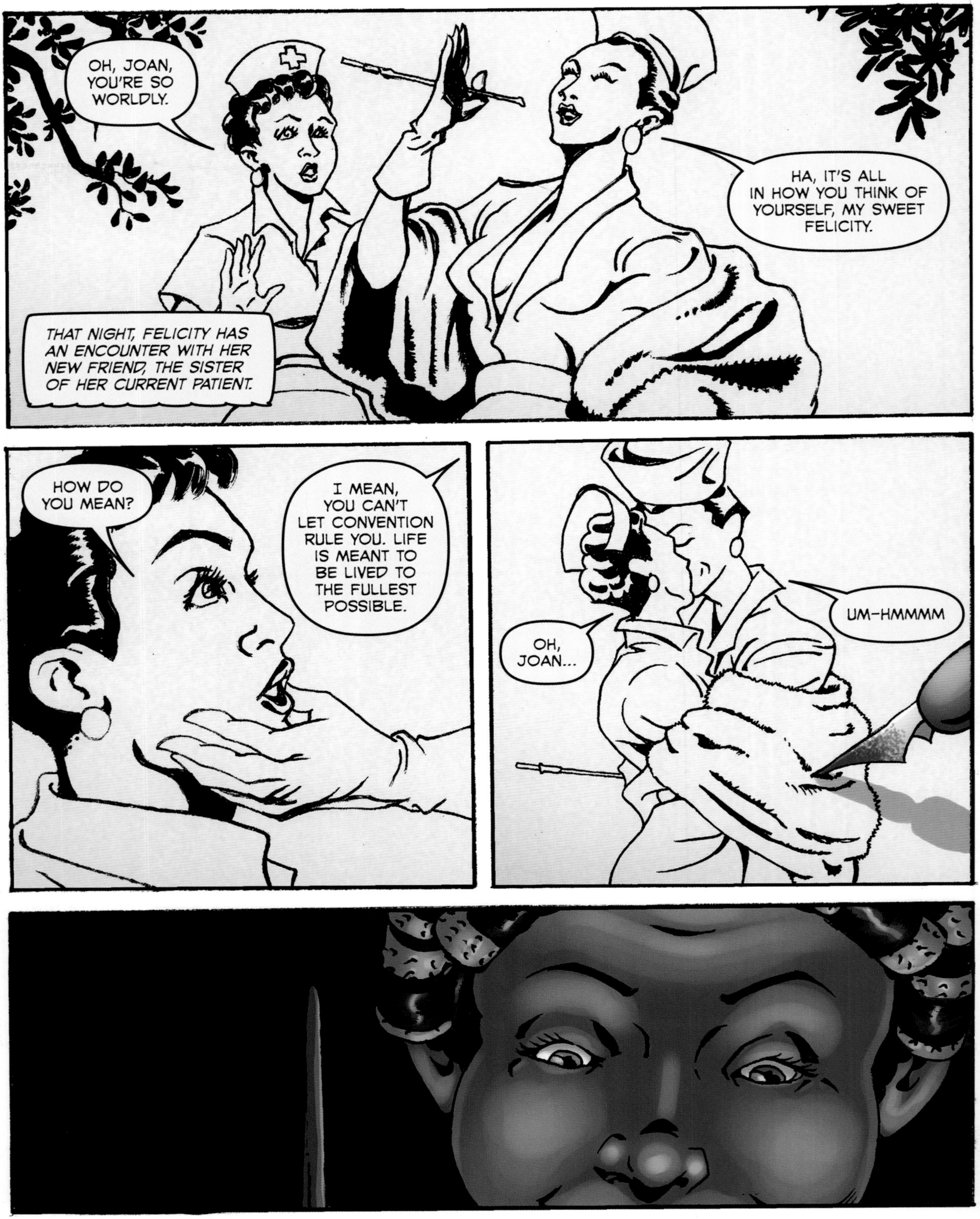
OH, JOAN, YOU'RE SO WORLDLY.
HA, IT'S ALL IN HOW YOU THINK OF YOURSELF, MY SWEET FELICITY.
THAT NIGHT, FELICITY HAS AN ENCOUNTER WITH HER NEW FRIEND, THE SISTER OF HER CURRENT PATIENT.
HOW DO YOU MEAN?
I MEAN, YOU CAN'T LET CONVENTION RULE YOU. LIFE IS MEANT TO BE LIVED TO THE FULLEST POSSIBLE.
OH, JOAN...
UM-HMMMM

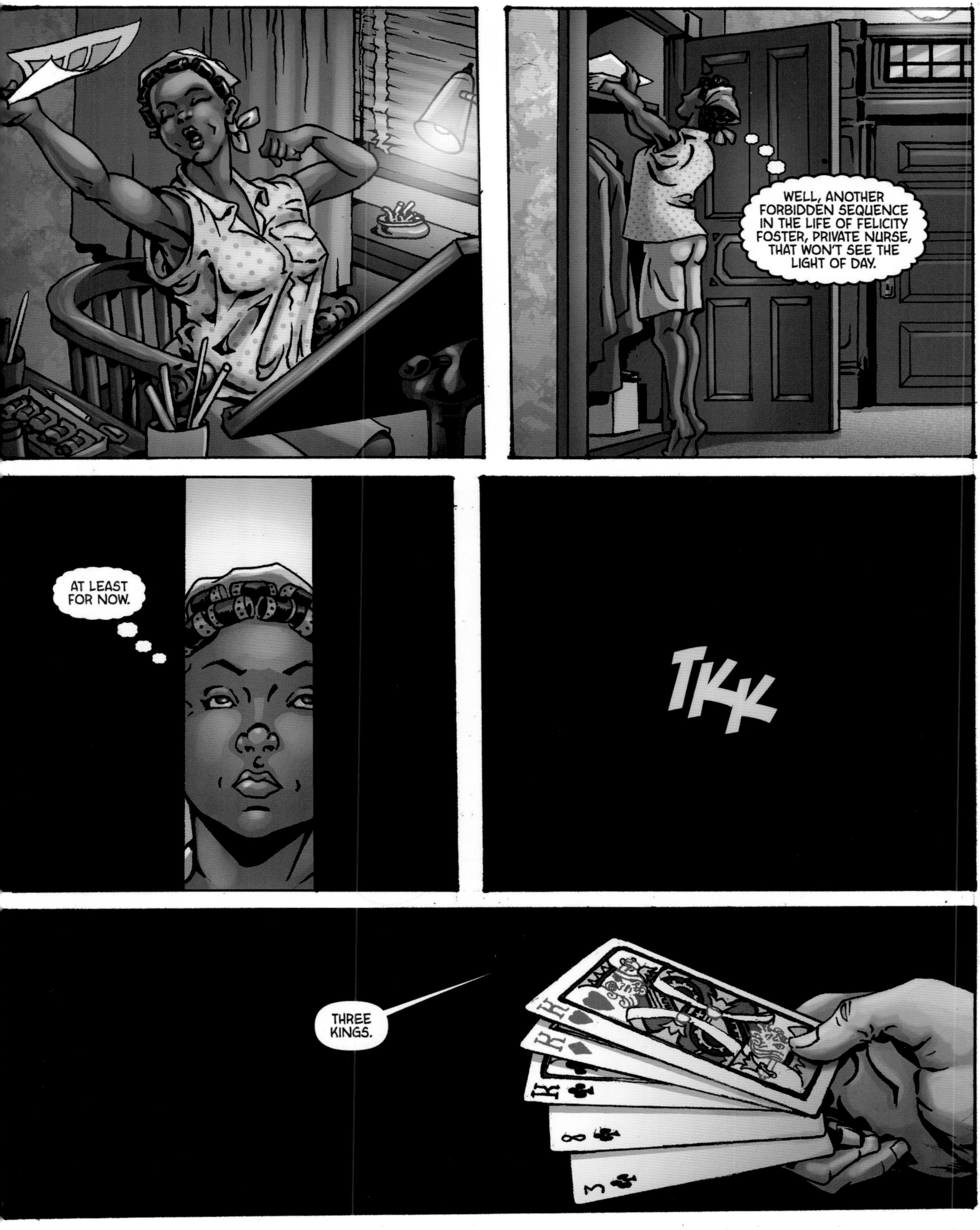
WELL, ANOTHER FORBIDDEN SEQUENCE IN THE LIFE OF FELICITY FOSTER, PRIVATE NURSE, THAT WON'T SEE THE LIGHT OF DAY.
AT LEAST FOR NOW.
TKK
THREE KINGS.

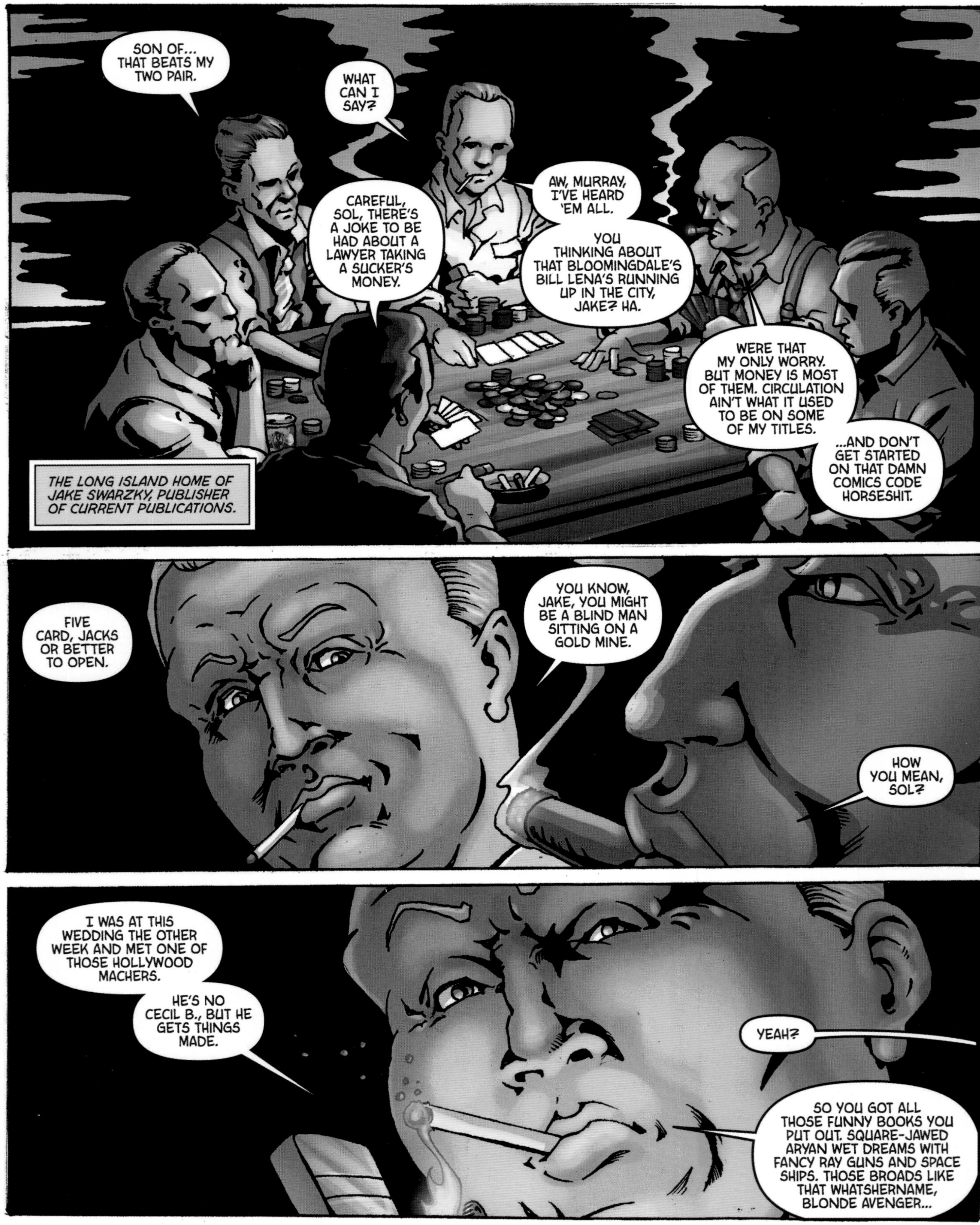
THE LONG ISLAND HOME OF JAKE SWARZKY, PUBLISHER OF CURRENT PUBLICATIONS.
SON OF... THAT BEATS MY TWO PAIR.
WHAT CAN I SAY?
CAREFUL, SOL, THERE'S A JOKE TO BE HAD ABOUT A LAWYER TAKING A SUCKER'S MONEY.
AW, MURRAY, I'VE HEARD 'EM ALL.
YOU THINKING ABOUT THAT BLOOMINGDALE'S BILL LENA'S RUNNING UP IN THE CITY, JAKE? HA.
WERE THAT MY ONLY WORRY. BUT MONEY IS MOST OF THEM. CIRCULATION AIN'T WHAT IT USED TO BE ON SOME OF MY TITLES.
...AND DON'T GET STARTED ON THAT DAMN COMICS CODE HORSESHIT.
FIVE CARD, JACKS OR BETTER TO OPEN.
YOU KNOW, JAKE, YOU MIGHT BE A BLIND MAN SITTING ON A GOLD MINE.
HOW YOU MEAN, SOL?
I WAS AT THIS WEDDING THE OTHER WEEK AND MET ONE OF THOSE HOLLYWOOD MACHERS.
HE'S NO CECIL B., BUT HE GETS THINGS MADE.
YEAH?
SO YOU GOT ALL THOSE FUNNY BOOKS YOU PUT OUT. SQUARE-JAWED ARYAN WET DREAMS WITH FANCY RAY GUNS AND SPACE SHIPS. THOSE BROADS LIKE THAT WHATSHERNAME, BLONDE AVENGER...

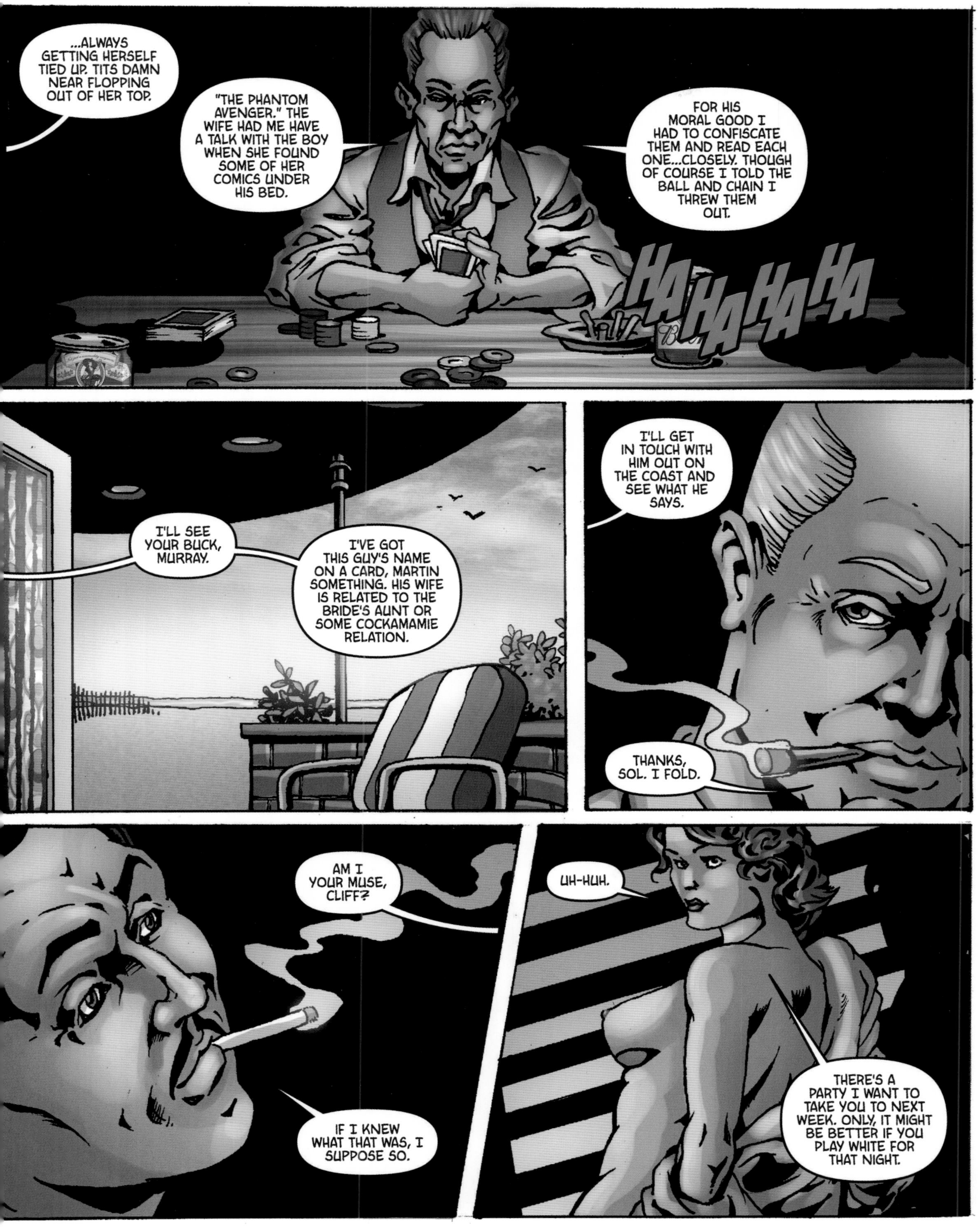
...ALWAYS GETTING HERSELF TIED UP. TITS DAMN NEAR FLOPPING OUT OF HER TOP.
"THE PHANTOM AVENGER." THE WIFE HAD ME HAVE A TALK WITH THE BOY WHEN SHE FOUND SOME OF HER COMICS UNDER HIS BED.
FOR HIS MORAL GOOD I HAD TO CONFISCATE THEM AND READ EACH ONE...CLOSELY. THOUGH OF COURSE I TOLD THE BALL AND CHAIN I THREW THEM OUT.
HAHAHAHAHA
I'LL SEE YOUR BUCK, MURRAY.
I'VE GOT THIS GUY'S NAME ON A CARD, MARTIN SOMETHING. HIS WIFE IS RELATED TO THE BRIDE'S AUNT OR SOME COCKAMAMIE RELATION.
I'LL GET IN TOUCH WITH HIM OUT ON THE COAST AND SEE WHAT HE SAYS.
THANKS, SOL. I FOLD.
AM I YOUR MUSE, CLIFF?
IF I KNEW WHAT THAT WAS, I SUPPOSE SO.
UH-HUH.
THERE'S A PARTY I WANT TO TAKE YOU TO NEXT WEEK. ONLY, IT MIGHT BE BETTER IF YOU PLAY WHITE FOR THAT NIGHT.

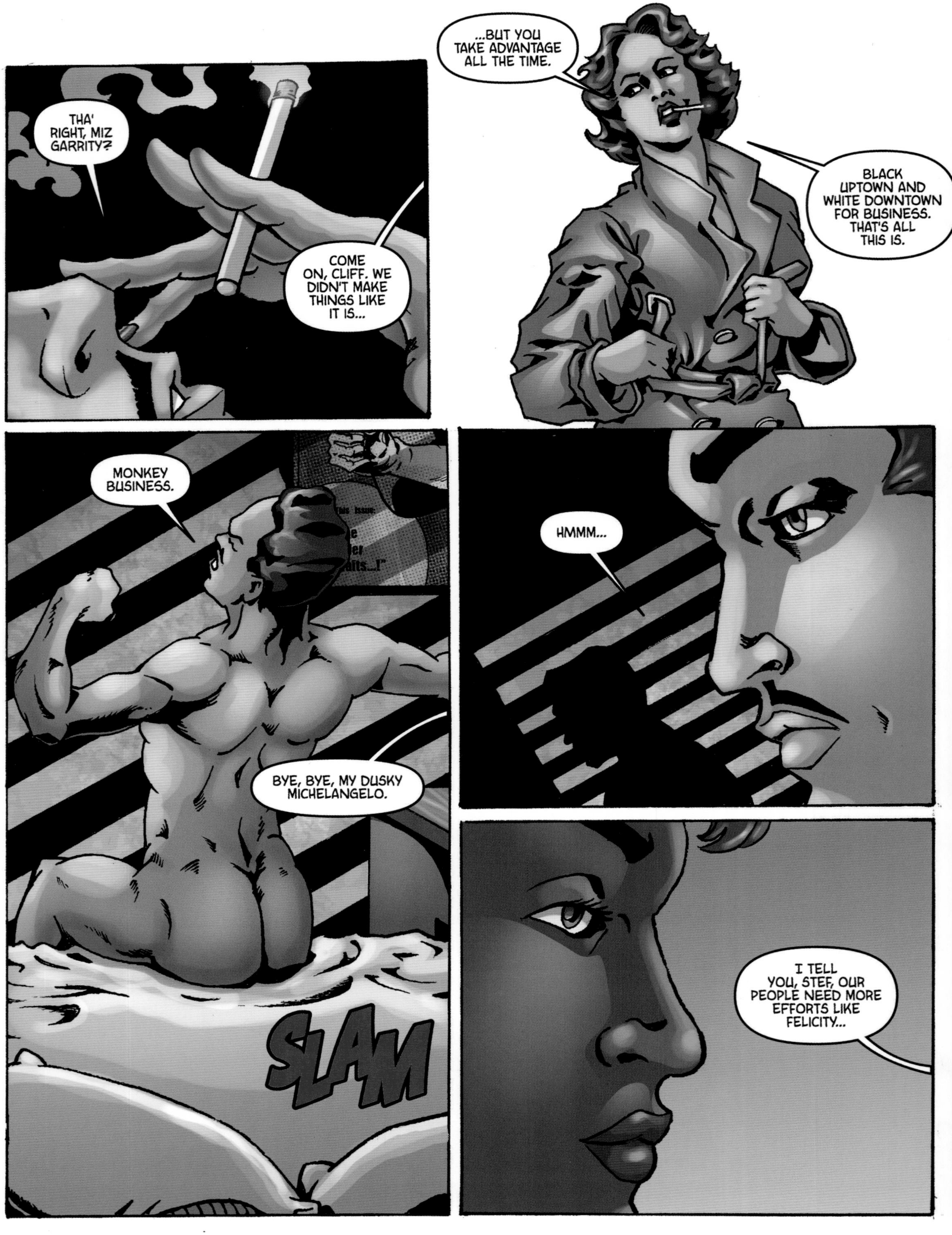
THA' RIGHT, MIZ GARRITY?
COME ON, CLIFF. WE DIDN'T MAKE THINGS LIKE IT IS...
...BUT YOU TAKE ADVANTAGE ALL THE TIME.
BLACK UPTOWN AND WHITE DOWNTOWN FOR BUSINESS. THAT'S ALL THIS IS.
MONKEY BUSINESS.
BYE, BYE, MY DUSKY MICHELANGELO.
SLAM
HMMM...
I TELL YOU, STEF, OUR PEOPLE NEED MORE EFFORTS LIKE FELICITY...

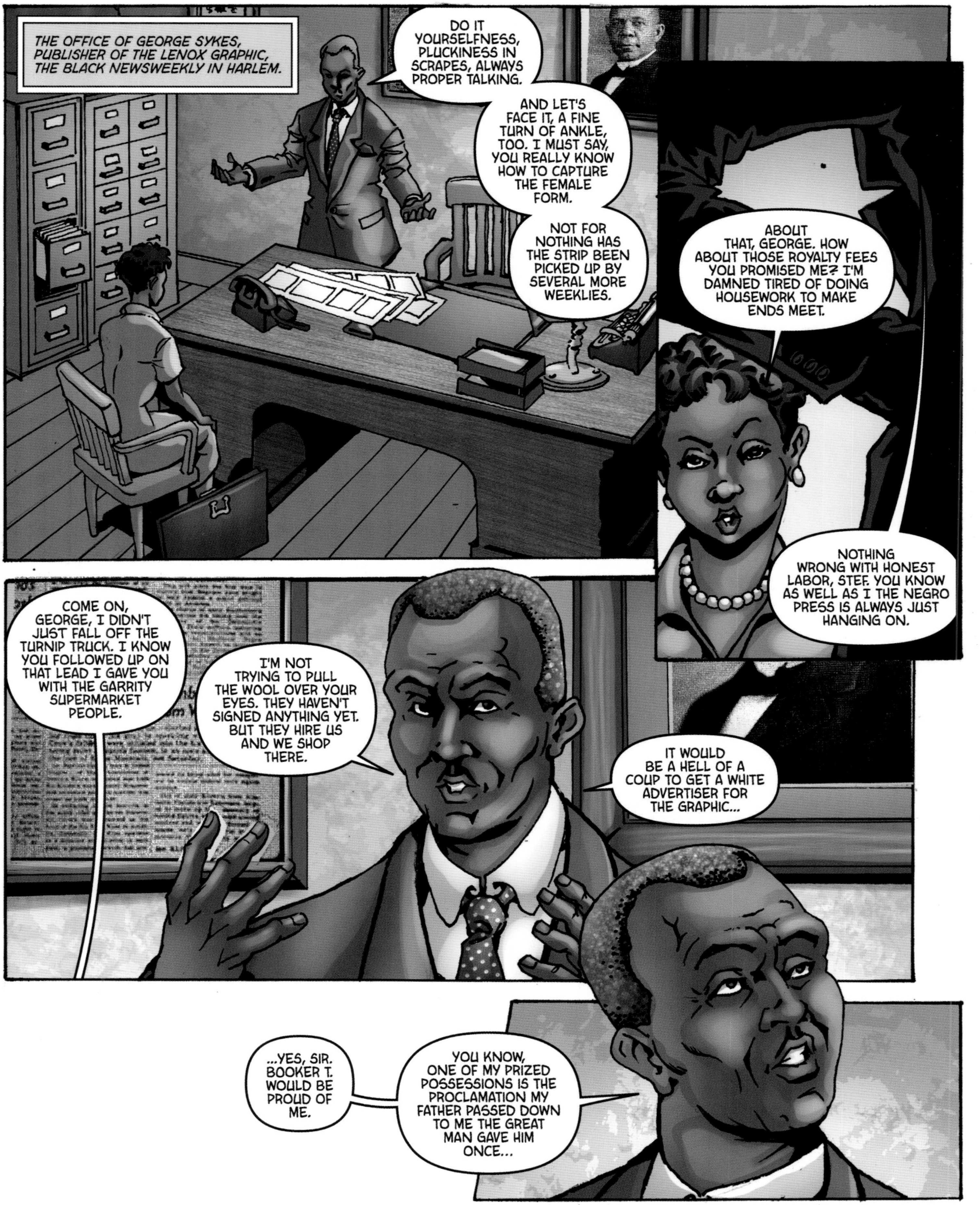
THE OFFICE OF GEORGE SYKES, PUBLISHER OF THE LENOX GRAPHIC, THE BLACK NEWSWEEKLY IN HARLEM.
DO IT YOURSELFNESS, PLUCKINESS IN SCRAPES, ALWAYS PROPER TALKING.
AND LET'S FACE IT, A FINE TURN OF ANKLE, TOO. I MUST SAY, YOU REALLY KNOW HOW TO CAPTURE THE FEMALE FORM.
NOT FOR NOTHING HAS THE STRIP BEEN PICKED UP BY SEVERAL MORE WEEKLIES.
ABOUT THAT, GEORGE. HOW ABOUT THOSE ROYALTY FEES YOU PROMISED ME? I'M DAMNED TIRED OF DOING HOUSEWORK TO MAKE ENDS MEET.
NOTHING WRONG WITH HONEST LABOR, STEF. YOU KNOW AS WELL AS I THE NEGRO PRESS IS ALWAYS JUST HANGING ON.
COME ON, GEORGE, I DIDN'T JUST FALL OFF THE TURNIP TRUCK. I KNOW YOU FOLLOWED UP ON THAT LEAD I GAVE YOU WITH THE GARRITY SUPERMARKET PEOPLE.
I'M NOT TRYING TO PULL THE WOOL OVER YOUR EYES. THEY HAVEN'T SIGNED ANYTHING YET. BUT THEY HIRE US AND WE SHOP THERE.
IT WOULD BE A HELL OF A COUP TO GET A WHITE ADVERTISER FOR THE GRAPHIC...
YOU KNOW, ONE OF MY PRIZED POSSESSIONS IS THE PROCLAMATION MY FATHER PASSED DOWN TO ME THE GREAT MAN GAVE HIM ONCE...
...YES, SIR. BOOKER T. WOULD BE PROUD OF ME.

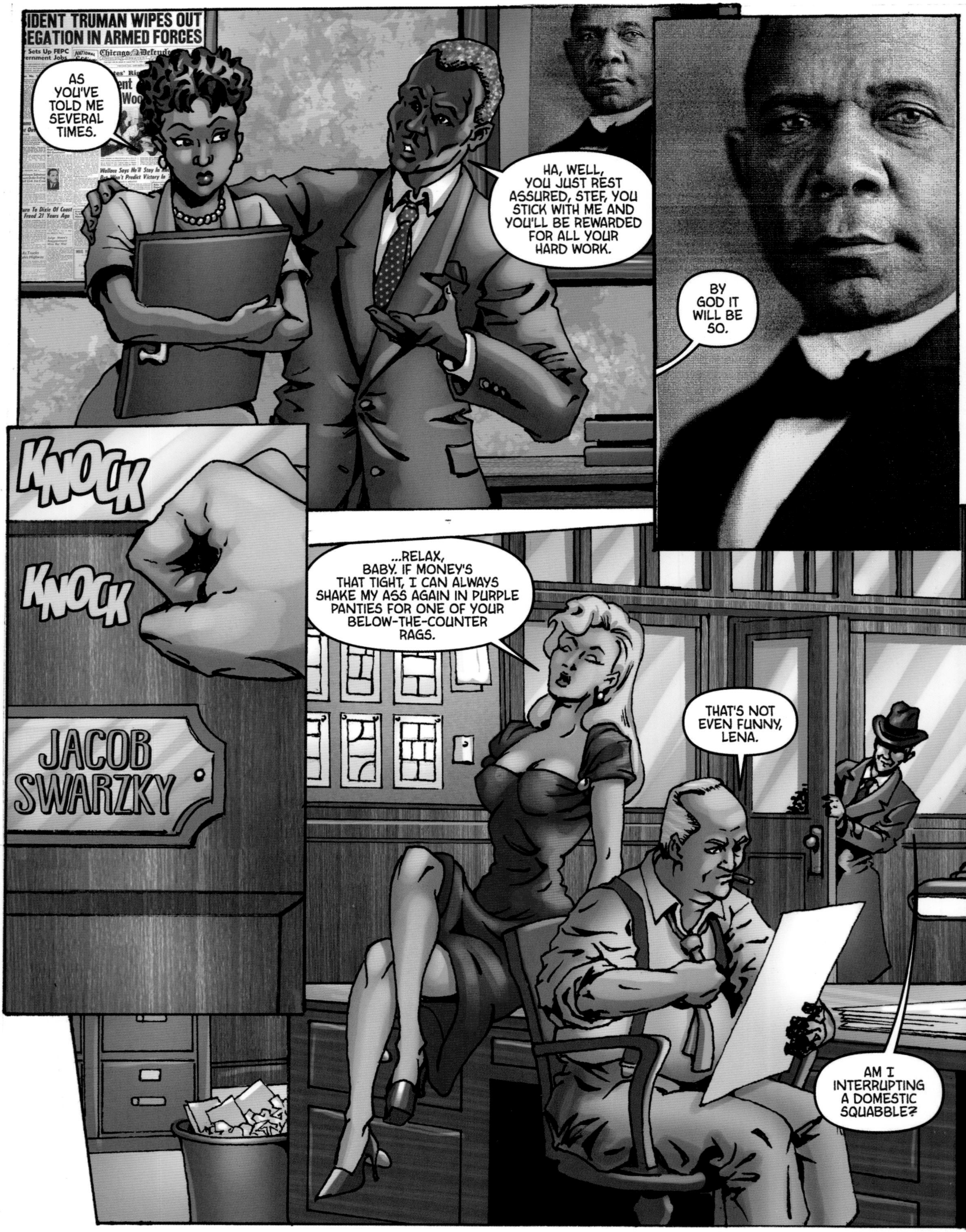
IDENT TRUMAN WIPES OUT
EGATION IN ARMED FORCES
AS YOU'VE TOLD ME SEVERAL TIMES.
HA, WELL, YOU JUST REST ASSURED, STEF, YOU STICK WITH ME AND YOU'LL BE REWARDED FOR ALL YOUR HARD WORK.
BY GOD IT WILL BE SO.
KNOCK
KNOCK
JACOB SWARZKY
...RELAX, BABY. IF MONEY'S THAT TIGHT, I CAN ALWAYS SHAKE MY ASS AGAIN IN PURPLE PANTIES FOR ONE OF YOUR BELOW-THE-COUNTER RAGS.
THAT'S NOT EVEN FUNNY, LENA.
AM I INTERRUPTING A DOMESTIC SQUABBLE?

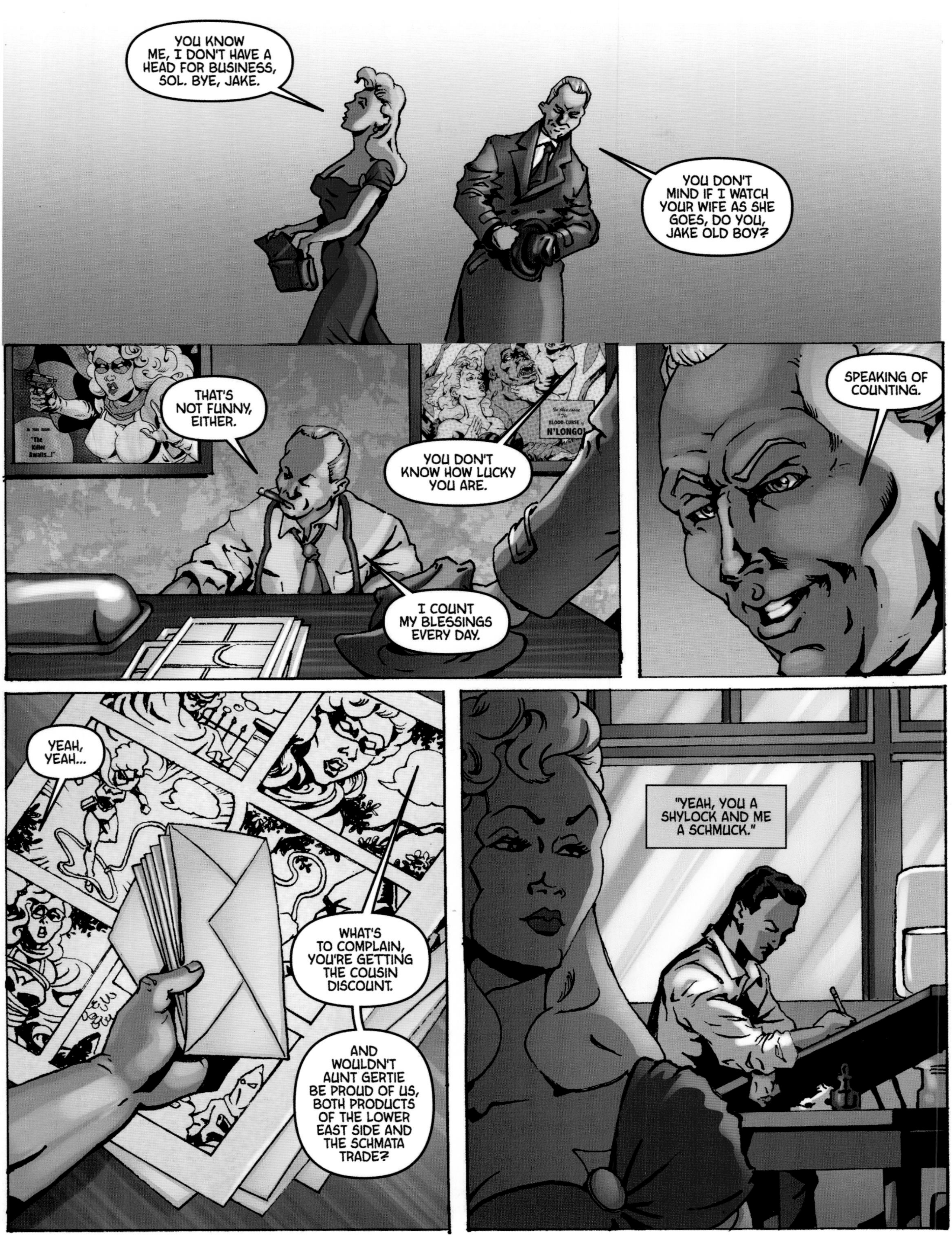
YOU KNOW ME, I DON'T HAVE A HEAD FOR BUSINESS, SOL. BYE, JAKE.
YOU DON'T MIND IF I WATCH YOUR WIFE AS SHE GOES, DO YOU, JAKE OLD BOY?
THAT'S NOT FUNNY, EITHER.
N'LONGO
YOU DON'T KNOW HOW LUCKY YOU ARE.
I COUNT MY BLESSINGS EVERY DAY.
SPEAKING OF COUNTING.
YEAH, YEAH...
WHAT'S TO COMPLAIN, YOU'RE GETTING THE COUSIN DISCOUNT.
AND WOULDN'T AUNT GERTIE BE PROUD OF US, BOTH PRODUCTS OF THE LOWER EAST SIDE AND THE SCHMATA TRADE?
"YEAH, YOU A SHYLOCK AND ME A SCHMUCK."

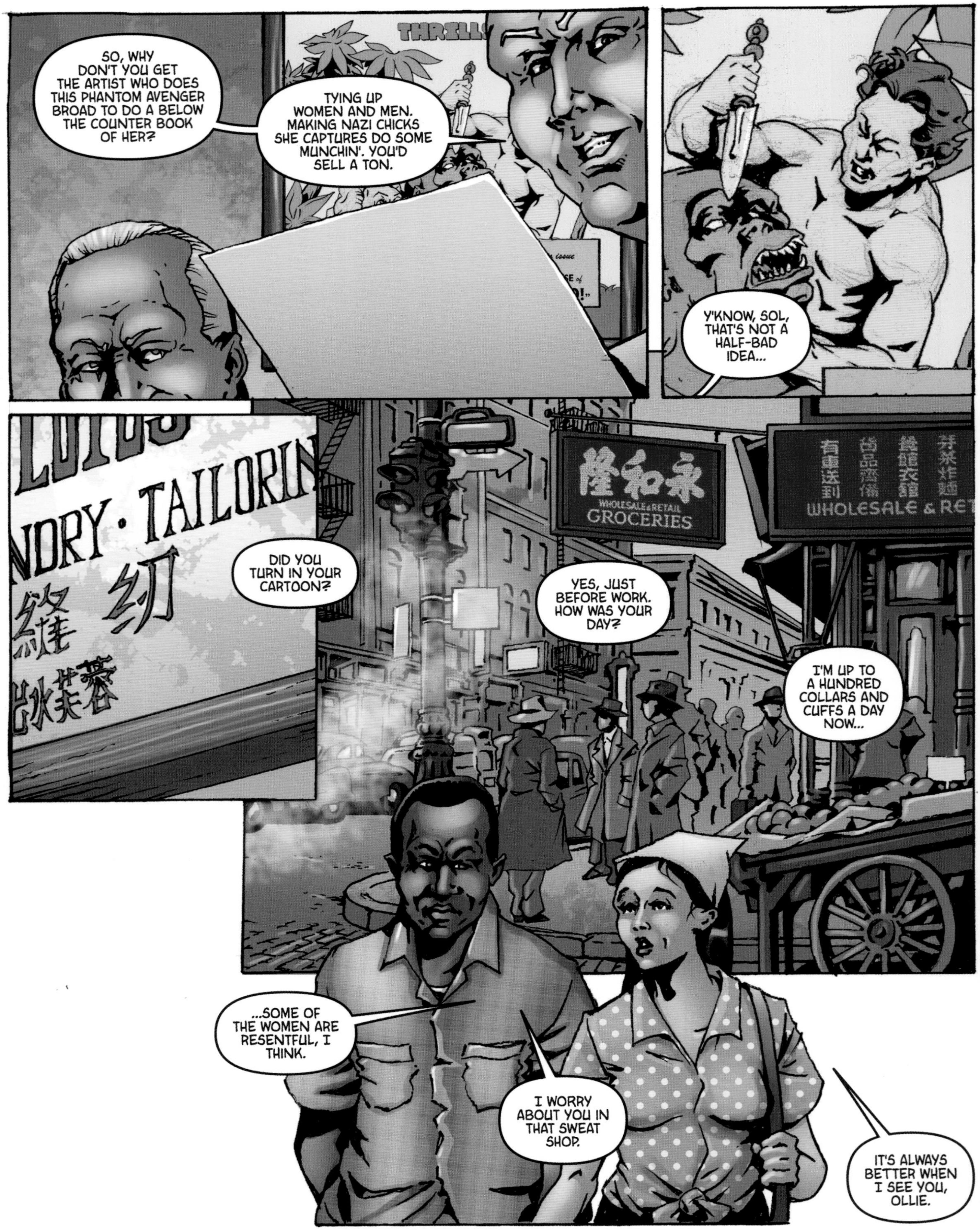
SO, WHY DON'T YOU GET THE ARTIST WHO DOES THIS PHANTOM AVENGER BROAD TO DO A BELOW THE COUNTER BOOK OF HER?
TYING UP WOMEN AND MEN. MAKING NAZI CHICKS SHE CAPTURES DO SOME MUNCHIN'. YOU'D SELL A TON.
Y'KNOW, SOL, THAT'S NOT A HALF-BAD IDEA...
NDRY · TAILORIN
WHOLESALE & RETAIL GROCERIES
WHOLESALE & RET
DID YOU TURN IN YOUR CARTOON?
YES, JUST BEFORE WORK. HOW WAS YOUR DAY?
I'M UP TO A HUNDRED COLLARS AND CUFFS A DAY NOW...
...SOME OF THE WOMEN ARE RESENTFUL, I THINK.
I WORRY ABOUT YOU IN THAT SWEAT SHOP.
IT'S ALWAYS BETTER WHEN I SEE YOU, OLLIE.

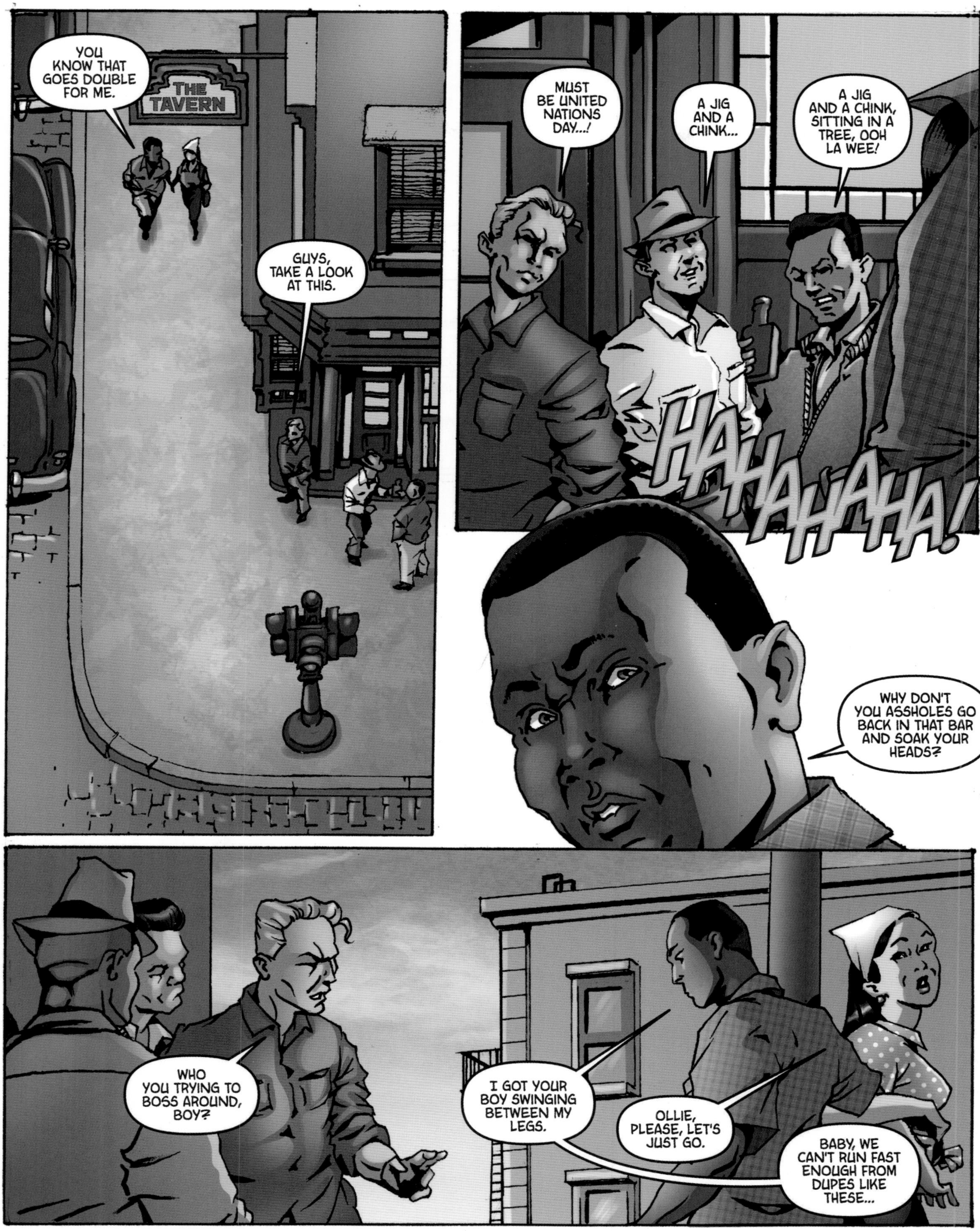
YOU KNOW THAT GOES DOUBLE FOR ME.
THE TAVERN
GUYS, TAKE A LOOK AT THIS.
MUST BE UNITED NATIONS DAY...!
A JIG AND A CHINK...
A JIG AND A CHINK, SITTING IN A TREE, OOH LA WEE!
HAHAHAHAHA!
WHY DON'T YOU ASSHOLES GO BACK IN THAT BAR AND SOAK YOUR HEADS?
WHO YOU TRYING TO BOSS AROUND, BOY?
I GOT YOUR BOY SWINGING BETWEEN MY LEGS.
OLLIE, PLEASE, LET'S JUST GO.
BABY, WE CAN'T RUN FAST ENOUGH FROM DUPES LIKE THESE...

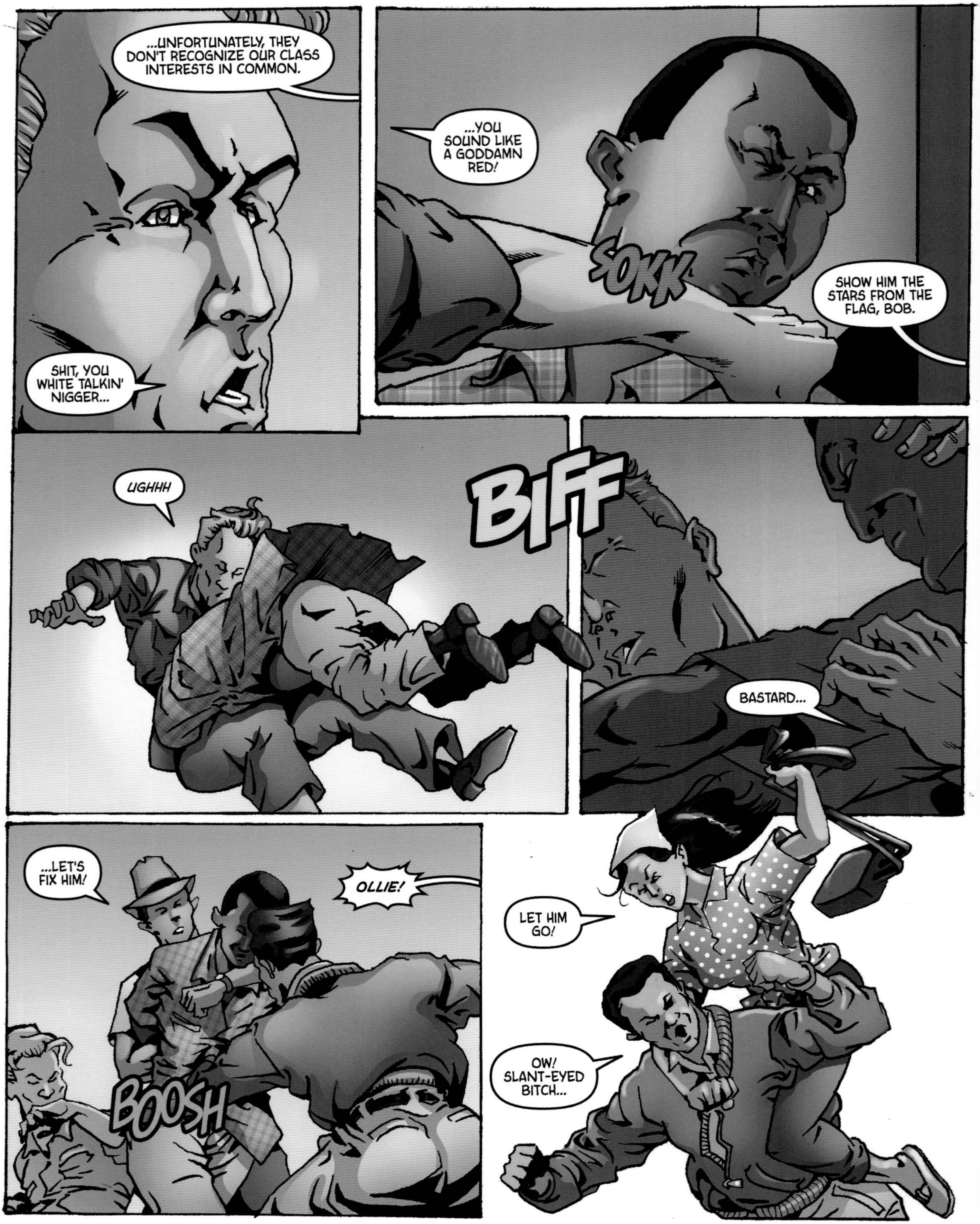
...UNFORTUNATELY, THEY DON'T RECOGNIZE OUR CLASS INTERESTS IN COMMON.
SHIT, YOU WHITE TALKIN' NIGGER...
...YOU SOUND LIKE A GODDAMN RED!
SOKK
SHOW HIM THE STARS FROM THE FLAG, BOB.
UGHHH
BIFF
BASTARD...
...LET'S FIX HIM!
OLLIE!
BOOSH
LET HIM GO!
OW! SLANT-EYED BITCH...

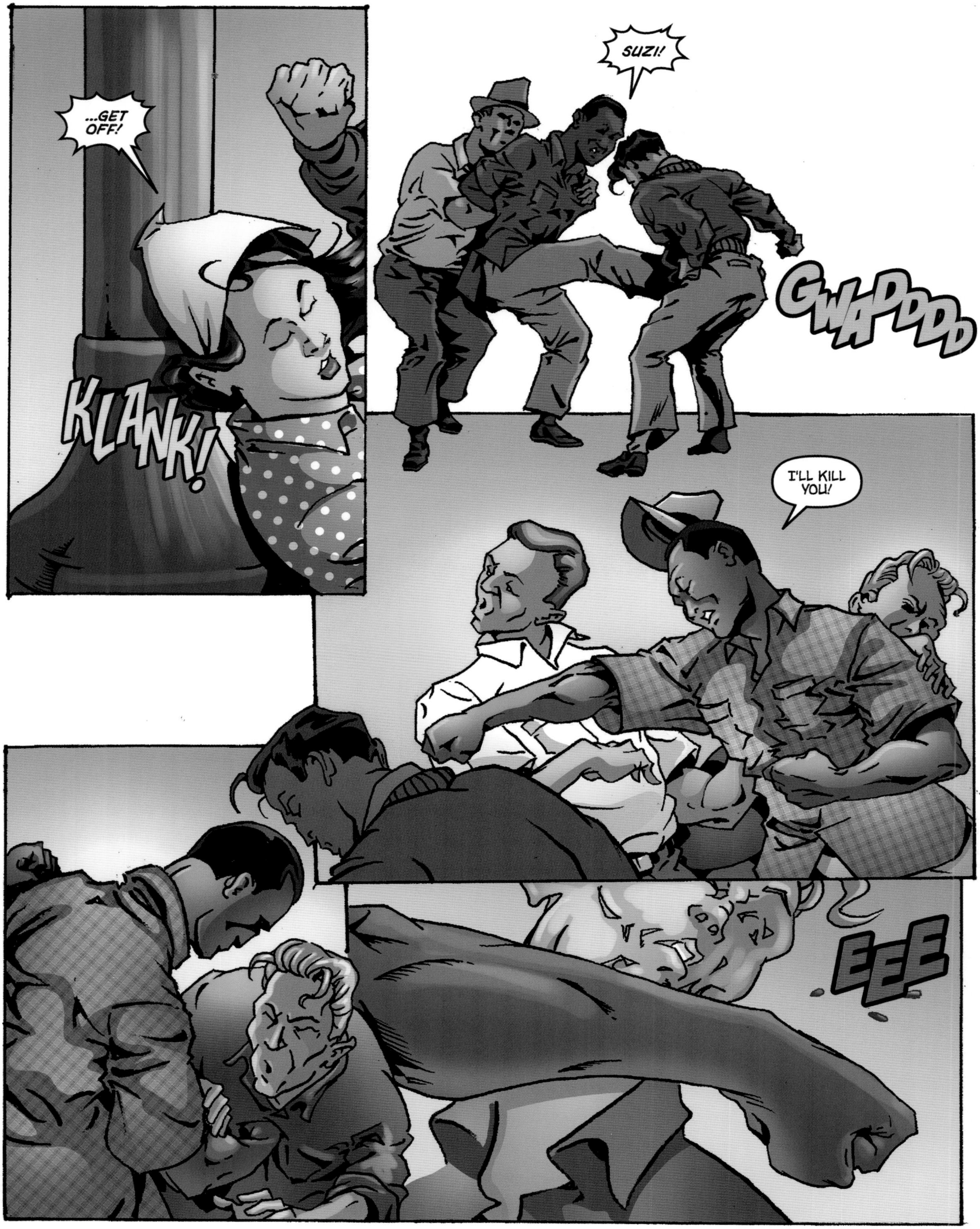
...GET OFF!
KLANK!
SUZI!
GWADDDD
I'LL KILL YOU!
EEE

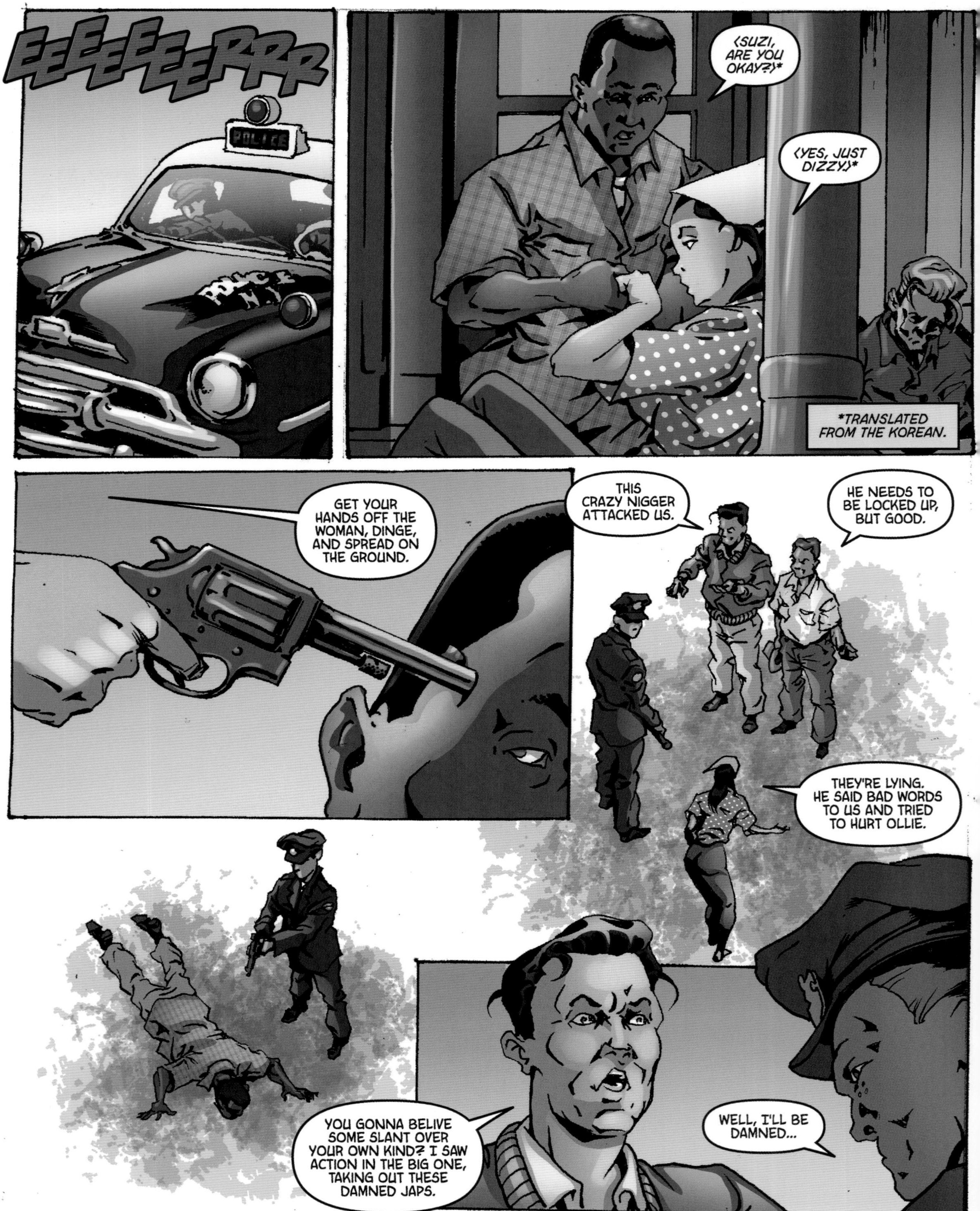
EEEEEEEERRR
POLICE
‹SUZI, ARE YOU OKAY?›*
‹YES, JUST DIZZY.›*
*TRANSLATED FROM THE KOREAN.
GET YOUR HANDS OFF THE WOMAN, DINGE, AND SPREAD ON THE GROUND.
THIS CRAZY NIGGER ATTACKED US.
HE NEEDS TO BE LOCKED UP, BUT GOOD.
THEY'RE LYING. HE SAID BAD WORDS TO US AND TRIED TO HURT OLLIE.
YOU GONNA BELIVE SOME SLANT OVER YOUR OWN KIND? I SAW ACTION IN THE BIG ONE, TAKING OUT THESE DAMNED JAPS.
WELL, I'LL BE DAMNED...

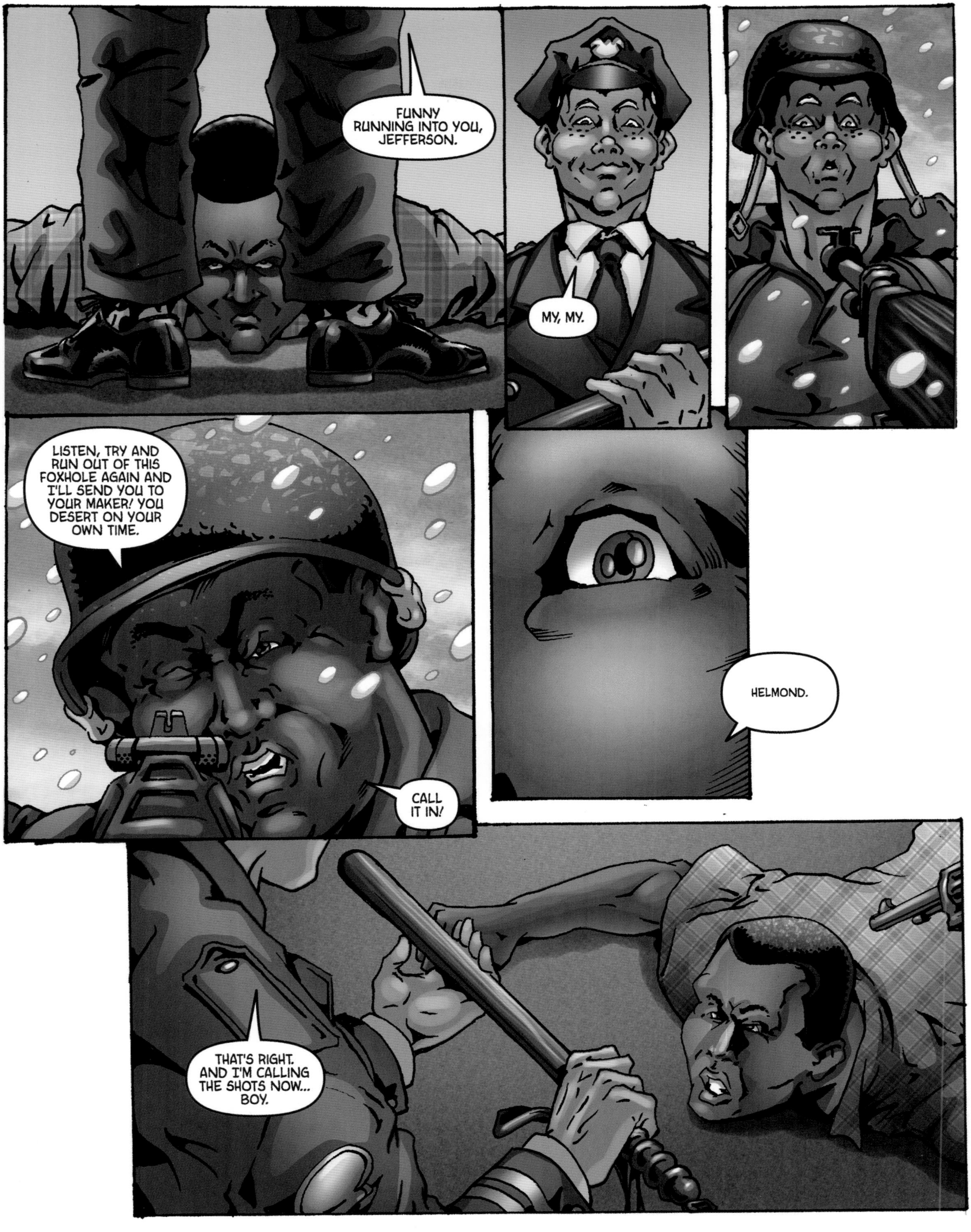
FUNNY RUNNING INTO YOU, JEFFERSON.
MY, MY.
LISTEN, TRY AND RUN OUT OF THIS FOXHOLE AGAIN AND I'LL SEND YOU TO YOUR MAKER! YOU DESERT ON YOUR OWN TIME.
CALL IT IN!
HELMOND.
THAT'S RIGHT. AND I'M CALLING THE SHOTS NOW... BOY.

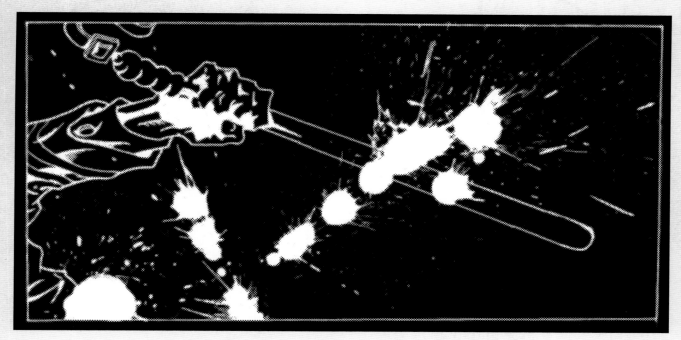

DAVE HELMOND GRINNED and said to the other officer who had his Police Special pointed at Ollie Jefferson, "Get his black ass up."

"What about these guys?" he said, indicating the drunks.

"Write down the war hero's name and address." Then, pointing his nightstick at the drunk veteran, Helond said, "After that, you all get the fuck on home and dry out."

"I want to press charges," the ex-serviceman said.

"Hey, asshole," Helmond shot back, "how about I throw you and your buddies in the drunk tank? Or better yet, drive you over to Harlem and let you out in the jungle so the natives can deal with you. How would that be, Audie Murphy?"

The man exchanged a look with his friend, who was standing up. He said, "Aw, the hell with it." Together they helped the third one get off the ground while the veteran told the cop his information. Thereafter grumbling under their breaths, the trio walked away on unsteady feet.

"You better run along too, missy," the other cop said to Suzi Bahn, tucking his notepad away in his flapped shirt pocket.

"I'm not going anywhere," she said defiantly. "I'm not going to let you hurt Ollie."

"It's okay, Suzi. Go on. I don't want these buzzards putting their hands on you. Call Irwin, honey."

"Yeah, honey," Helmond mocked, "you run along now and go call Irwin, which is a funny name for a spade." He chuckled at his witticism.

The other cop cast a nervous glance at her then back on Helmond.

"Ollie," Bahn began.

Jefferson, who was now back on his feet, cut her off with a meaningful look and grim smile. "It's going to be fine. I won't let them get the best of me."

"See, he's got the world by the tail." Helmond spread his arms wide, nightstick held tight in his knotted fist.

Wiping at her eye, Suzi Bahn turned away and walked stiffly toward the corner. As soon as she was out of sight she'd run until she found a pay phone. But she wasn't going to show any sign that these bastards had rattled her.

Helmond poked the end of his billy club into Jefferson's stomach. "Like I said, I'm the top dog now."

"Bow-wow."

The first blow from the nightstick caused Jefferson to grit his teeth but he didn't buckle. They would have to do a lot more damage than that, he determined. "Pussies," he snarled at the two cops as they shoved him around some and got handcuffs on him. They roughly loaded him into the rear of the prowl car.

While it was unlikely anyone would intervene as a negro got what was probably coming to him, beaten senseless on a city street, Helmond wanted Jefferson to really feel trapped. At the station there was privacy and bars. He would instill hopelessness in him but good.

MILLIE HANKS PICKED up the receiver on the second ring. "Hello," she said.

"Millie, it's Irwin. We need your help." Irwin Silver was the managing editor of the *Daily Struggle*, the daily newspaper put out by the Communist Party U.S.A.

"One of your Bolsheviks getting evicted again?"

"This is serious, Millie. One of our staff has been arrested on trumped up charges. He's a colored man."

"That supposed to make me all weak in the knees, Irwin?" she teased. As soon as she heard his voice, she knew the matter would be low or no pay and an uphill battle. Was she ever going to be able to afford a secretary? Or even an office where her hand-me-down desk didn't take up most of the room?

Silver was saying, "He goes by the nom de guerre of Atticus in the paper."

"The one that does those editorial cartoons?"

"Yes. We knew we had to hide his identity given the incendiary nature of his anti-capitalist work."

"Uh-huh," the lawyer replied. "That and he had to keep a day job as the people don't exactly pay a living wage."

Silver drew in breath. "I don't want to sound like an exploiter, but this case could be big. Ollie's a decorated Korean War vet, a self-taught artist, a working class intellectual. Dig?"

"Go on you smooth devil, you."

"We think money can be raised for his defense fund across this city and beyond."

"You've had that hope before. And we both got our teeth kicked in."

"I hear you. No one's saying this will have the momentum of what happened in Montgomery, but this for sure could give the struggle locally a big shot in the arm."

She asked, "Where's he being held?" She stood. The receiver's spiral cord was stretched from the phone, the device cradled between her shoulder and ear as she reached for her camel-hair coat hanging from her coat rack. Her one extravagance.

"At the 24th Precinct. We've already started making calls to gather the troops for a show of solidarity, and it's looking good to raise the bail. And there's his fiancée. She witnessed his mistreatment. There's some sort of history between one of the cops and Ollie, she said."

"That's his real name?"

"Yeah, Ollie . . . Oliver Jefferson. He works at the school district's textbook warehouse."

"I should have my head examined, but okay, I'm on my way."

"You're the best. See you shortly," Silver rang off on his end.

Hanks settled the receiver and shrugged into her coat. She also carefully put her felt tilt cap on her recently refreshed, marcelled hair, holding it in place with a hair pin. She quickly took in her modest third-floor office that, in addition to the standing coat rack and desk and chair, had a bookcase with some law books on it, her framed law degree on the wall, and a stack of newspapers, including a few issues of the Party's paper on a side table.

Muttering, she said, "Lonely is the champion of the underclass." She shook her head and turned out the overhead lights on her way out.

IN THE HOLDING cell at the 24th Precinct, Ollie Jefferson stood with his arms folded against the wall. The bitter aroma of the unwashed and urine was strong. Several men, black and white, were in the cell, with a few of them taking up residence on the one built-in bunk bed. One of the men sitting on the crowded cot was leafing through a copy of the *Daily Struggle*. Somehow the cops missed that, Jefferson noted, for surely they would have confiscated the paper. And it was with muted pleasure that the man had paused to take in his editorial cartoon done under his Atticus name. This one depicted two figures dressed stylishly like jazz musicians as they rolled craps in an alleyway. One was a skeleton in a fedora with a large brim and feather sticking out of the crown. The other was what a typical moneybags-type would look like, complete with a lit cigar, jowls, and a top hat. The dice were large as they came at the viewer in the foreground. On their sides weren't dots but the continents of the world.

The caption read: They Gamble with Our Future.

Familiar footfalls sounding on the concrete floor refocused Jefferson's attention.

"You didn't think I'd forgotten about you?" Helmond stood at the cell, leering in at him. His hand gripped the bar, the skin around the knuckles white as he tightened his fist in anticipation.

"Why don't you get over yourself, Helmond?" He tried not to show his anxiety. They hadn't touched him on the way over here after that first blow out on the street. But he knew the other shoe had to drop. "I certainly have."

Everyone else in the cell incredulously regarded the lippy prisoner. He was either brave or stupid or both, they estimated.

Helmond now had both hands on the bars, an unpleasant grin on his face like a demented clown. "Come on, you and I got us some catching up to do . . . Sarge." Helmond unlocked the cell door, standing back a pace, hand on the butt of his holstered revolver.

Jefferson straightened up, eyes front, and without hesitating marched out of the cell into the recess of the precinct, Officer Helmond directly behind him, whistling. The black men in the cell and even one of the whites looked ashen.

TOWARD EVENING IN Harlem, Stef Rawls sprinkled water on the maid's uniform she was ironing. She checked the time on her clock on the wall and with a flourish of the wrist, got the crease

precisely as she wanted to, the short sleeve cuffed in white against the uniform's gray. Draped on her one plush chair was the white apron, pristine and unwrinkled, like it had just been bought even though it was in fact more than five years old. As she finished up, she considered having a belt from the scotch in her kitchenette's cabinet but knew better. It would not do to have booze on her breath before she went to work at "Miz Lady's" function, she smiled.

In the bathroom she undid the handkerchief around her hair and took out her rollers. She then brushed her hair, noting a trip to the beauty parlor was due but then so was the electric bill and she had yet to master drawing in the dark. She got dressed. Rawls also put on her cloth coat, which was getting thin at the elbows, the hem ragged. She then went down to the street. The shoe repairman was standing outside his compact shop, his ring of keys jingling as he locked his door.

"Mr. Monkalla," she said.

"Miss Stephanie," the Ethiopian immigrant said in return.

"One day you will be so famous, you will have your own maid."

"Bless, you, Mr. Monkalla, bless you." She touched his shoulder as she headed for the bus stop. The shoe man had a twelve-year-old daughter who was a fan of her strip. If Rawls wasn't exactly overjoyed to have to be heading off to do yet another bend-and-grin gig, she reflected, at least she only had to get over to Jackson Heights and not, say, way out on Long Island or some damn faraway place.

And while the work was demanding, not physically but putting up with the caprice of well-off white folks who considered her little more than a trained idiot the way they talked to her, it did at times provide material she incorporated in the adventures of Felicity Foster.

"Now, you do understand what I've told you, my dear," the middle-aged woman with the off-white pearls said. She lightly touched Rawls's hand with hers as if trans-

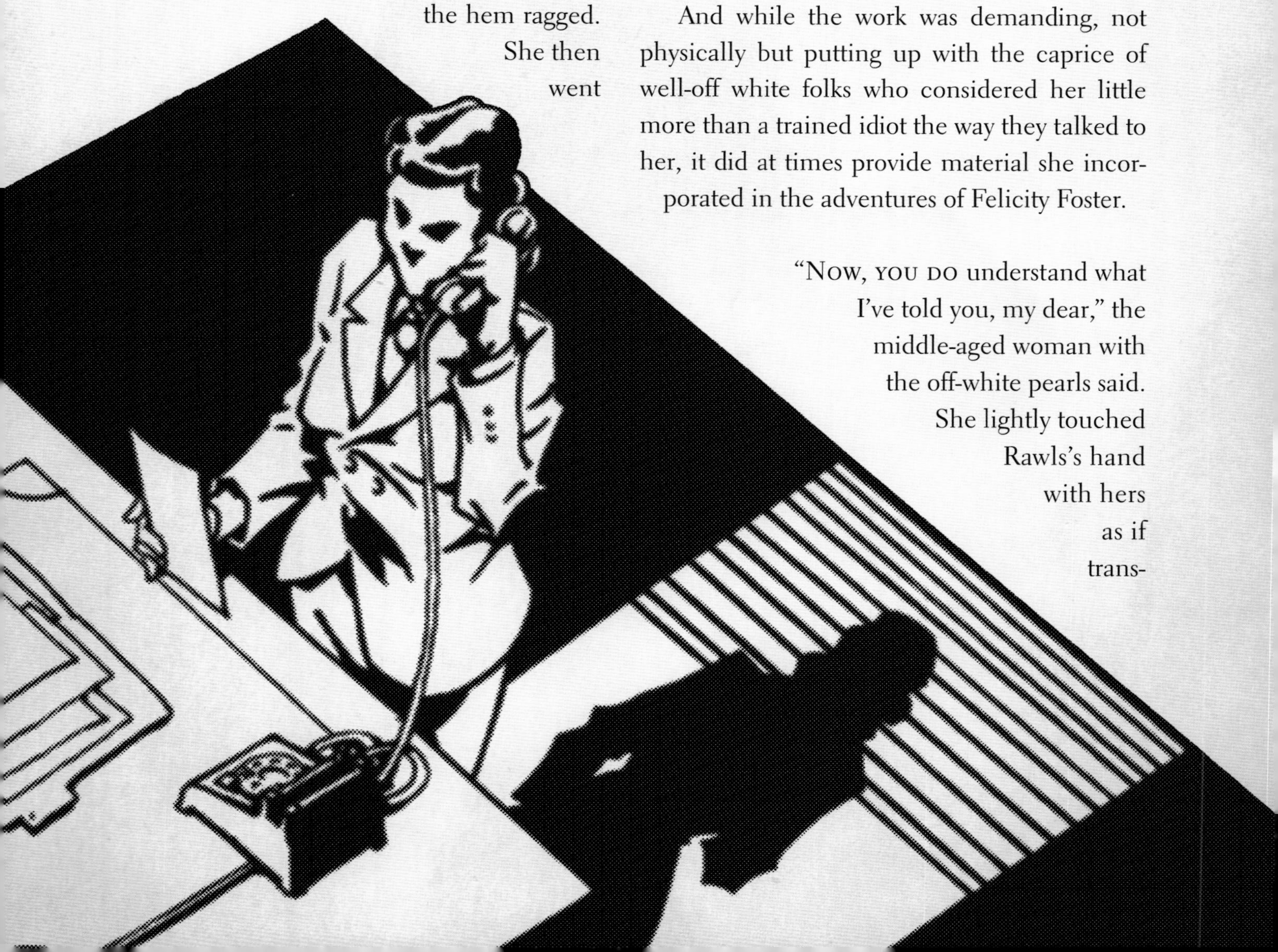

mitting the instructions via her fingertips as well as verbally. She leaned toward her some, wine on her breath. They stood in the woman's well-appointed kitchen in her well-appointed brownstone. Behind her the regular colored maid dared to bug her eyes at Rawls then resume her practiced placid expression.

"Yes, ma'am, I understand."

"Good, good, Matilda."

Rawls didn't dare give this woman a sharp look. She'd told her twice what her name was, and she knew it was in the paperwork the agency had sent over. Was her calling her "Matilda" like when white passengers called all black train porters "George" because of George Pullman, who had built the sleeping cars for trains? Ah well.

The dinner party the woman was having, as she was some sort of opera buff, Rawls surmised, was for the Central Queens Music Appreciation Society. While those in attendance were mostly woman mirroring the hostess's age and class, or aspiring to such, there were a fair amount of men in attendance too. Several males puffed on pipes and nodded their heads thoughtfully as they blew smoke out of the sides of their mouths. Rawls moved in and around them, picking up empty glasses or ferrying appetizers out of the kitchen prepared by the chef brought on for tonight's soiree.

"Oh, it was dreadful what he went through," one woman in a silvery dress was saying to another as they sat near one another on one of the couches. They each had a martini glass in hand.

"But this psychiatrist he saw really helped your brother make a breakthrough?"

"Yes," she said, taking a swallow from her glass then placing it empty on an end table. Rawls hovered into view, taking up the glass but lingering.

"He was fantastic," the woman was saying.

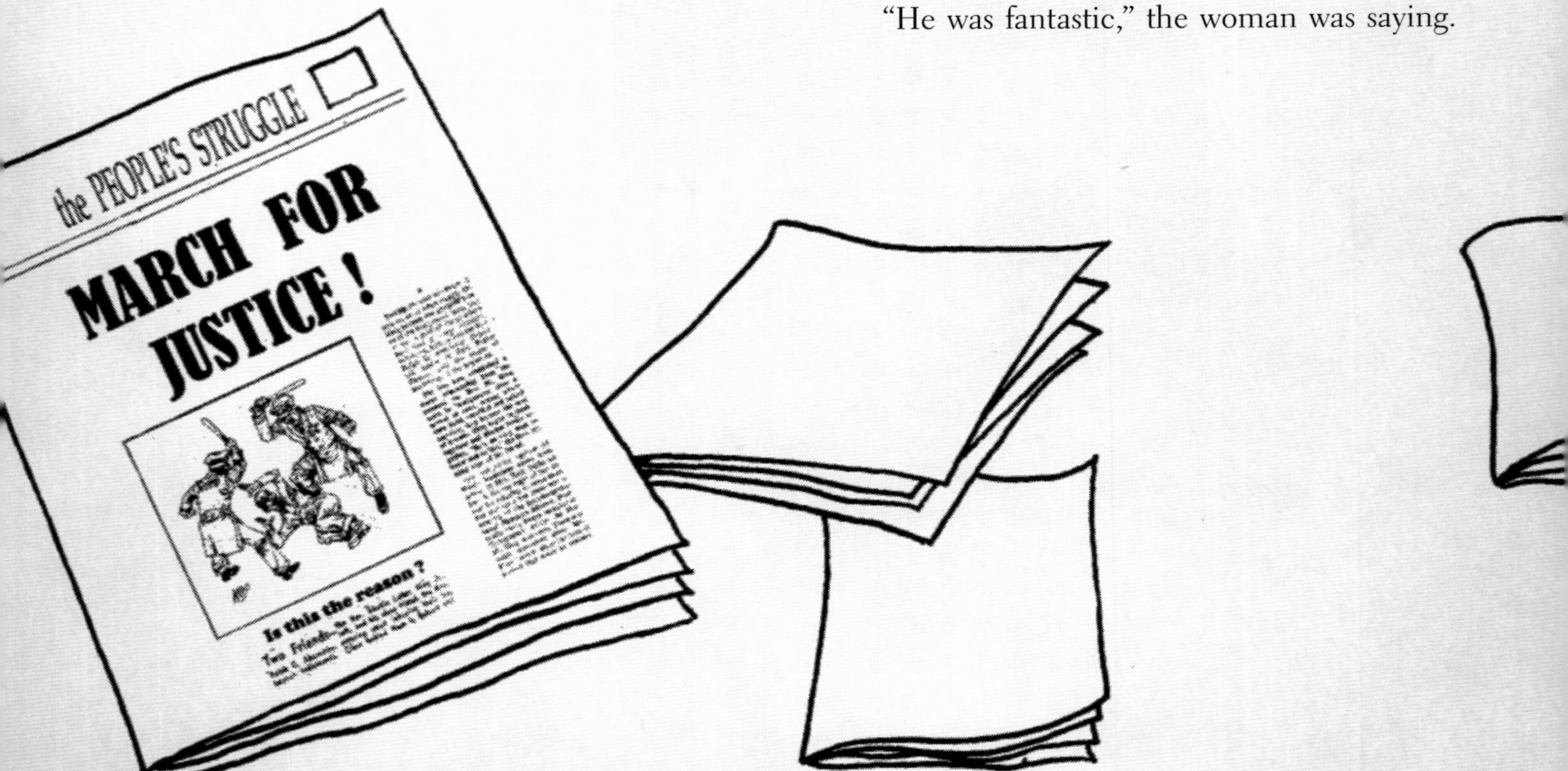
the PEOPLE'S STRUGGLE
MARCH FOR JUSTICE !
Is this the reason ?

"He got through to Rob's subconsciousness and his sleepwalking is a thing of the past."

"The mind is such a fascinating study, isn't it?"

"Indeed, indeed." Silvery dress turned abruptly, snapping her fingers. "You there, fetch me another vodka martini, would you, my girl?"

"Yes'um," Rawls said, putting some Southern in her voice for kicks.

Later when she got home, she was tired but also inspired. Rawls got into comfortable clothes and got some coffee percolating. Doing a few stretches to get the creative juices flowing, she put down a fresh sheet of Bristol on her draft table and got to work. She was ahead in terms of where the latest published episode of Felicity was at. But rather than write down notes in terms of new avenues to explore in the strip, she liked to at times draw them out, visualize what her ideas were. Using her T-square and triangle, her Number 2 pencil dulled down as she liked it, she plotted out the panels on the page. In the

first panel was an outside shot of the woman's house in Jackson Heights. Not it per se, but her impression of the place. Then in the second panel, now sipping coffee laced with scotch, she did an interior shot of the people gathered for the party. In the third panel, she sketched out two of the maids talking as they took a smoke break outside the kitchen door. Then the fourth panel, which was good-sized, was a shot of the women looking stylish on the couch. Only one of them was now her heroine, Felicity Foster.

The white woman in the silvery dress, younger, tauter, was saying to her, "Oh, Felicity, I can't thank you enough for what you did for my shell-shocked brother."

"I was glad I could help."

She smiled at her handiwork. Yes, she estimated, this was going to be an interesting storyline. She sipped more of her strong coffee and made notes in the margins of the page.

Down below, standing outside a several-years-old DeSoto Fireflite, a man in a fedora

and a trench coat cinched against the cold stood and smoked. He'd been sitting in the car but had to take a leak and had gone around the corner to go behind a clutch of bushes to do so. He promptly returned to keeping an eye on the muted light seen from Stef Rawls's apartment. He was one of the two who'd been keeping tabs on her friend, Cliff Murphy.

"THIS IS A goddamn outrage."

"Hey, watch that mouth."

"Not ladylike, am I?" Millie Hanks said to the police captain, jabbing a finger at him. They stood in a hallway off the main entrance to the precinct. After more than half an hour of wrangling with the police, she'd had Ollie Jefferson brought out of his cell.

Hanks continued. "I should be all demure and whatnot with all you big, strong men around. Swooning I suppose. Or maybe you want to have a couple of your officers work me over like they did Ollie with their nigger-be-good sticks."

The captain pointed back. "You better watch your mouth, girly."

Hanks put her hands on her hips, smartly dressed in a grey suit and matching cap. "And maybe you better take a look outside." She looked from him over to her client, Ollie Jefferson. His face was swollen and the beating he'd taken was mapped on his face. But like his lawyer, defiance lay behind his eyes.

The captain and two of his officers standing with him went to the windows looking out on the avenue. At the front desk, a man insisted to the seen-it-all sergeant sitting there that President Eisenhower was speaking to him in Japanese through his radio at exactly 11:40 each

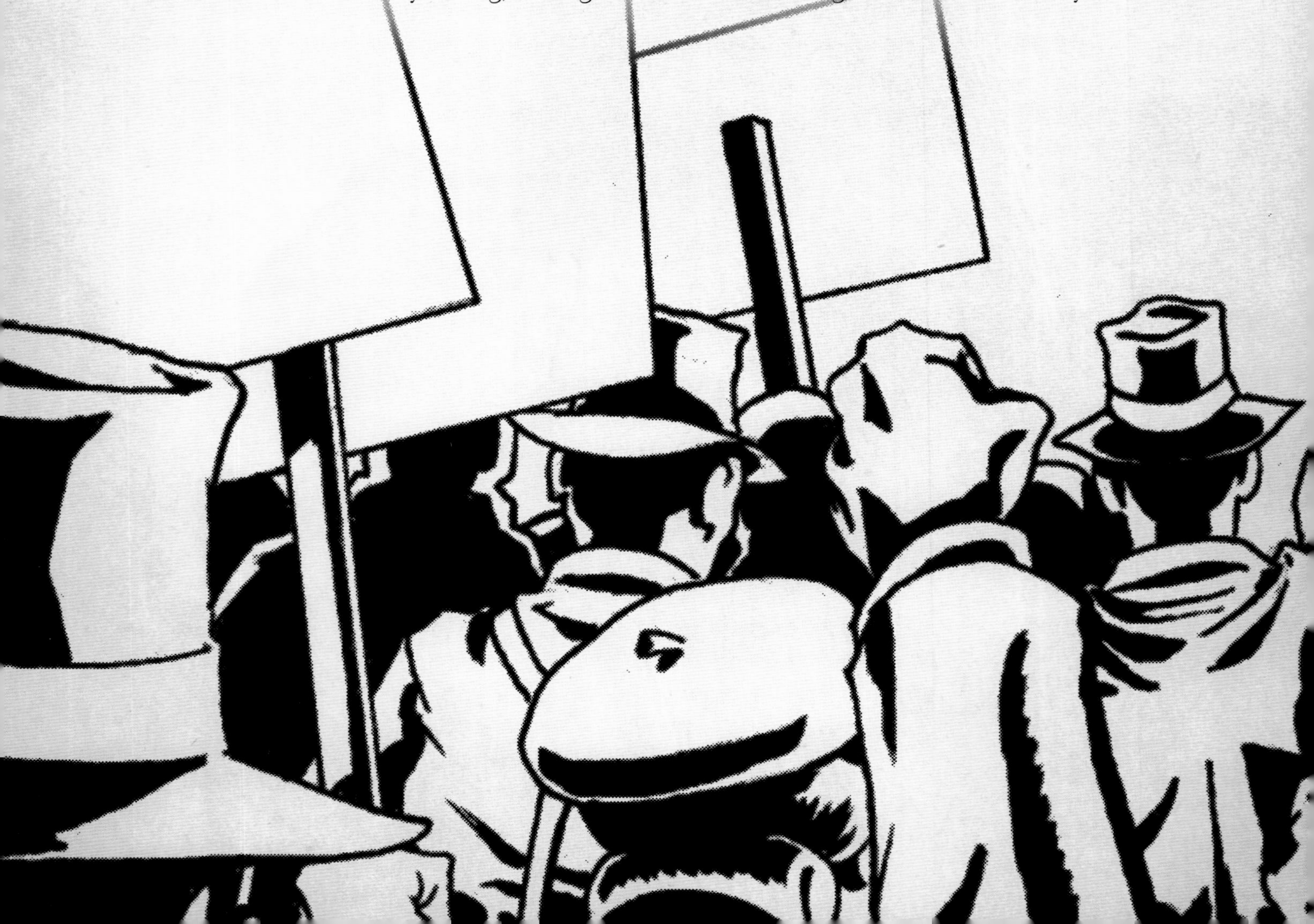

ight. He seemed like a pleasant fellow and talked ratio- ally.

"Shit," the captain muttered.

Outside was a sizable crowd of people, at least three undred or so, the cops at the window estimated. They vere black and white and there were plenty of them olding signs that ranged from wording like "EQUAL REATMENT" and "MORE NEGRO POLICE" to "STOP OLICE ABUSE" and "AIN'T I A MAN TOO?" Some of hem walked back and forth hoisting their placards and ome stood and talked to each other. Several looked up t the precinct house. Suzi Bahn, Irwin Silver, and Cliff Murphy stood together, Murphy smoking a cigarette. tef Rawls was one of the ones walking in a circle with a ign. Hers read: "JAIL KILLER COPS."

"That's an illegal formation," the captain said, having ecovered his calm, turning toward Hanks and Jefferson. I have the right to disperse such an assembly."

"Then go ahead and deploy your officers to break them up," Hanks challenged. "There's a few reporters out there too, and not just from the *Lenox Graphic*."

The captain ground his teeth, the muscles in his jaw pulsing. He glared at one of his officers. "Process Jefferson's release and get him the hell out of here."

"Yes, sir," he said, walking off.

"This isn't over," Hanks said. "I will be bringing charges against Officer Helmond and you for letting this barbarity occur."

The captain pointed toward the station house's double doors. "Bring your goddamn charges. I will not tolerate anarchy, Miss Lawyer. There's several reds out there known to us and we know how they love to feed on the plight of the poor ol' put-upon negro to advance their anti-American agenda."

"We'll be waiting right here, captain," Hanks said.

With a guttural sound in his throat, the captain also walked off.

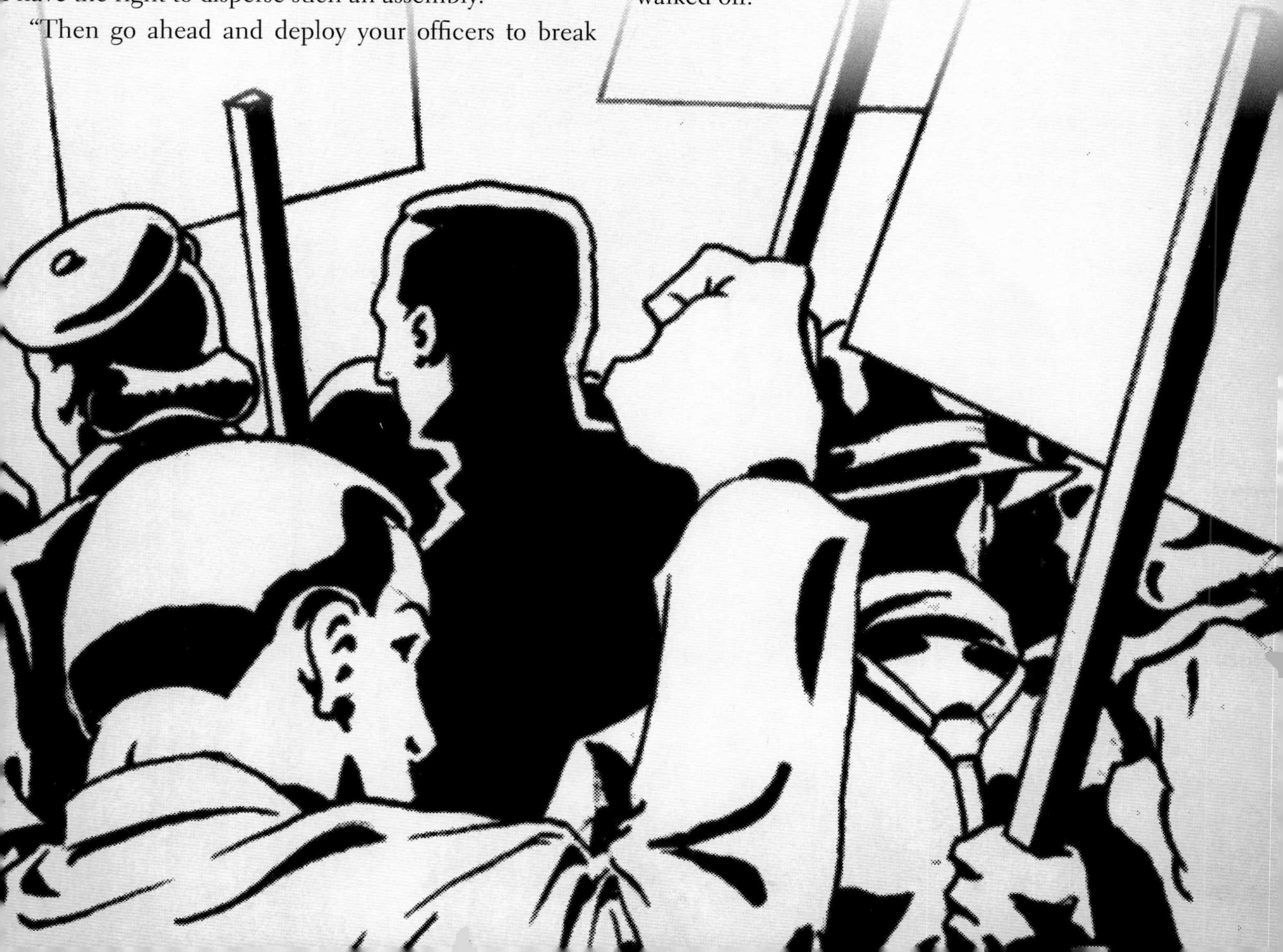

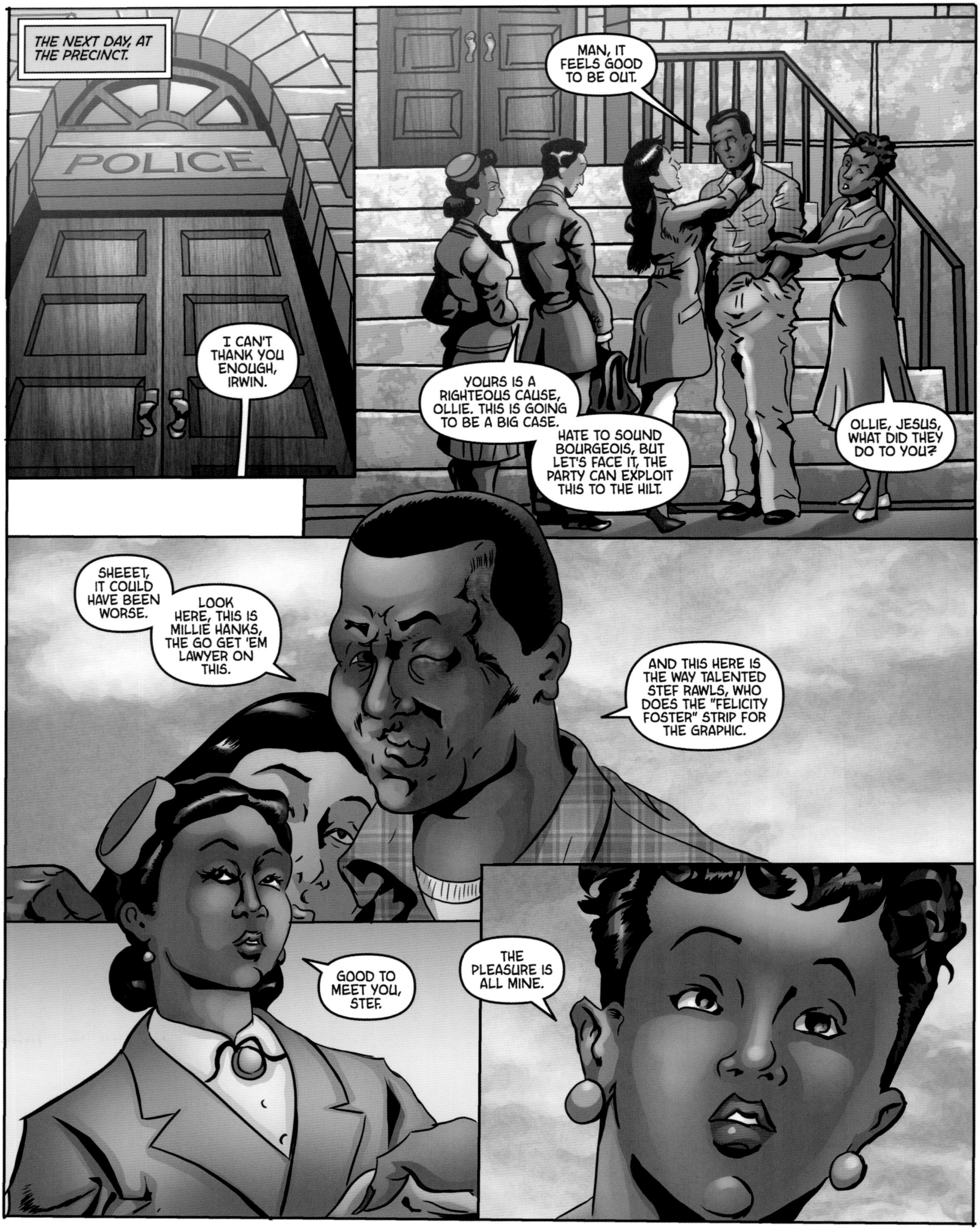
THE NEXT DAY, AT THE PRECINCT.
POLICE
I CAN'T THANK YOU ENOUGH, IRWIN.
MAN, IT FEELS GOOD TO BE OUT.
YOURS IS A RIGHTEOUS CAUSE, OLLIE. THIS IS GOING TO BE A BIG CASE.
HATE TO SOUND BOURGEOIS, BUT LET'S FACE IT, THE PARTY CAN EXPLOIT THIS TO THE HILT.
OLLIE, JESUS, WHAT DID THEY DO TO YOU?
SHEEET, IT COULD HAVE BEEN WORSE.
LOOK HERE, THIS IS MILLIE HANKS, THE GO GET 'EM LAWYER ON THIS.
AND THIS HERE IS THE WAY TALENTED STEF RAWLS, WHO DOES THE "FELICITY FOSTER" STRIP FOR THE GRAPHIC.
GOOD TO MEET YOU, STEF.
THE PLEASURE IS ALL MINE.

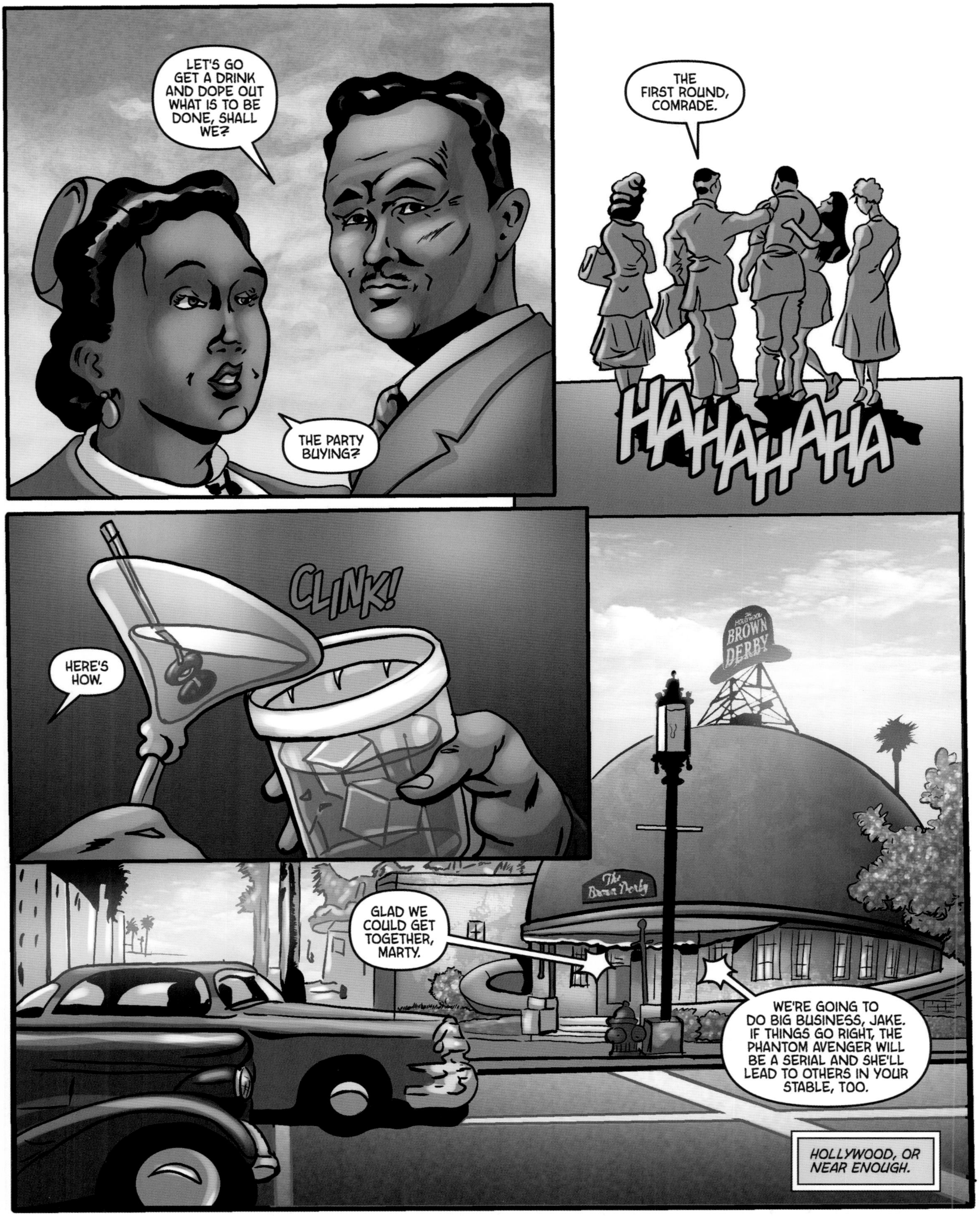

LET'S GO GET A DRINK AND DOPE OUT WHAT IS TO BE DONE, SHALL WE?
THE PARTY BUYING?
THE FIRST ROUND, COMRADE.
HAHAHAHAHA
CLINK!
HERE'S HOW.
BROWN DERBY
HOLLYWOOD, OR NEAR ENOUGH.
GLAD WE COULD GET TOGETHER, MARTY.
WE'RE GOING TO DO BIG BUSINESS, JAKE. IF THINGS GO RIGHT, THE PHANTOM AVENGER WILL BE A SERIAL AND SHE'LL LEAD TO OTHERS IN YOUR STABLE, TOO.

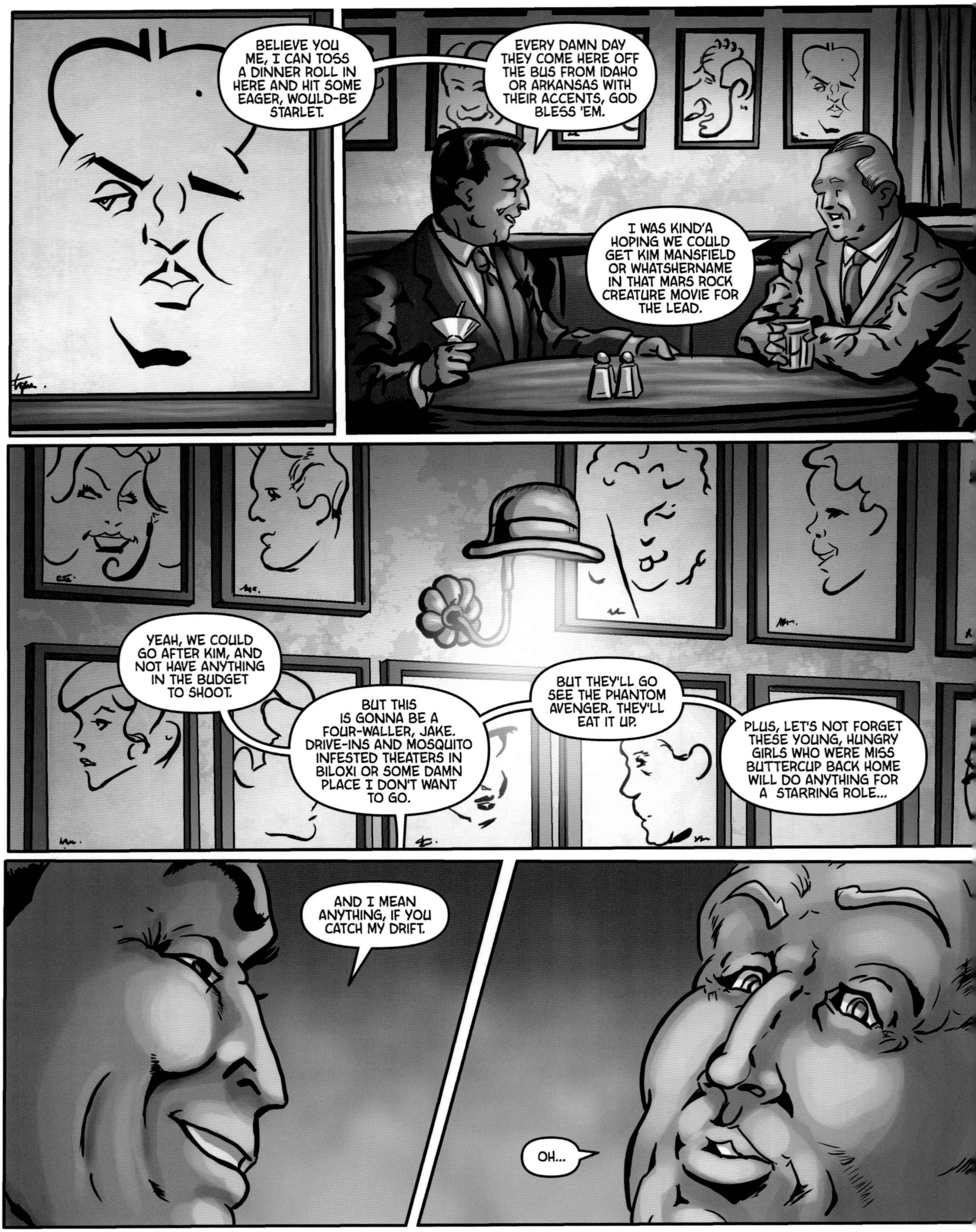
BELIEVE YOU ME, I CAN TOSS A DINNER ROLL IN HERE AND HIT SOME EAGER, WOULD-BE STARLET.
EVERY DAMN DAY THEY COME HERE OFF THE BUS FROM IDAHO OR ARKANSAS WITH THEIR ACCENTS, GOD BLESS 'EM.
I WAS KIND'A HOPING WE COULD GET KIM MANSFIELD OR WHATSHERNAME IN THAT MARS ROCK CREATURE MOVIE FOR THE LEAD.
YEAH, WE COULD GO AFTER KIM, AND NOT HAVE ANYTHING IN THE BUDGET TO SHOOT.
BUT THIS IS GONNA BE A FOUR-WALLER, JAKE. DRIVE-INS AND MOSQUITO INFESTED THEATERS IN BILOXI OR SOME DAMN PLACE I DON'T WANT TO GO.
BUT THEY'LL GO SEE THE PHANTOM AVENGER. THEY'LL EAT IT UP.
PLUS, LET'S NOT FORGET THESE YOUNG, HUNGRY GIRLS WHO WERE MISS BUTTERCUP BACK HOME WILL DO ANYTHING FOR A STARRING ROLE...
AND I MEAN ANYTHING, IF YOU CATCH MY DRIFT.
OH...

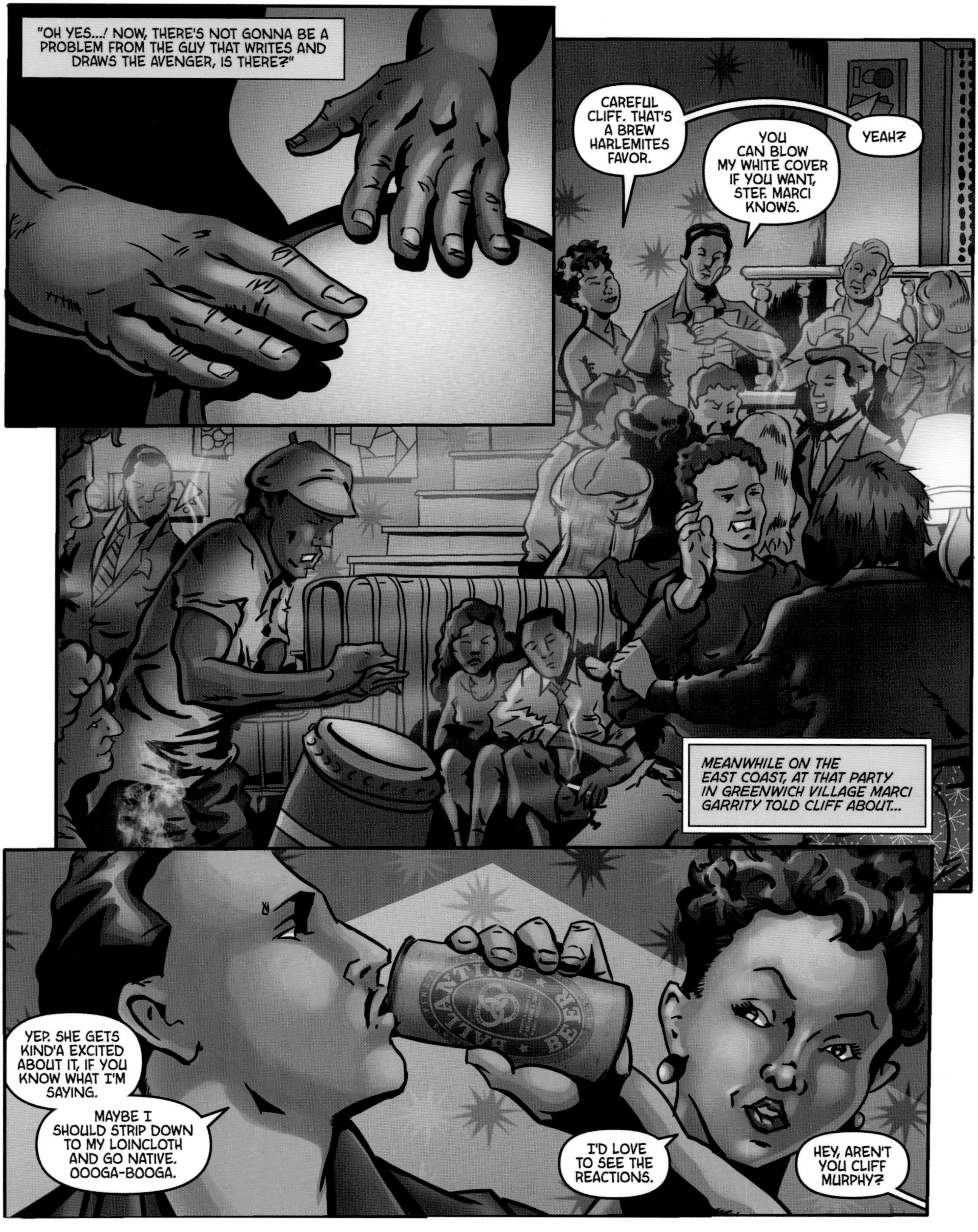
"OH YES...! NOW, THERE'S NOT GONNA BE A PROBLEM FROM THE GUY THAT WRITES AND DRAWS THE AVENGER, IS THERE?"
CAREFUL CLIFF. THAT'S A BREW HARLEMITES FAVOR.
YOU CAN BLOW MY WHITE COVER IF YOU WANT, STEF. MARCI KNOWS.
YEAH?
MEANWHILE ON THE EAST COAST, AT THAT PARTY IN GREENWICH VILLAGE MARCI GARRITY TOLD CLIFF ABOUT...
YEP. SHE GETS KIND'A EXCITED ABOUT IT, IF YOU KNOW WHAT I'M SAYING.
MAYBE I SHOULD STRIP DOWN TO MY LOINCLOTH AND GO NATIVE. OOOGA-BOOGA.
I'D LOVE TO SEE THE REACTIONS.
HEY, AREN'T YOU CLIFF MURPHY?

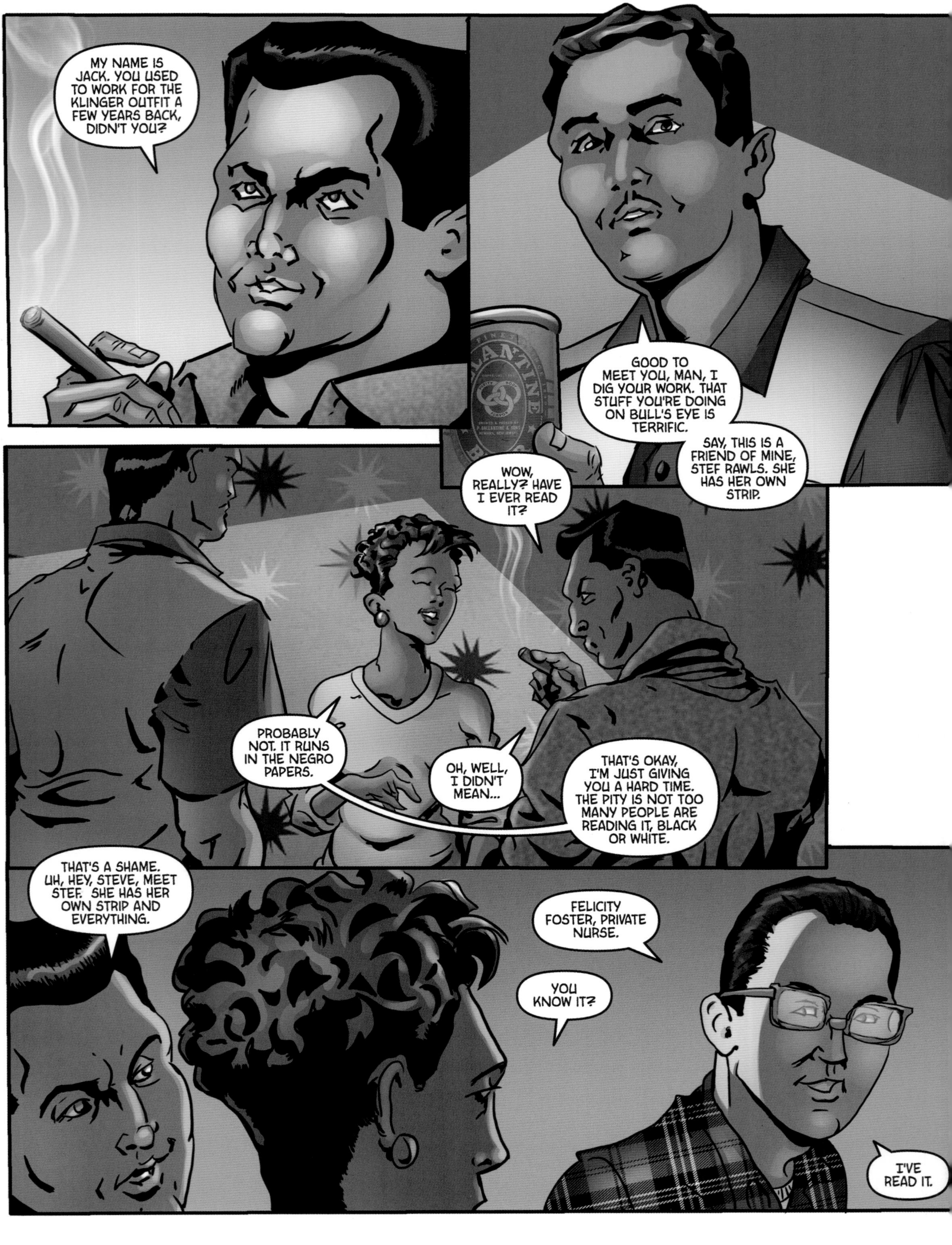
MY NAME IS JACK. YOU USED TO WORK FOR THE KLINGER OUTFIT A FEW YEARS BACK, DIDN'T YOU?
GOOD TO MEET YOU, MAN, I DIG YOUR WORK. THAT STUFF YOU'RE DOING ON BULL'S EYE IS TERRIFIC.
SAY, THIS IS A FRIEND OF MINE, STEF RAWLS. SHE HAS HER OWN STRIP.
WOW, REALLY? HAVE I EVER READ IT?
PROBABLY NOT. IT RUNS IN THE NEGRO PAPERS.
OH, WELL, I DIDN'T MEAN...
THAT'S OKAY, I'M JUST GIVING YOU A HARD TIME. THE PITY IS NOT TOO MANY PEOPLE ARE READING IT, BLACK OR WHITE.
THAT'S A SHAME. UH, HEY, STEVE, MEET STEF. SHE HAS HER OWN STRIP AND EVERYTHING.
FELICITY FOSTER, PRIVATE NURSE.
YOU KNOW IT?
I'VE READ IT.

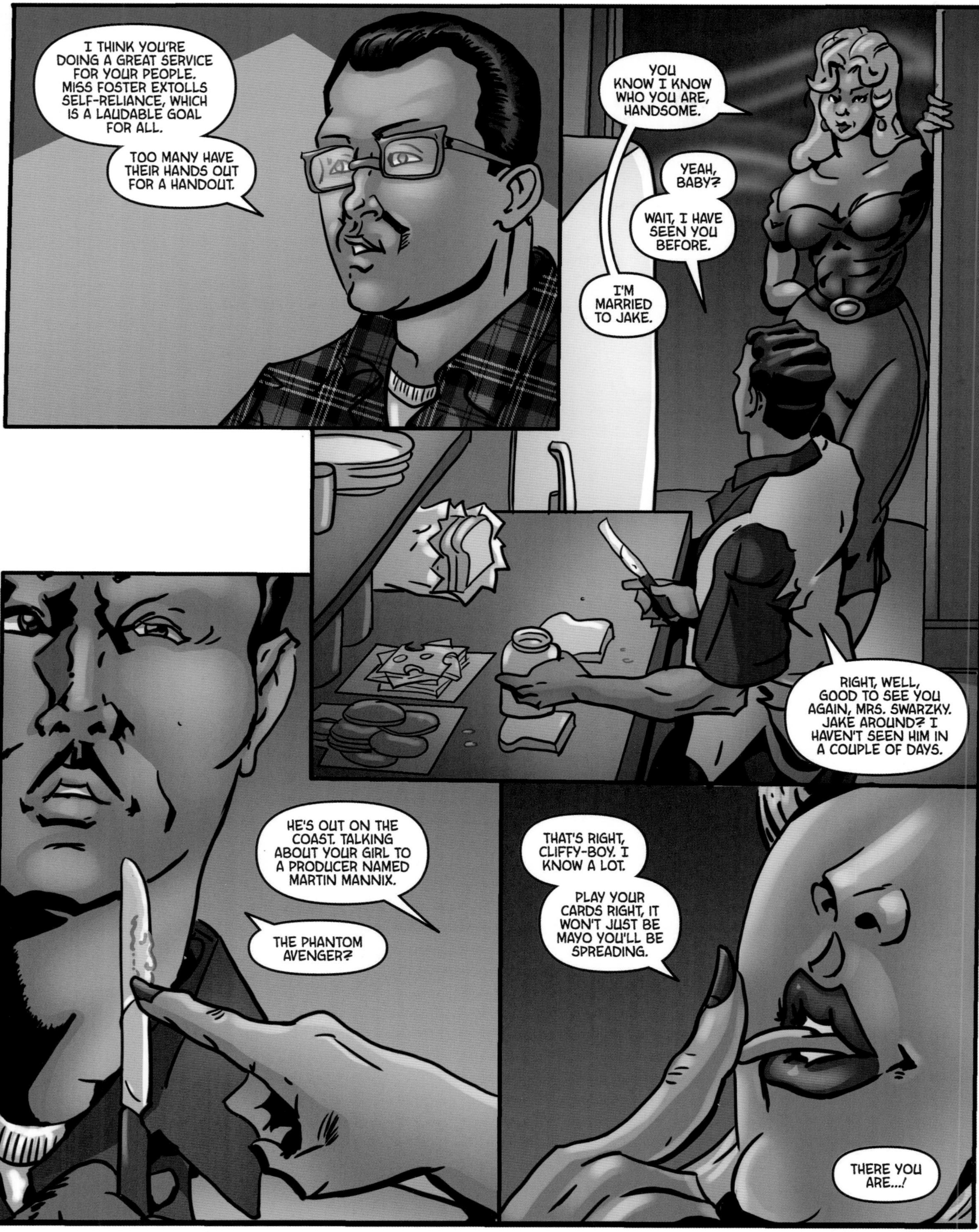
I THINK YOU'RE DOING A GREAT SERVICE FOR YOUR PEOPLE. MISS FOSTER EXTOLLS SELF-RELIANCE, WHICH IS A LAUDABLE GOAL FOR ALL.
TOO MANY HAVE THEIR HANDS OUT FOR A HANDOUT.
YOU KNOW I KNOW WHO YOU ARE, HANDSOME.
YEAH, BABY?
WAIT, I HAVE SEEN YOU BEFORE.
I'M MARRIED TO JAKE.
RIGHT, WELL, GOOD TO SEE YOU AGAIN, MRS. SWARZKY. JAKE AROUND? I HAVEN'T SEEN HIM IN A COUPLE OF DAYS.
HE'S OUT ON THE COAST. TALKING ABOUT YOUR GIRL TO A PRODUCER NAMED MARTIN MANNIX.
THE PHANTOM AVENGER?
THAT'S RIGHT, CLIFFY-BOY. I KNOW A LOT.
PLAY YOUR CARDS RIGHT, IT WON'T JUST BE MAYO YOU'LL BE SPREADING.
THERE YOU ARE...!

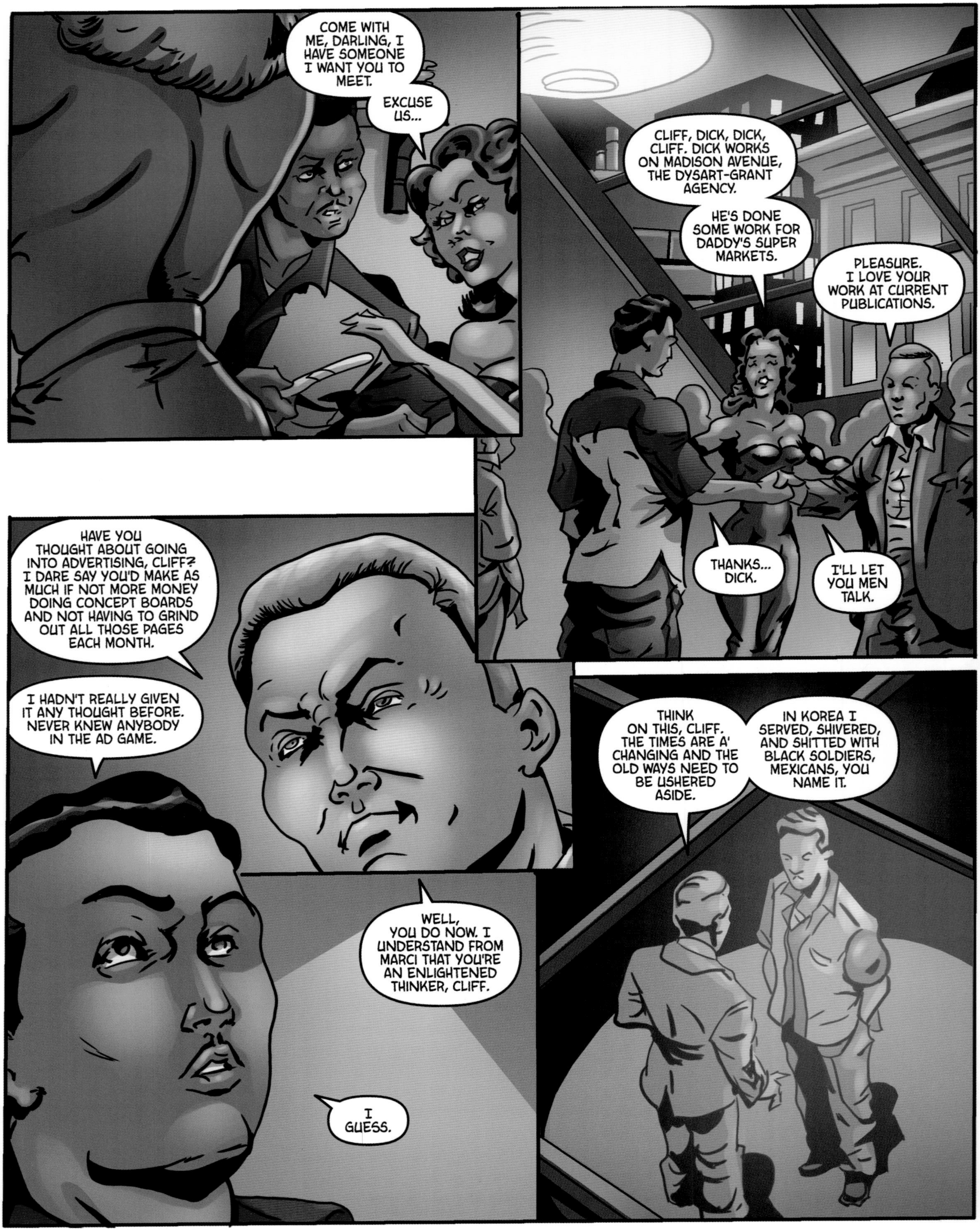
COME WITH ME, DARLING, I HAVE SOMEONE I WANT YOU TO MEET.
EXCUSE US...
CLIFF, DICK, DICK, CLIFF. DICK WORKS ON MADISON AVENUE, THE DYSART-GRANT AGENCY.
HE'S DONE SOME WORK FOR DADDY'S SUPER MARKETS.
PLEASURE. I LOVE YOUR WORK AT CURRENT PUBLICATIONS.
THANKS... DICK.
I'LL LET YOU MEN TALK.
HAVE YOU THOUGHT ABOUT GOING INTO ADVERTISING, CLIFF? I DARE SAY YOU'D MAKE AS MUCH IF NOT MORE MONEY DOING CONCEPT BOARDS AND NOT HAVING TO GRIND OUT ALL THOSE PAGES EACH MONTH.
I HADN'T REALLY GIVEN IT ANY THOUGHT BEFORE. NEVER KNEW ANYBODY IN THE AD GAME.
WELL, YOU DO NOW. I UNDERSTAND FROM MARCI THAT YOU'RE AN ENLIGHTENED THINKER, CLIFF.
I GUESS.
THINK ON THIS, CLIFF. THE TIMES ARE A' CHANGING AND THE OLD WAYS NEED TO BE USHERED ASIDE.
IN KOREA I SERVED, SHIVERED, AND SHITTED WITH BLACK SOLDIERS, MEXICANS, YOU NAME IT.

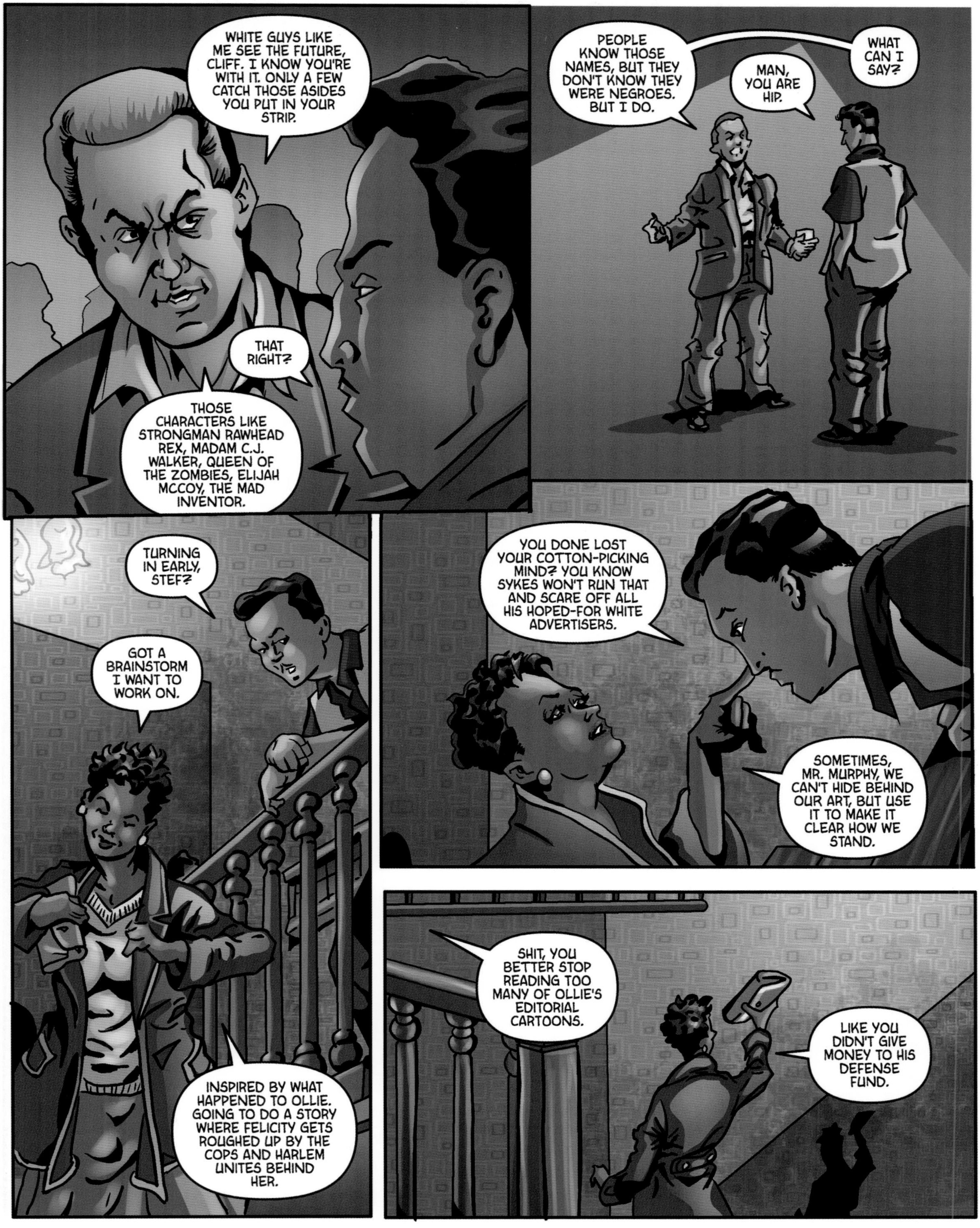
WHITE GUYS LIKE ME SEE THE FUTURE, CLIFF. I KNOW YOU'RE WITH IT. ONLY A FEW CATCH THOSE ASIDES YOU PUT IN YOUR STRIP.
THAT RIGHT?
THOSE CHARACTERS LIKE STRONGMAN RAWHEAD REX, MADAM C.J. WALKER, QUEEN OF THE ZOMBIES, ELIJAH MCCOY, THE MAD INVENTOR.
PEOPLE KNOW THOSE NAMES, BUT THEY DON'T KNOW THEY WERE NEGROES. BUT I DO.
MAN, YOU ARE HIP.
WHAT CAN I SAY?
TURNING IN EARLY, STEF?
GOT A BRAINSTORM I WANT TO WORK ON.
INSPIRED BY WHAT HAPPENED TO OLLIE. GOING TO DO A STORY WHERE FELICITY GETS ROUGHED UP BY THE COPS AND HARLEM UNITES BEHIND HER.
YOU DONE LOST YOUR COTTON-PICKING MIND? YOU KNOW SYKES WON'T RUN THAT AND SCARE OFF ALL HIS HOPED-FOR WHITE ADVERTISERS.
SOMETIMES, MR. MURPHY, WE CAN'T HIDE BEHIND OUR ART, BUT USE IT TO MAKE IT CLEAR HOW WE STAND.
SHIT, YOU BETTER STOP READING TOO MANY OF OLLIE'S EDITORIAL CARTOONS.
LIKE YOU DIDN'T GIVE MONEY TO HIS DEFENSE FUND.

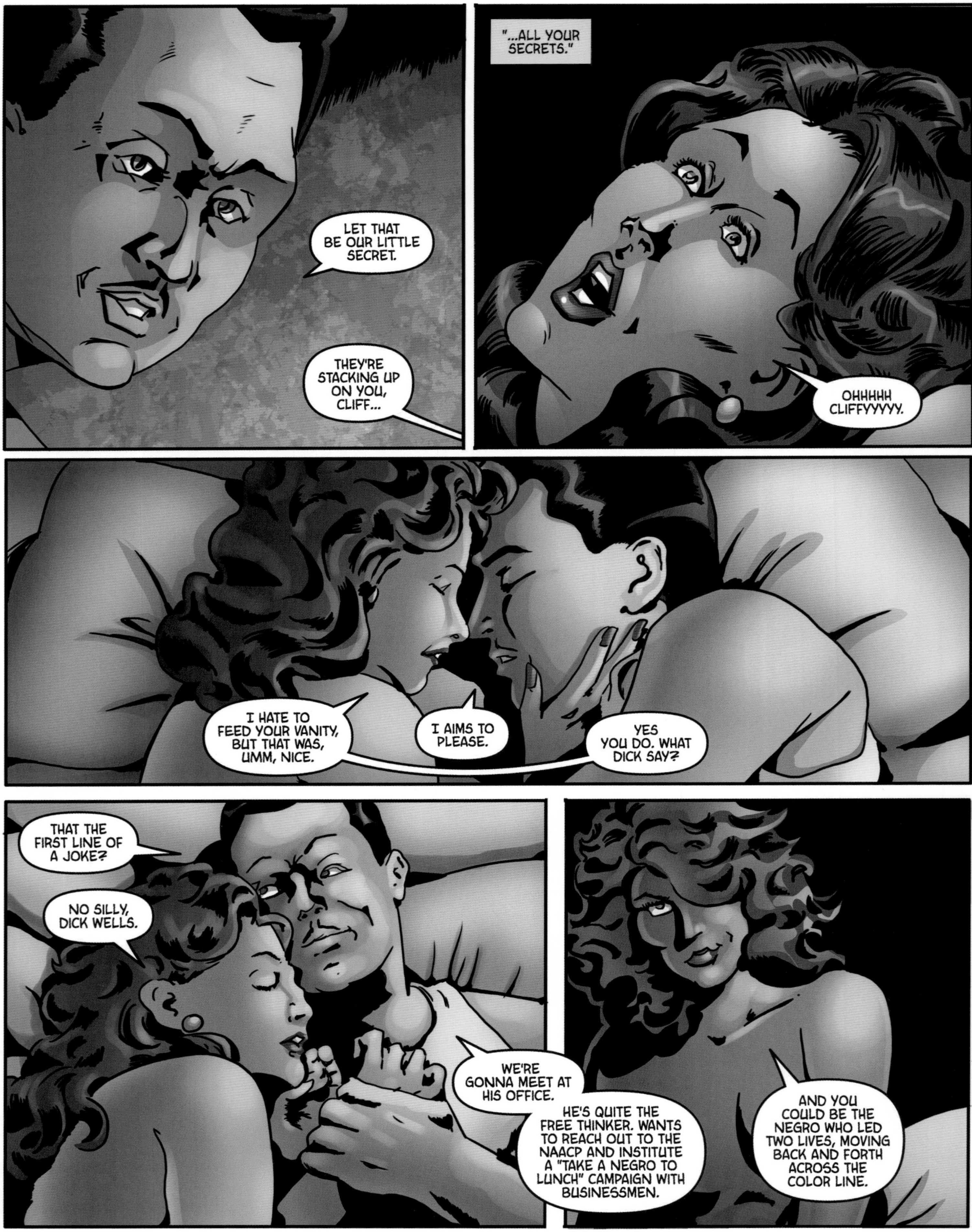
LET THAT BE OUR LITTLE SECRET.
THEY'RE STACKING UP ON YOU, CLIFF...
"...ALL YOUR SECRETS."
OHHHHH CLIFFYYYYY.
I HATE TO FEED YOUR VANITY, BUT THAT WAS, UMM, NICE.
I AIMS TO PLEASE.
YES YOU DO. WHAT DICK SAY?
THAT THE FIRST LINE OF A JOKE?
NO SILLY, DICK WELLS.
WE'RE GONNA MEET AT HIS OFFICE.
HE'S QUITE THE FREE THINKER. WANTS TO REACH OUT TO THE NAACP AND INSTITUTE A "TAKE A NEGRO TO LUNCH" CAMPAIGN WITH BUSINESSMEN.
AND YOU COULD BE THE NEGRO WHO LED TWO LIVES, MOVING BACK AND FORTH ACROSS THE COLOR LINE.

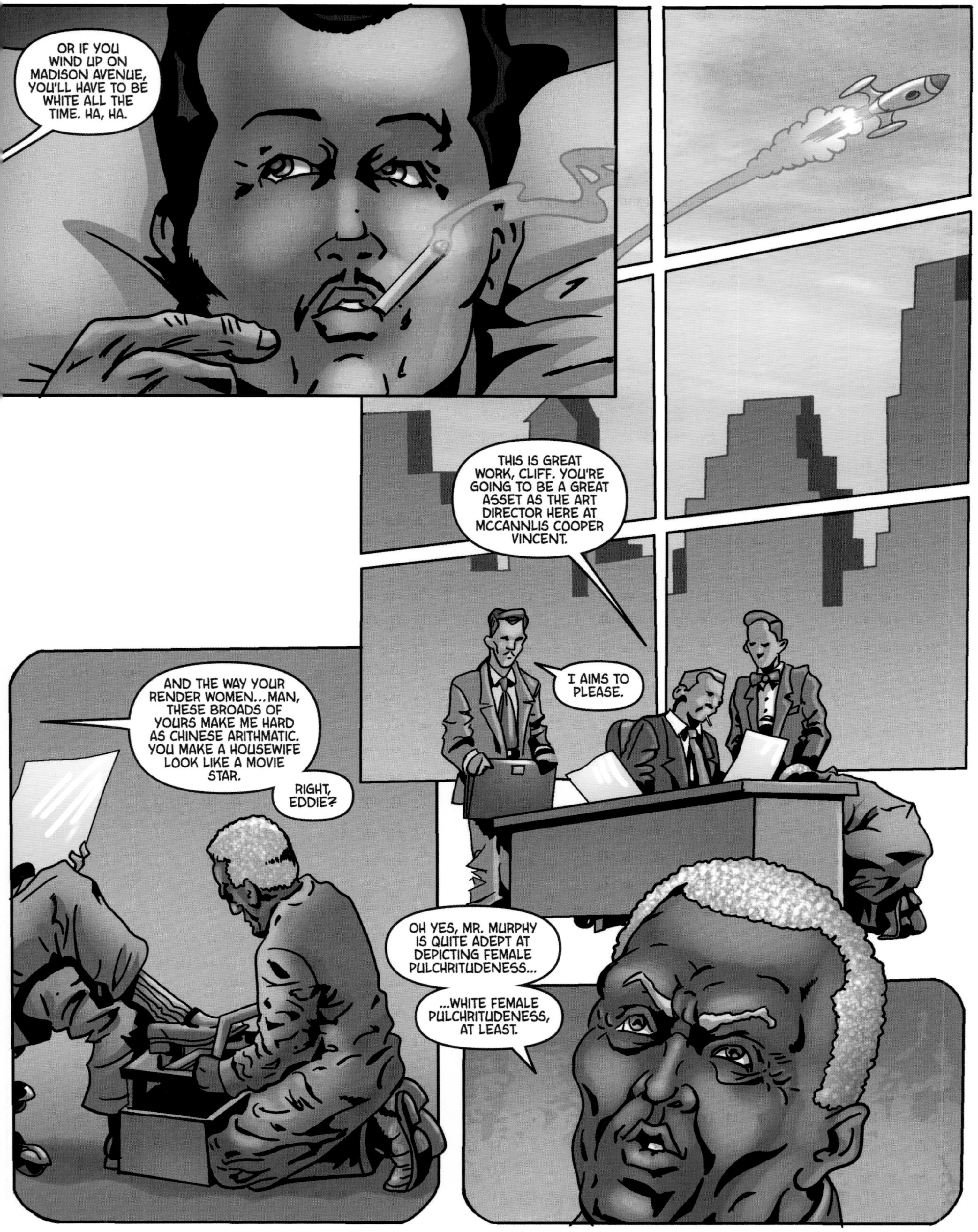
OR IF YOU WIND UP ON MADISON AVENUE, YOU'LL HAVE TO BE WHITE ALL THE TIME. HA, HA.
THIS IS GREAT WORK, CLIFF. YOU'RE GOING TO BE A GREAT ASSET AS THE ART DIRECTOR HERE AT MCCANNLIS COOPER VINCENT.
I AIMS TO PLEASE.
AND THE WAY YOUR RENDER WOMEN...MAN, THESE BROADS OF YOURS MAKE ME HARD AS CHINESE ARITHMATIC. YOU MAKE A HOUSEWIFE LOOK LIKE A MOVIE STAR.
RIGHT, EDDIE?
OH YES, MR. MURPHY IS QUITE ADEPT AT DEPICTING FEMALE PULCHRITUDENESS...
...WHITE FEMALE PULCHRITUDENESS, AT LEAST.

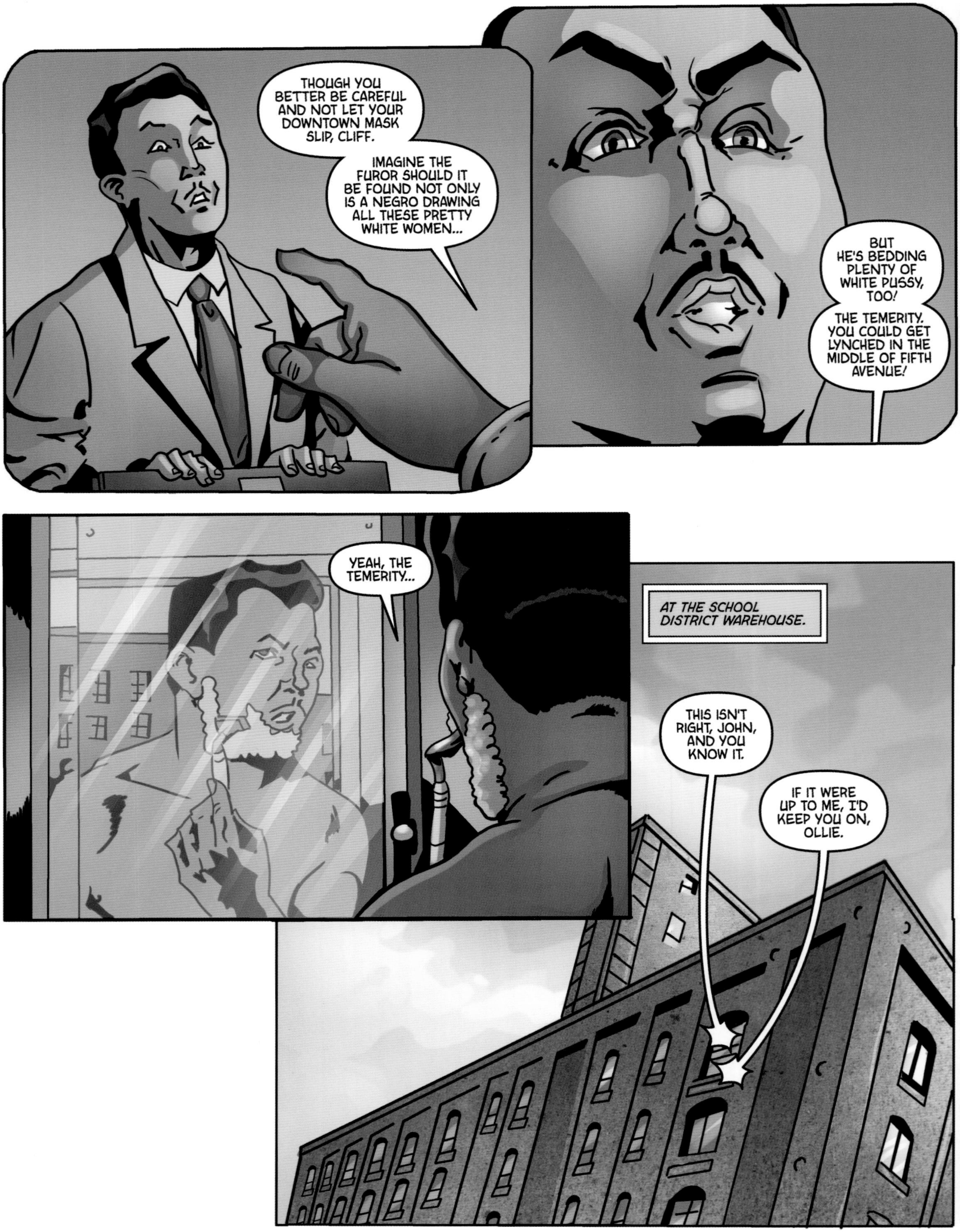
THOUGH YOU BETTER BE CAREFUL AND NOT LET YOUR DOWNTOWN MASK SLIP, CLIFF.
IMAGINE THE FUROR SHOULD IT BE FOUND NOT ONLY IS A NEGRO DRAWING ALL THESE PRETTY WHITE WOMEN...
BUT HE'S BEDDING PLENTY OF WHITE PUSSY, TOO!
THE TEMERITY. YOU COULD GET LYNCHED IN THE MIDDLE OF FIFTH AVENUE!
YEAH, THE TEMERITY...
AT THE SCHOOL DISTRICT WAREHOUSE.
THIS ISN'T RIGHT, JOHN, AND YOU KNOW IT.
IF IT WERE UP TO ME, I'D KEEP YOU ON, OLLIE.

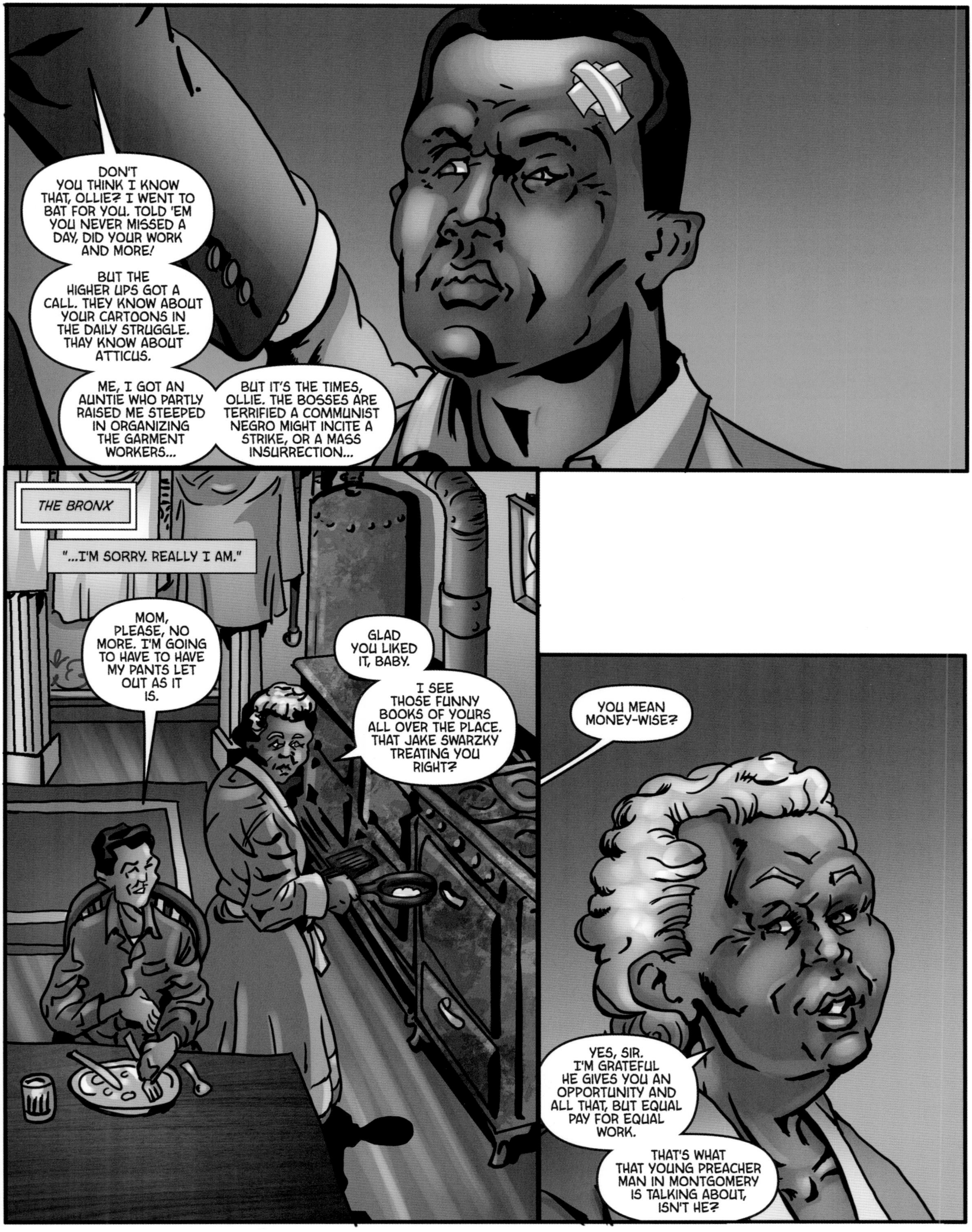
DON'T YOU THINK I KNOW THAT, OLLIE? I WENT TO BAT FOR YOU. TOLD 'EM YOU NEVER MISSED A DAY, DID YOUR WORK AND MORE!
BUT THE HIGHER UPS GOT A CALL. THEY KNOW ABOUT YOUR CARTOONS IN THE DAILY STRUGGLE. THAY KNOW ABOUT ATTICUS.
ME, I GOT AN AUNTIE WHO PARTLY RAISED ME STEEPED IN ORGANIZING THE GARMENT WORKERS...
BUT IT'S THE TIMES, OLLIE. THE BOSSES ARE TERRIFIED A COMMUNIST NEGRO MIGHT INCITE A STRIKE, OR A MASS INSURRECTION...
THE BRONX
"...I'M SORRY. REALLY I AM."
MOM, PLEASE, NO MORE. I'M GOING TO HAVE TO HAVE MY PANTS LET OUT AS IT IS.
GLAD YOU LIKED IT, BABY.
I SEE THOSE FUNNY BOOKS OF YOURS ALL OVER THE PLACE. THAT JAKE SWARZKY TREATING YOU RIGHT?
YOU MEAN MONEY-WISE?
YES, SIR. I'M GRATEFUL HE GIVES YOU AN OPPORTUNITY AND ALL THAT, BUT EQUAL PAY FOR EQUAL WORK.
THAT'S WHAT THAT YOUNG PREACHER MAN IN MONTGOMERY IS TALKING ABOUT, ISN'T HE?

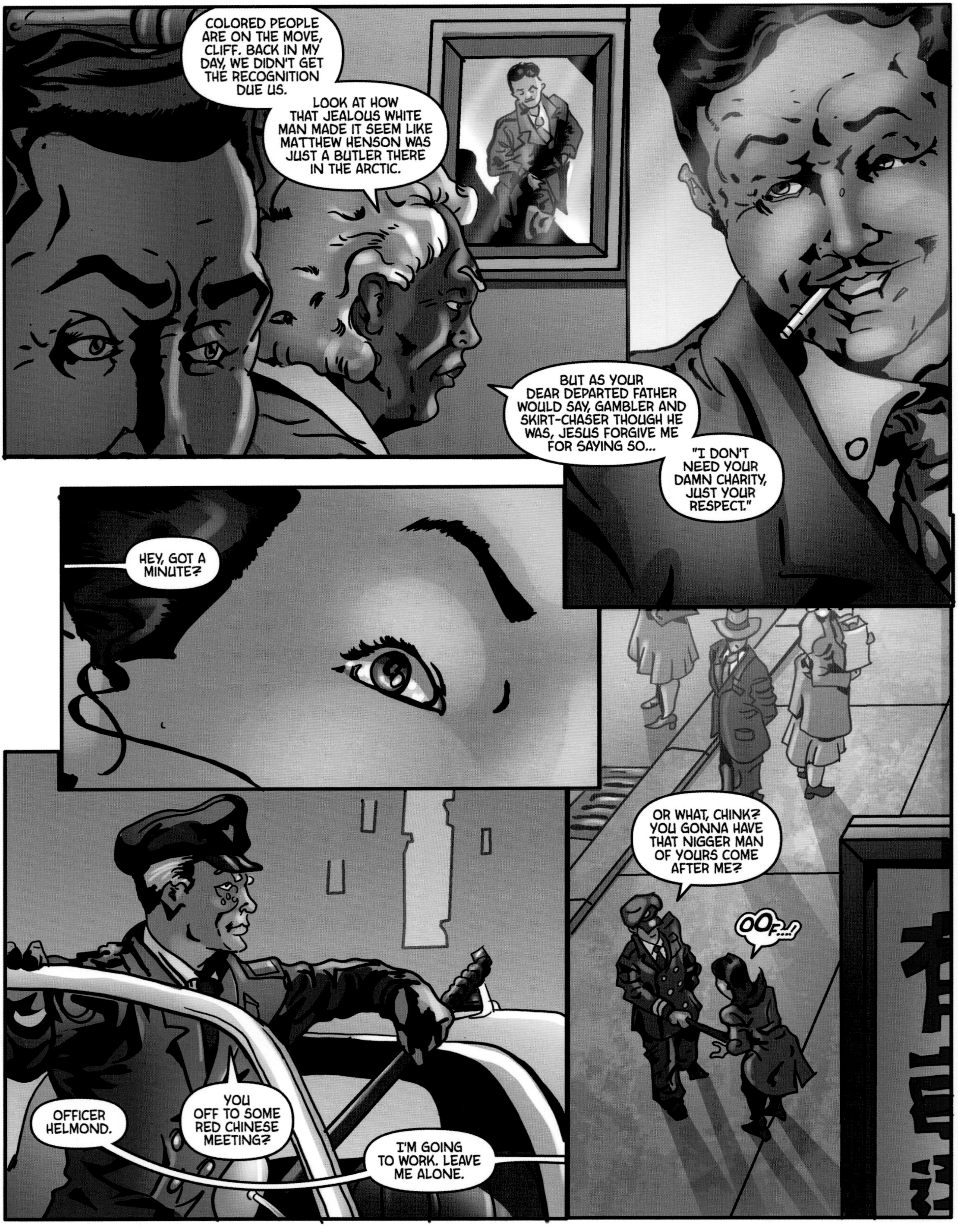

COLORED PEOPLE ARE ON THE MOVE, CLIFF. BACK IN MY DAY, WE DIDN'T GET THE RECOGNITION DUE US.
LOOK AT HOW THAT JEALOUS WHITE MAN MADE IT SEEM LIKE MATTHEW HENSON WAS JUST A BUTLER THERE IN THE ARCTIC.
BUT AS YOUR DEAR DEPARTED FATHER WOULD SAY, GAMBLER AND SKIRT-CHASER THOUGH HE WAS, JESUS FORGIVE ME FOR SAYING SO...
"I DON'T NEED YOUR DAMN CHARITY, JUST YOUR RESPECT."
HEY, GOT A MINUTE?
OFFICER HELMOND.
YOU OFF TO SOME RED CHINESE MEETING?
I'M GOING TO WORK. LEAVE ME ALONE.
OR WHAT, CHINK? YOU GONNA HAVE THAT NIGGER MAN OF YOURS COME AFTER ME?
OOF...!

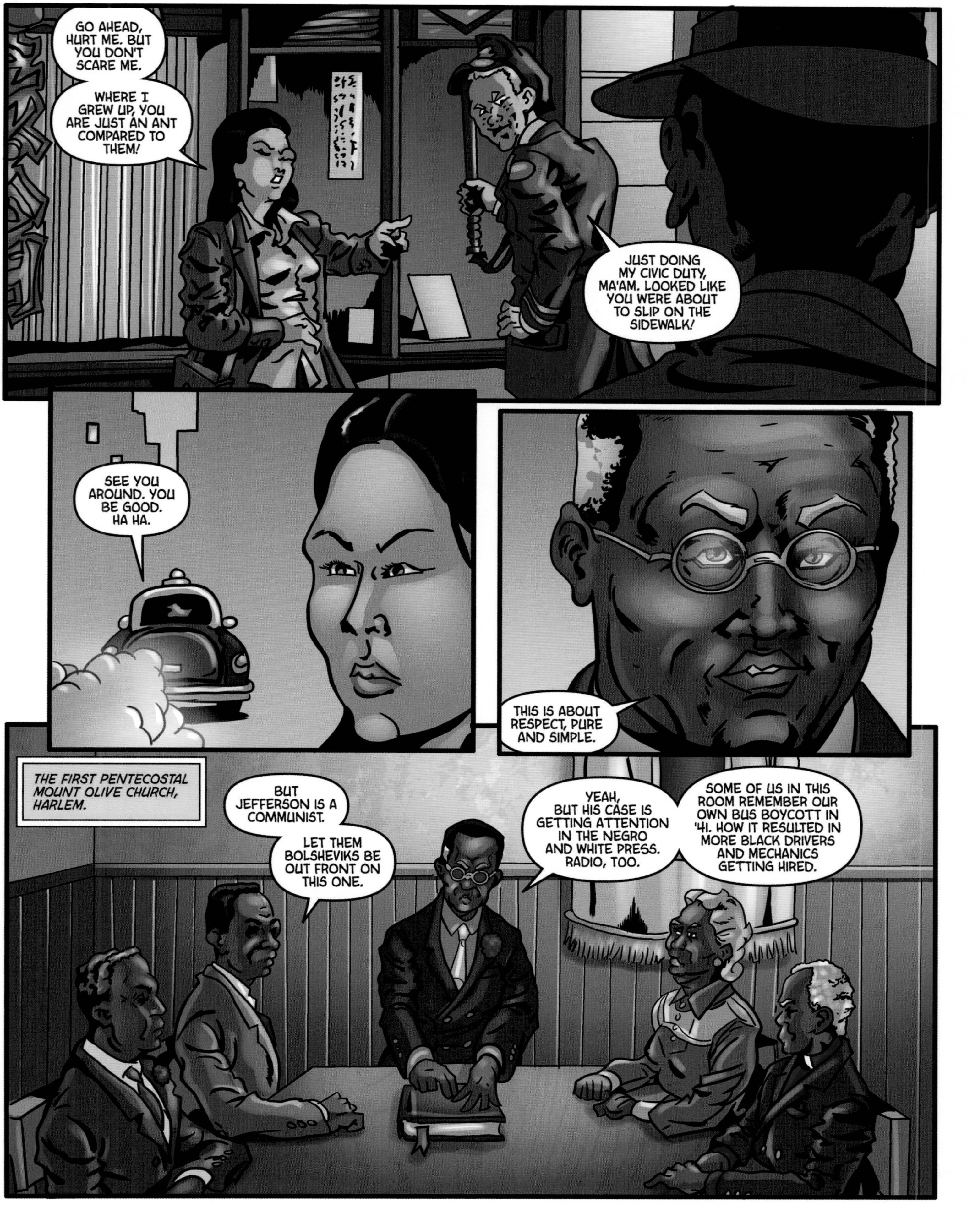
GO AHEAD, HURT ME. BUT YOU DON'T SCARE ME.
WHERE I GREW UP, YOU ARE JUST AN ANT COMPARED TO THEM!
JUST DOING MY CIVIC DUTY, MA'AM. LOOKED LIKE YOU WERE ABOUT TO SLIP ON THE SIDEWALK!
SEE YOU AROUND. YOU BE GOOD. HA HA.
THIS IS ABOUT RESPECT, PURE AND SIMPLE.
THE FIRST PENTECOSTAL MOUNT OLIVE CHURCH, HARLEM.
BUT JEFFERSON IS A COMMUNIST.
LET THEM BOLSHEVIKS BE OUT FRONT ON THIS ONE.
YEAH, BUT HIS CASE IS GETTING ATTENTION IN THE NEGRO AND WHITE PRESS. RADIO, TOO.
SOME OF US IN THIS ROOM REMEMBER OUR OWN BUS BOYCOTT IN '41. HOW IT RESULTED IN MORE BLACK DRIVERS AND MECHANICS GETTING HIRED.

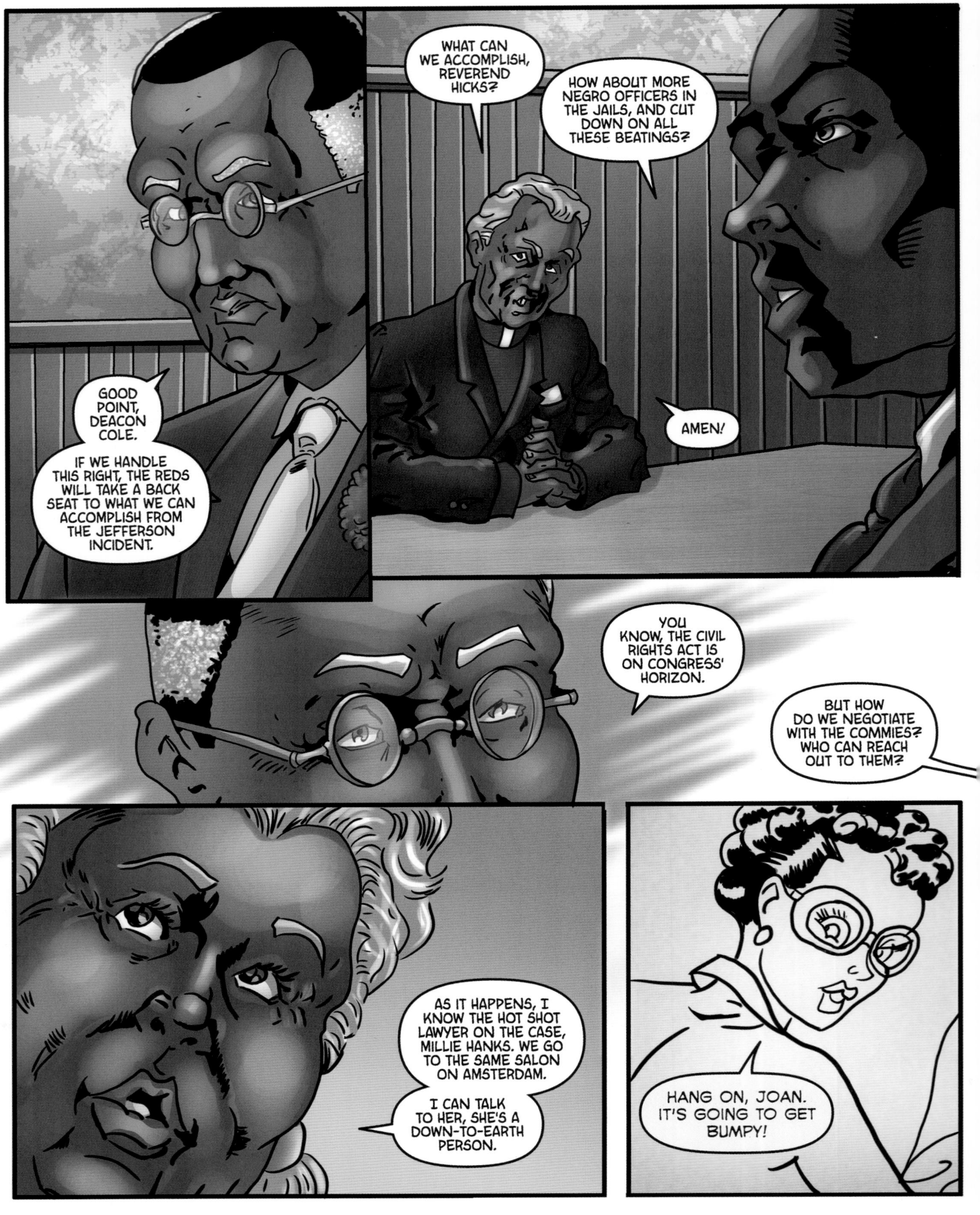
WHAT CAN WE ACCOMPLISH, REVEREND HICKS?
HOW ABOUT MORE NEGRO OFFICERS IN THE JAILS, AND CUT DOWN ON ALL THESE BEATINGS?
AMEN!
GOOD POINT, DEACON COLE.
IF WE HANDLE THIS RIGHT, THE REDS WILL TAKE A BACK SEAT TO WHAT WE CAN ACCOMPLISH FROM THE JEFFERSON INCIDENT.
YOU KNOW, THE CIVIL RIGHTS ACT IS ON CONGRESS' HORIZON.
BUT HOW DO WE NEGOTIATE WITH THE COMMIES? WHO CAN REACH OUT TO THEM?
AS IT HAPPENS, I KNOW THE HOT SHOT LAWYER ON THE CASE, MILLIE HANKS. WE GO TO THE SAME SALON ON AMSTERDAM.
I CAN TALK TO HER, SHE'S A DOWN-TO-EARTH PERSON.
HANG ON, JOAN. IT'S GOING TO GET BUMPY!

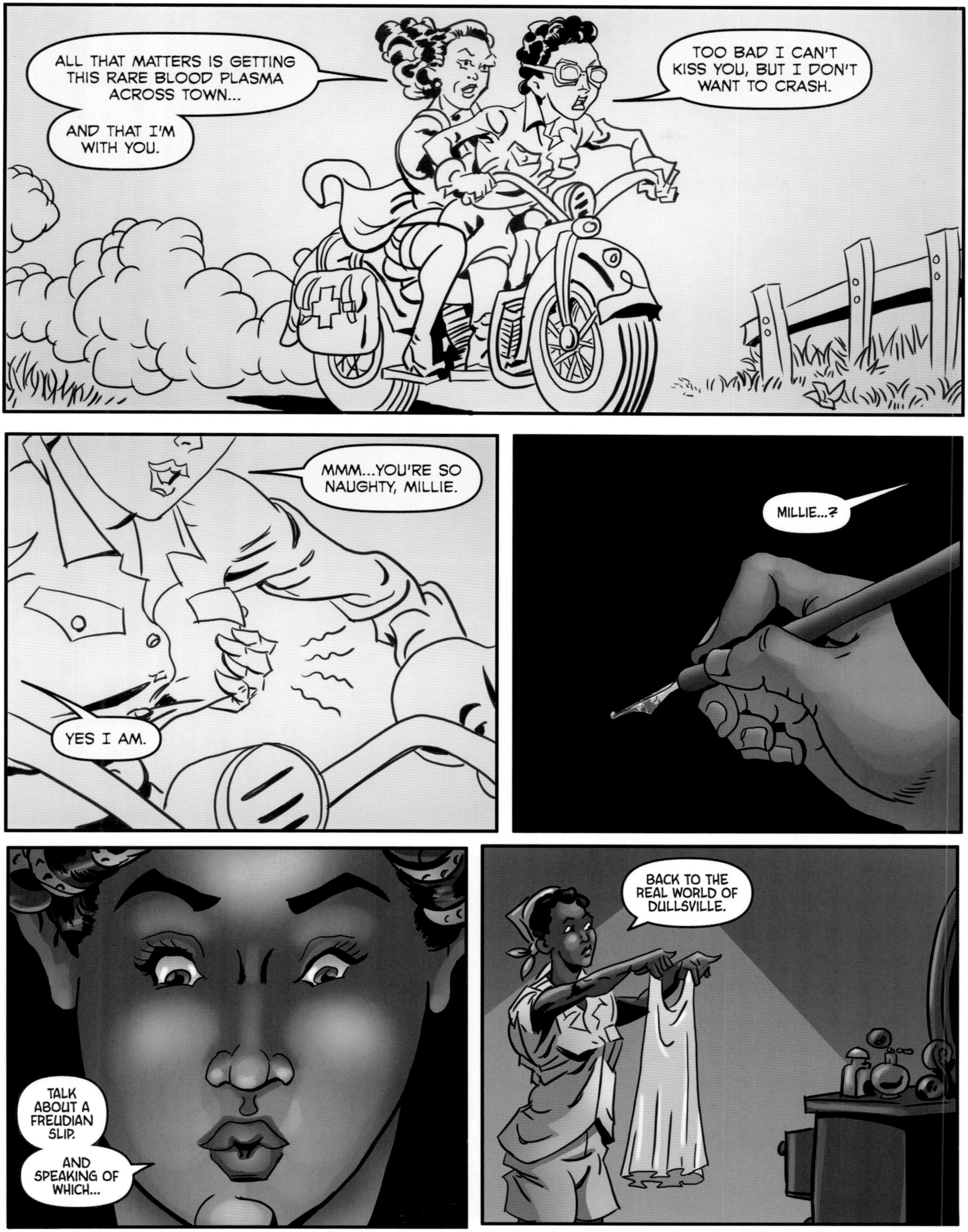
ALL THAT MATTERS IS GETTING THIS RARE BLOOD PLASMA ACROSS TOWN...
AND THAT I'M WITH YOU.
TOO BAD I CAN'T KISS YOU, BUT I DON'T WANT TO CRASH.
MMM...YOU'RE SO NAUGHTY, MILLIE.
YES I AM.
MILLIE...?
TALK ABOUT A FREUDIAN SLIP.
AND SPEAKING OF WHICH...
BACK TO THE REAL WORLD OF DULLSVILLE.

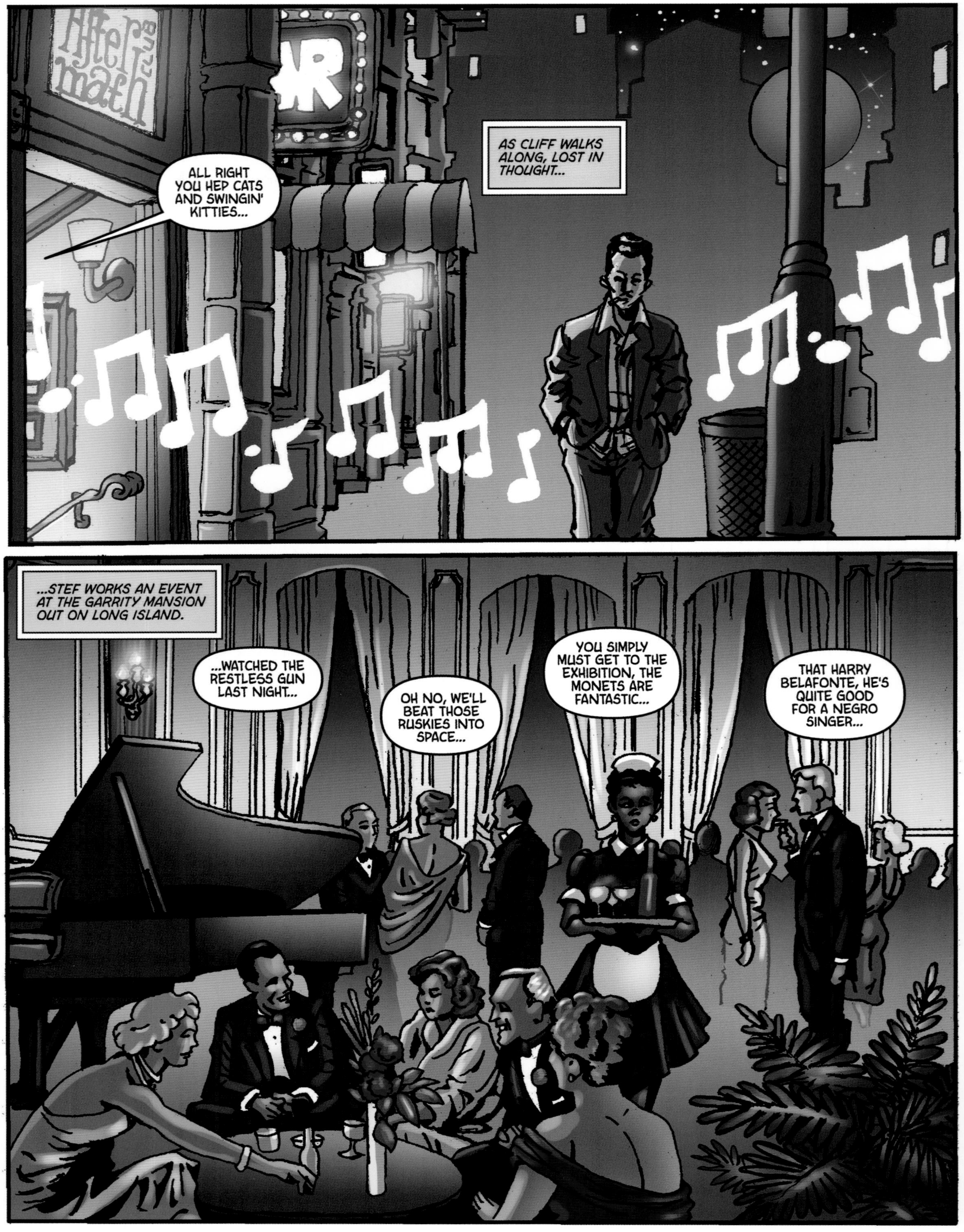

ALL RIGHT YOU HEP CATS AND SWINGIN' KITTIES...
AS CLIFF WALKS ALONG, LOST IN THOUGHT...
...STEF WORKS AN EVENT AT THE GARRITY MANSION OUT ON LONG ISLAND.
...WATCHED THE RESTLESS GUN LAST NIGHT...
OH NO, WE'LL BEAT THOSE RUSKIES INTO SPACE...
YOU SIMPLY MUST GET TO THE EXHIBITION, THE MONETS ARE FANTASTIC...
THAT HARRY BELAFONTE, HE'S QUITE GOOD FOR A NEGRO SINGER...

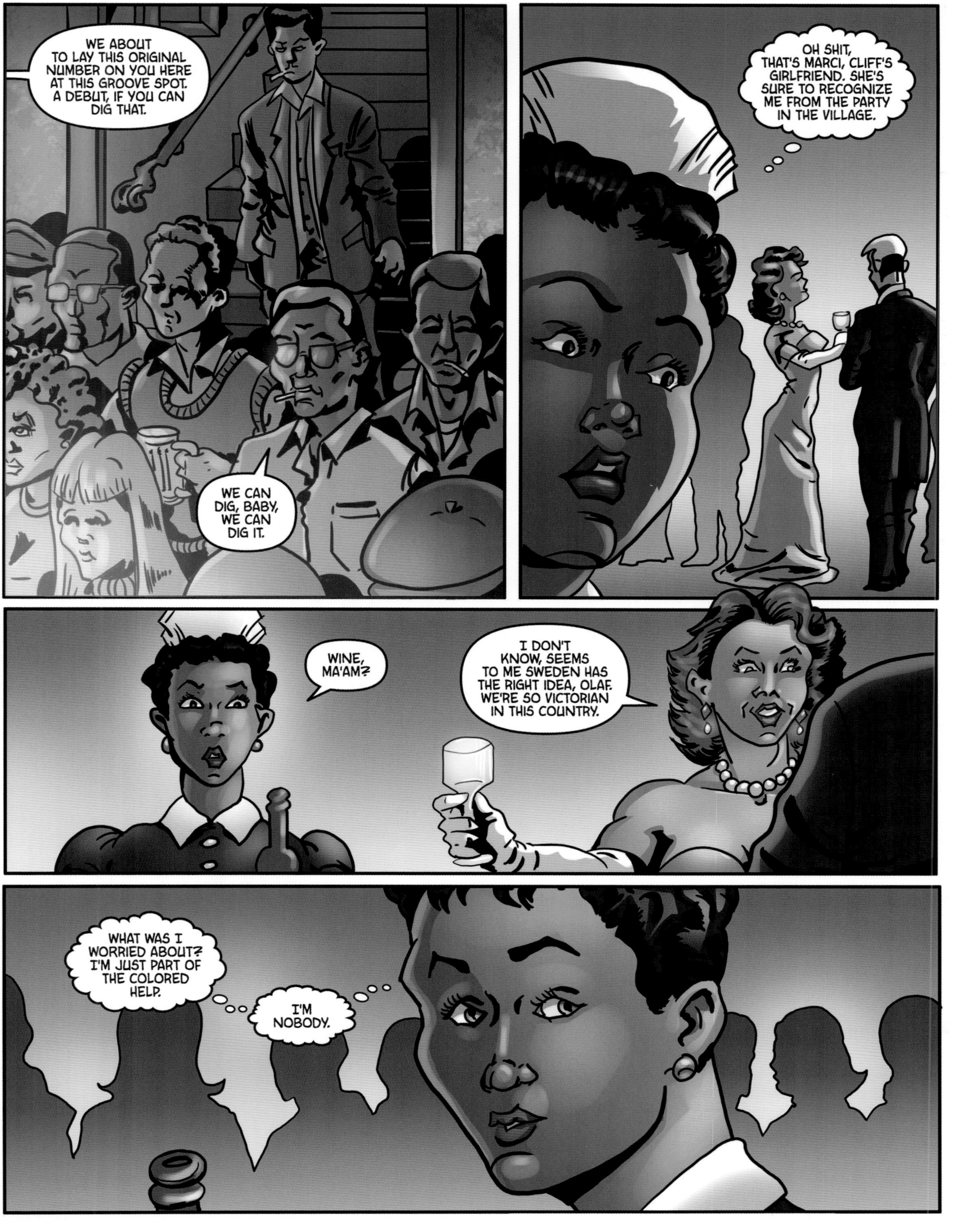
WE ABOUT TO LAY THIS ORIGINAL NUMBER ON YOU HERE AT THIS GROOVE SPOT. A DEBUT, IF YOU CAN DIG THAT.
WE CAN DIG, BABY, WE CAN DIG IT.
OH SHIT, THAT'S MARCI, CLIFF'S GIRLFRIEND. SHE'S SURE TO RECOGNIZE ME FROM THE PARTY IN THE VILLAGE.
WINE, MA'AM?
I DON'T KNOW, SEEMS TO ME SWEDEN HAS THE RIGHT IDEA, OLAF. WE'RE SO VICTORIAN IN THIS COUNTRY.
WHAT WAS I WORRIED ABOUT? I'M JUST PART OF THE COLORED HELP.
I'M NOBODY.

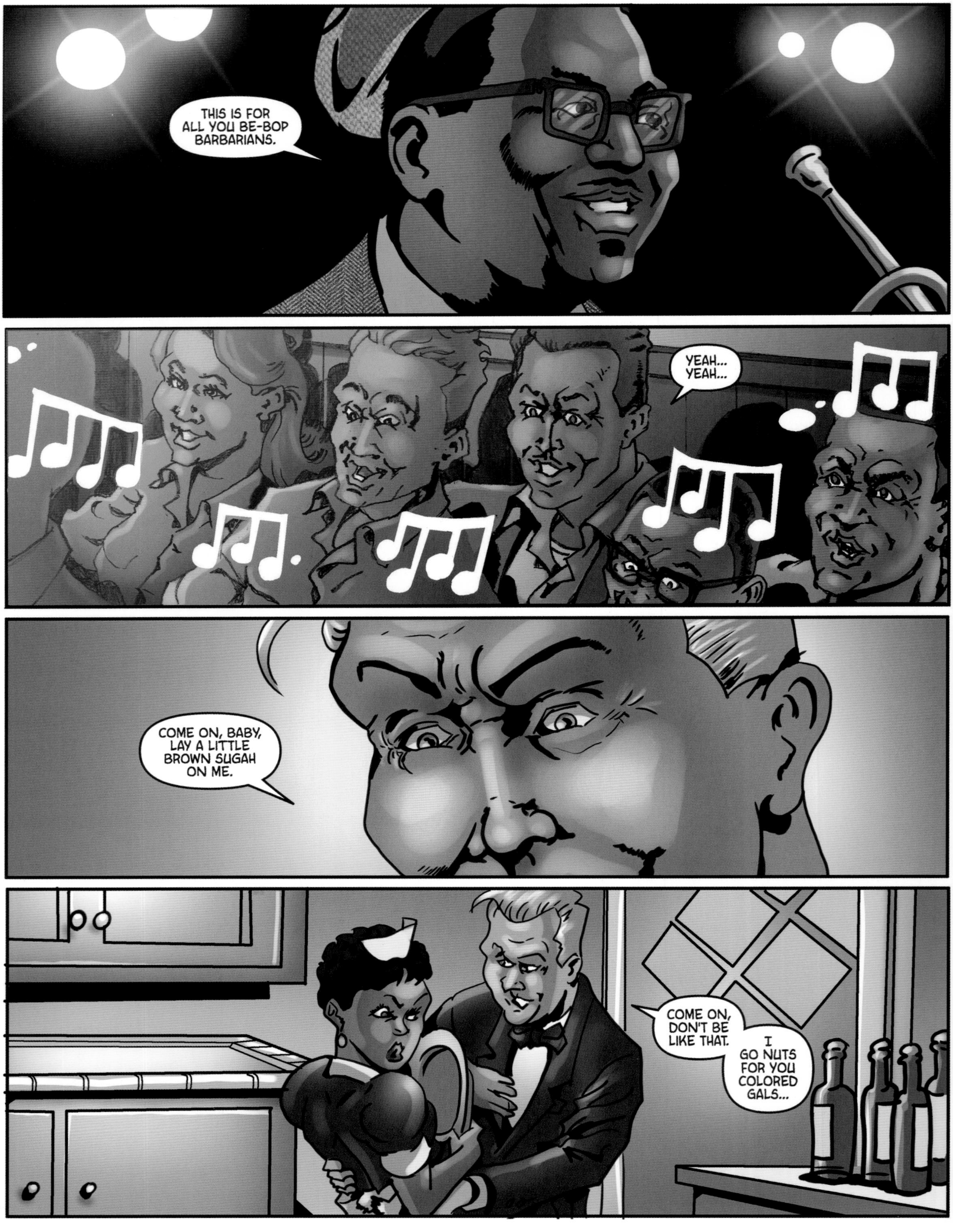
THIS IS FOR ALL YOU BE-BOP BARBARIANS.
YEAH... YEAH...
COME ON, BABY, LAY A LITTLE BROWN SUGAH ON ME.
COME ON, DON'T BE LIKE THAT.
I GO NUTS FOR YOU COLORED GALS...

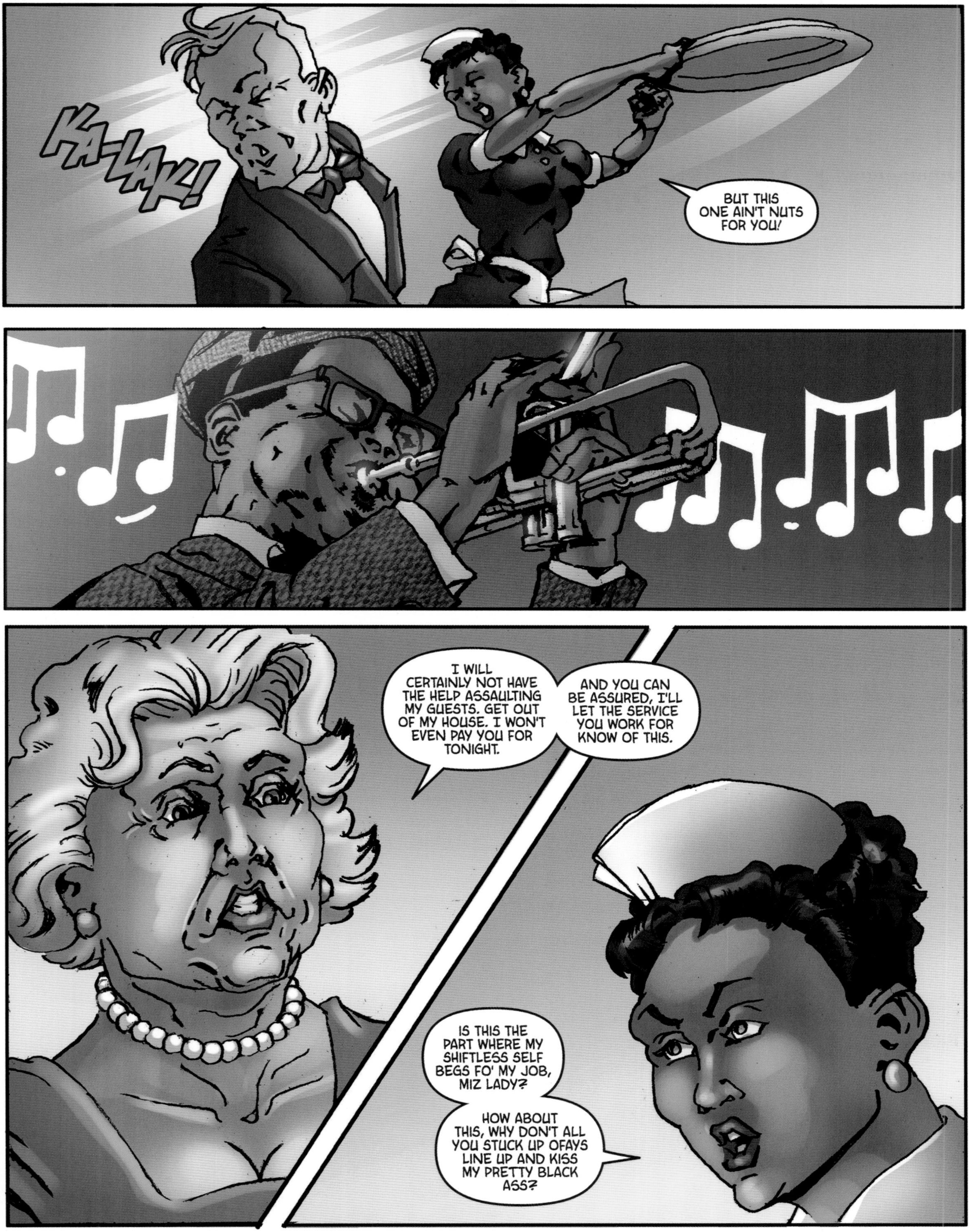
KA-LAK!
BUT THIS ONE AIN'T NUTS FOR YOU!
I WILL CERTAINLY NOT HAVE THE HELP ASSAULTING MY GUESTS. GET OUT OF MY HOUSE. I WON'T EVEN PAY YOU FOR TONIGHT.
AND YOU CAN BE ASSURED, I'LL LET THE SERVICE YOU WORK FOR KNOW OF THIS.
IS THIS THE PART WHERE MY SHIFTLESS SELF BEGS FO' MY JOB, MIZ LADY?
HOW ABOUT THIS, WHY DON'T ALL YOU STUCK UP OFAYS LINE UP AND KISS MY PRETTY BLACK ASS?

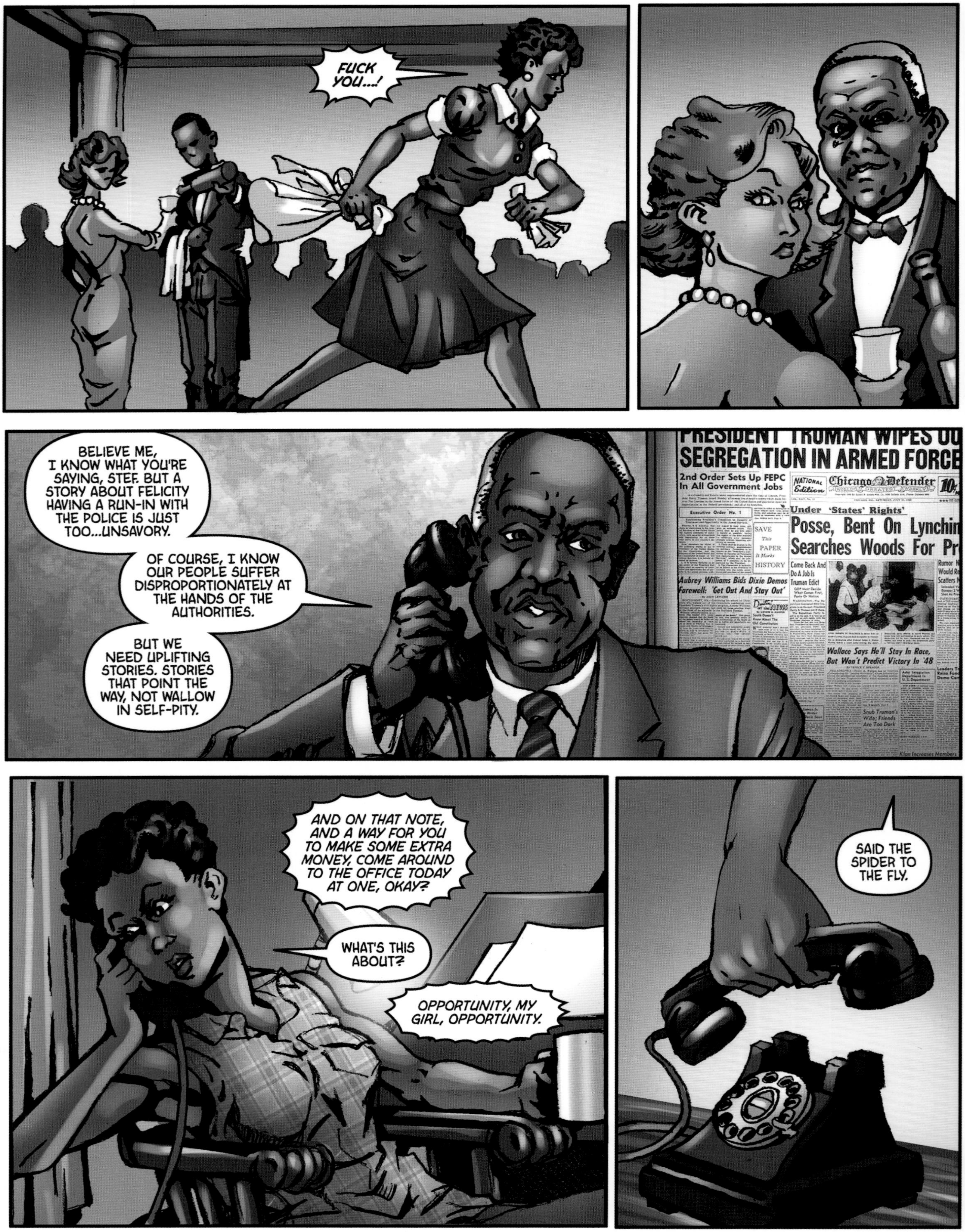
FUCK YOU...!
BELIEVE ME, I KNOW WHAT YOU'RE SAYING, STEF. BUT A STORY ABOUT FELICITY HAVING A RUN-IN WITH THE POLICE IS JUST TOO...UNSAVORY.
OF COURSE, I KNOW OUR PEOPLE SUFFER DISPROPORTIONATELY AT THE HANDS OF THE AUTHORITIES.
BUT WE NEED UPLIFTING STORIES. STORIES THAT POINT THE WAY, NOT WALLOW IN SELF-PITY.
2nd Order Sets Up FEPC In All Government Jobs
Chicago Defender
Under 'States' Rights'
SAVE This PAPER It Marks HISTORY
Come Back And Do A Job Is Truman Edict
Aubrey Williams Bids Dixie Demos Farewell: 'Get Out And Stay Out'
Wallace Says He'll Stay In Race, But Won't Predict Victory In '48
Snub Truman's Wife; Friends Are Too Dark
Klan Increases Members
AND ON THAT NOTE, AND A WAY FOR YOU TO MAKE SOME EXTRA MONEY, COME AROUND TO THE OFFICE TODAY AT ONE, OKAY?
WHAT'S THIS ABOUT?
OPPORTUNITY, MY GIRL, OPPORTUNITY.
SAID THE SPIDER TO THE FLY.

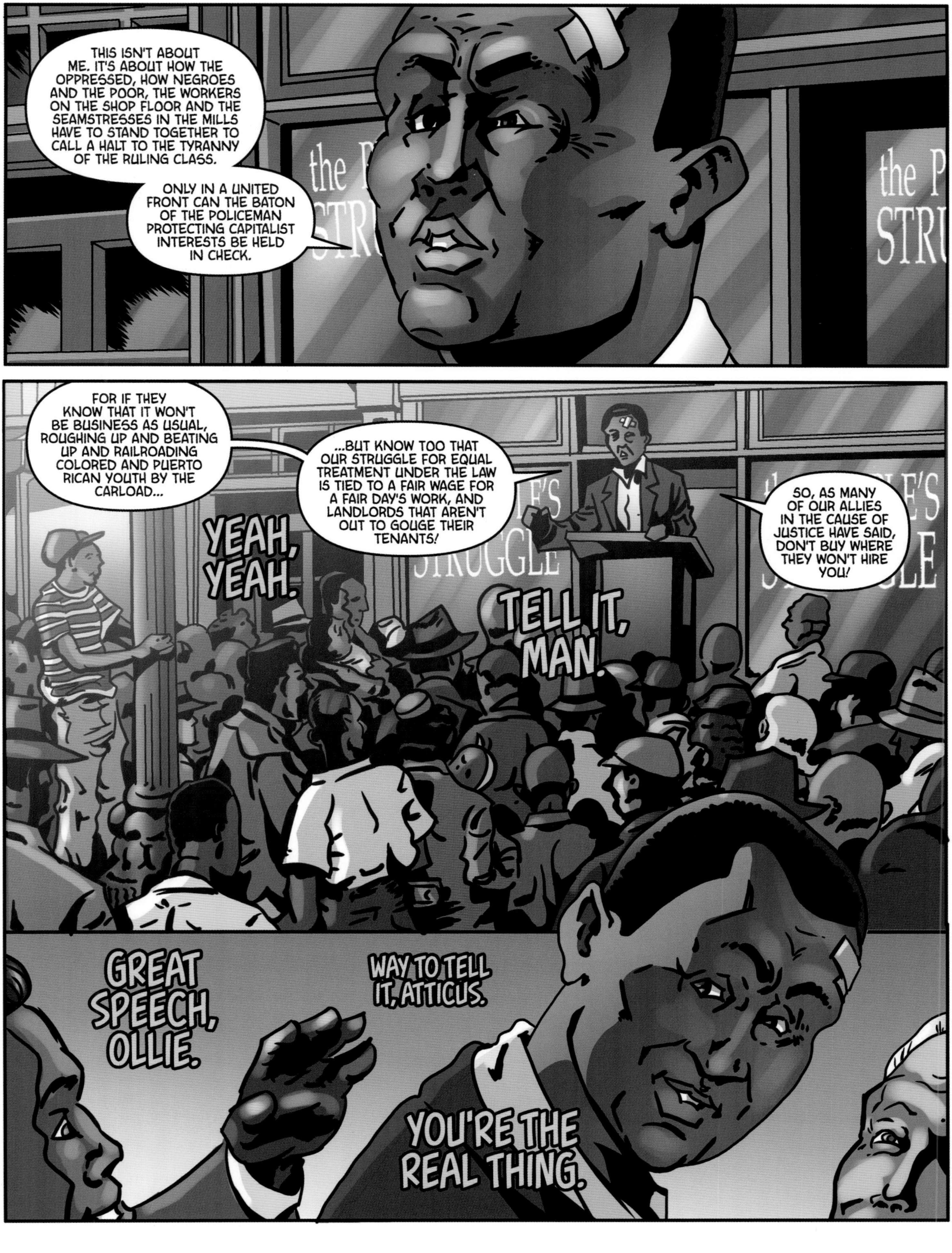
THIS ISN'T ABOUT ME. IT'S ABOUT HOW THE OPPRESSED, HOW NEGROES AND THE POOR, THE WORKERS ON THE SHOP FLOOR AND THE SEAMSTRESSES IN THE MILLS HAVE TO STAND TOGETHER TO CALL A HALT TO THE TYRANNY OF THE RULING CLASS.
ONLY IN A UNITED FRONT CAN THE BATON OF THE POLICEMAN PROTECTING CAPITALIST INTERESTS BE HELD IN CHECK.
FOR IF THEY KNOW THAT IT WON'T BE BUSINESS AS USUAL, ROUGHING UP AND BEATING UP AND RAILROADING COLORED AND PUERTO RICAN YOUTH BY THE CARLOAD...
...BUT KNOW TOO THAT OUR STRUGGLE FOR EQUAL TREATMENT UNDER THE LAW IS TIED TO A FAIR WAGE FOR A FAIR DAY'S WORK, AND LANDLORDS THAT AREN'T OUT TO GOUGE THEIR TENANTS!
SO, AS MANY OF OUR ALLIES IN THE CAUSE OF JUSTICE HAVE SAID, DON'T BUY WHERE THEY WON'T HIRE YOU!
YEAH, YEAH.
TELL IT, MAN.
GREAT SPEECH, OLLIE.
WAY TO TELL IT, ATTICUS.
YOU'RE THE REAL THING.

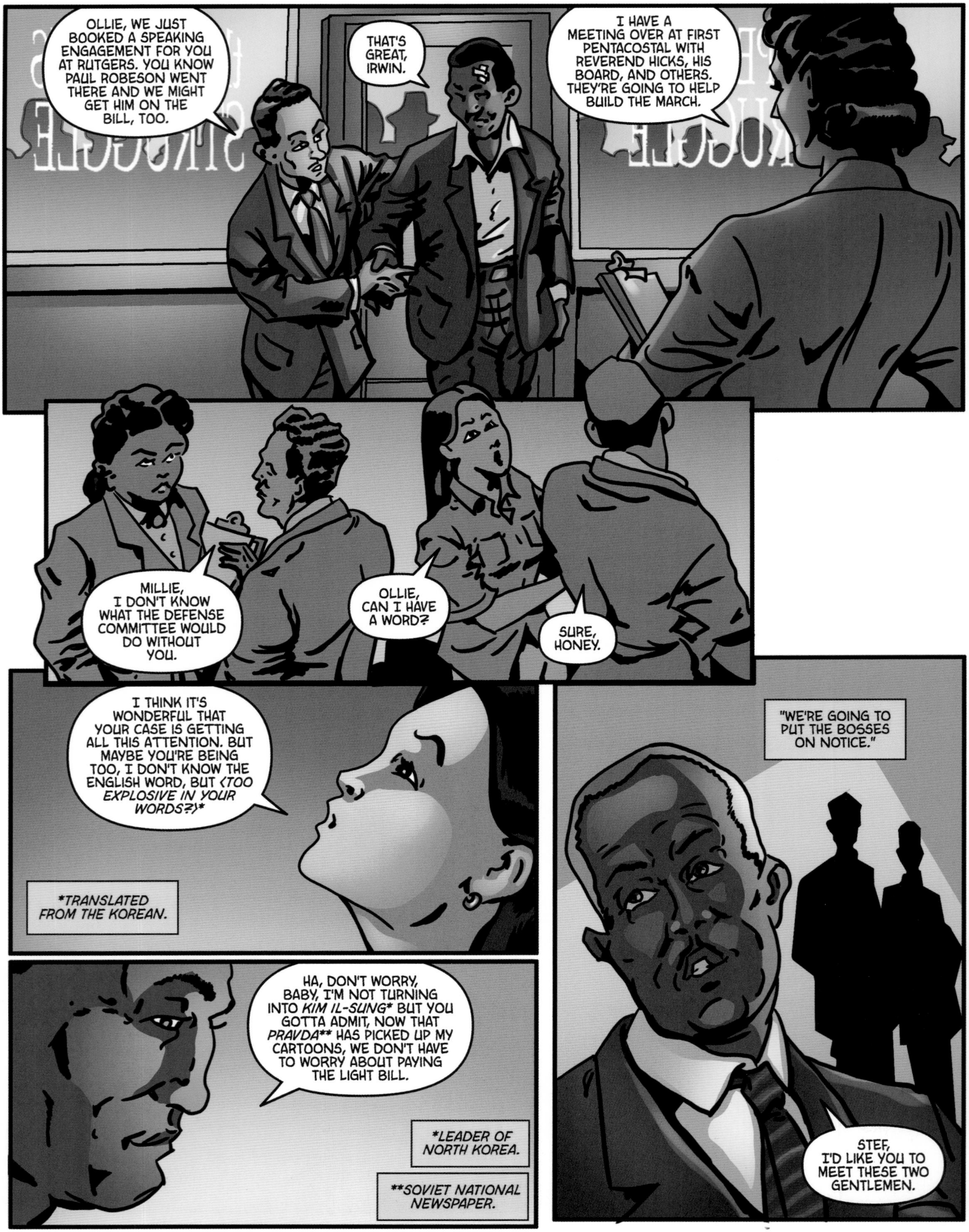
OLLIE, WE JUST BOOKED A SPEAKING ENGAGEMENT FOR YOU AT RUTGERS. YOU KNOW PAUL ROBESON WENT THERE AND WE MIGHT GET HIM ON THE BILL, TOO.
THAT'S GREAT, IRWIN.
I HAVE A MEETING OVER AT FIRST PENTACOSTAL WITH REVEREND HICKS, HIS BOARD, AND OTHERS. THEY'RE GOING TO HELP BUILD THE MARCH.
MILLIE, I DON'T KNOW WHAT THE DEFENSE COMMITTEE WOULD DO WITHOUT YOU.
OLLIE, CAN I HAVE A WORD?
SURE, HONEY.
I THINK IT'S WONDERFUL THAT YOUR CASE IS GETTING ALL THIS ATTENTION. BUT MAYBE YOU'RE BEING TOO, I DON'T KNOW THE ENGLISH WORD, BUT <TOO EXPLOSIVE IN YOUR WORDS?>*
*TRANSLATED FROM THE KOREAN.
HA, DON'T WORRY, BABY, I'M NOT TURNING INTO KIM IL-SUNG* BUT YOU GOTTA ADMIT, NOW THAT PRAVDA** HAS PICKED UP MY CARTOONS, WE DON'T HAVE TO WORRY ABOUT PAYING THE LIGHT BILL.
*LEADER OF NORTH KOREA.
**SOVIET NATIONAL NEWSPAPER.
"WE'RE GOING TO PUT THE BOSSES ON NOTICE."
STEF, I'D LIKE YOU TO MEET THESE TWO GENTLEMEN.

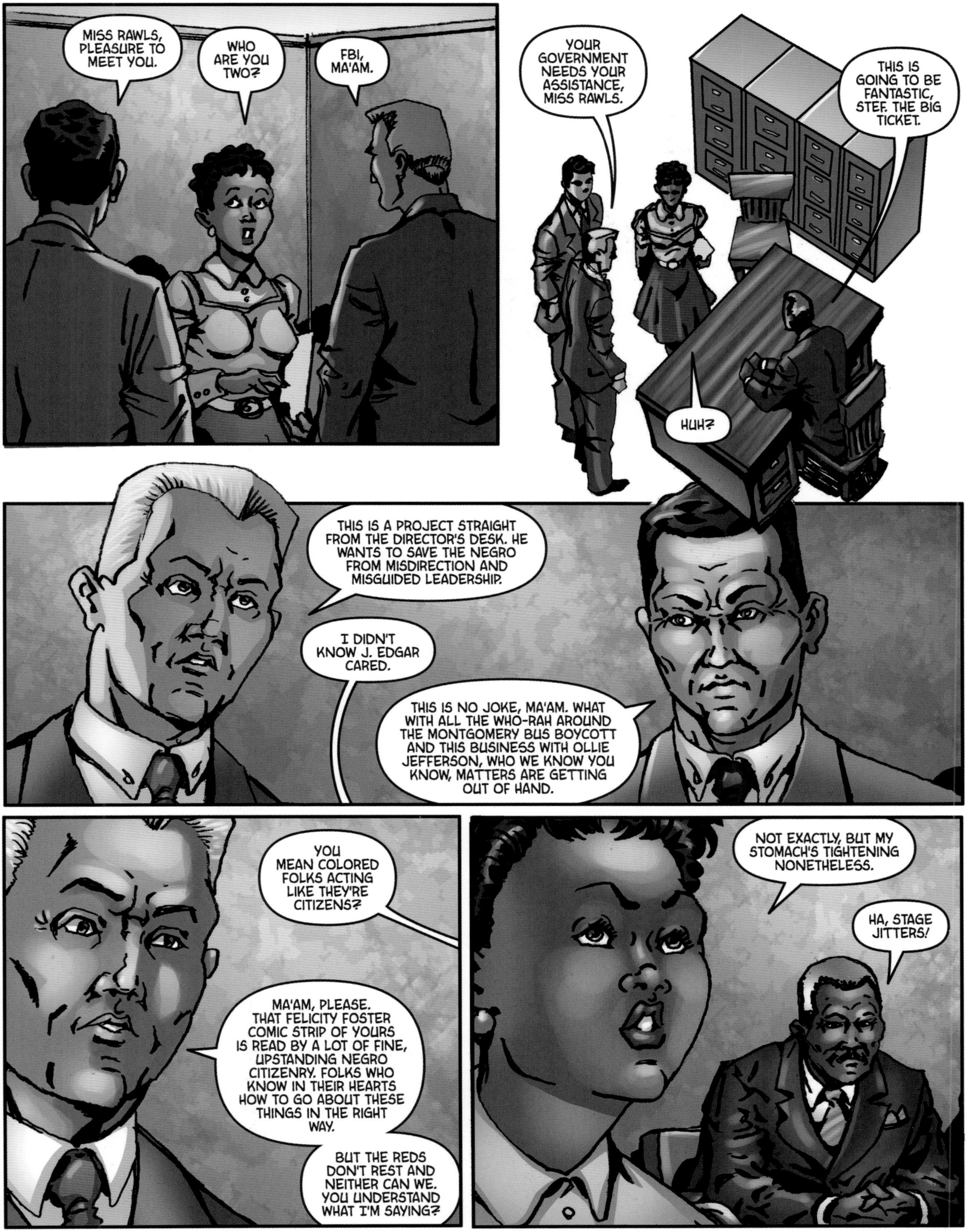
MISS RAWLS, PLEASURE TO MEET YOU.
WHO ARE YOU TWO?
FBI, MA'AM.
YOUR GOVERNMENT NEEDS YOUR ASSISTANCE, MISS RAWLS.
THIS IS GOING TO BE FANTASTIC, STEF. THE BIG TICKET.
HUH?
THIS IS A PROJECT STRAIGHT FROM THE DIRECTOR'S DESK. HE WANTS TO SAVE THE NEGRO FROM MISDIRECTION AND MISGUIDED LEADERSHIP.
I DIDN'T KNOW J. EDGAR CARED.
THIS IS NO JOKE, MA'AM. WHAT WITH ALL THE WHO-RAH AROUND THE MONTGOMERY BUS BOYCOTT AND THIS BUSINESS WITH OLLIE JEFFERSON, WHO WE KNOW YOU KNOW, MATTERS ARE GETTING OUT OF HAND.
YOU MEAN COLORED FOLKS ACTING LIKE THEY'RE CITIZENS?
MA'AM, PLEASE. THAT FELICITY FOSTER COMIC STRIP OF YOURS IS READ BY A LOT OF FINE, UPSTANDING NEGRO CITIZENRY. FOLKS WHO KNOW IN THEIR HEARTS HOW TO GO ABOUT THESE THINGS IN THE RIGHT WAY.
BUT THE REDS DON'T REST AND NEITHER CAN WE. YOU UNDERSTAND WHAT I'M SAYING?
NOT EXACTLY, BUT MY STOMACH'S TIGHTENING NONETHELESS.
HA, STAGE JITTERS!

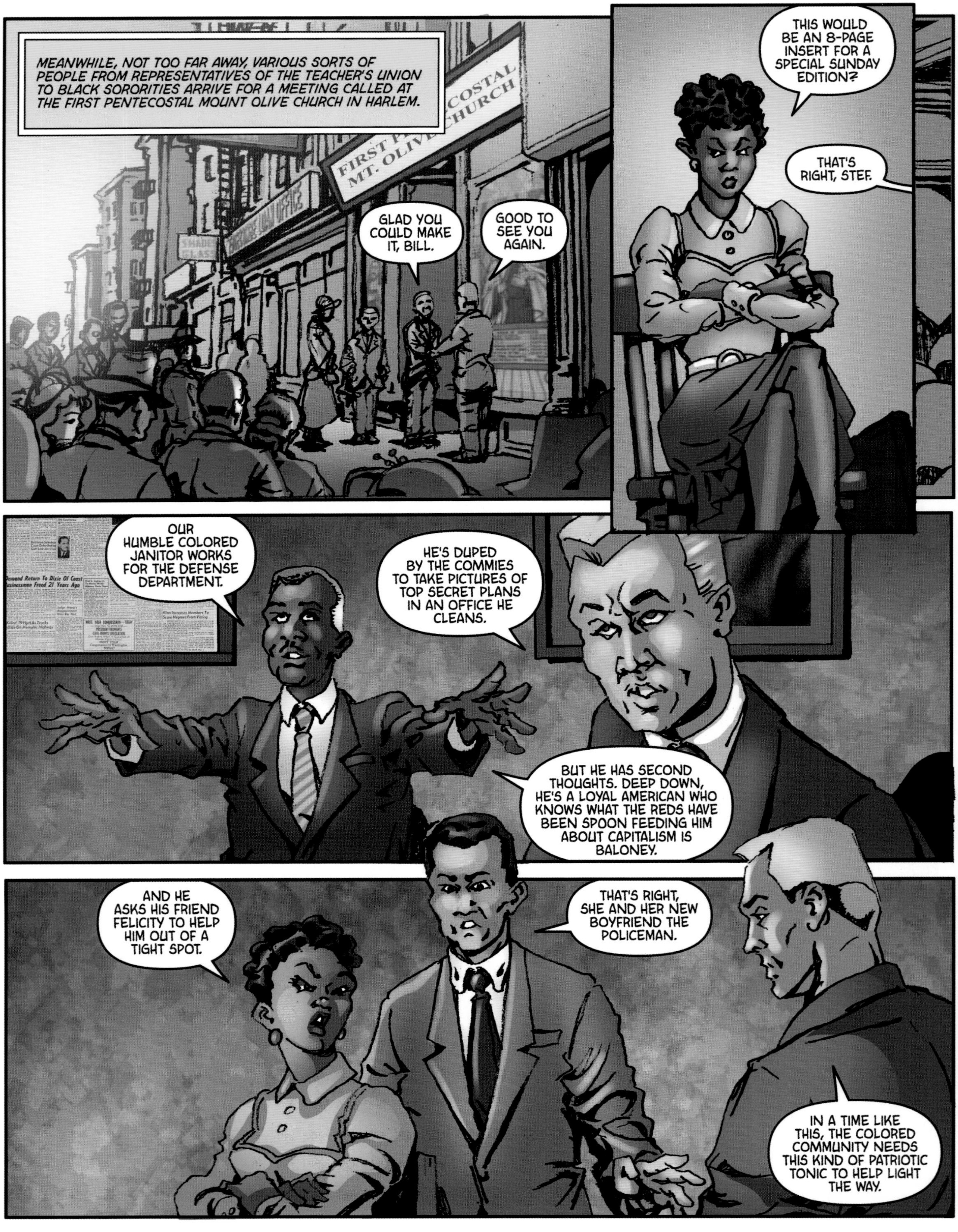
MEANWHILE, NOT TOO FAR AWAY, VARIOUS SORTS OF PEOPLE FROM REPRESENTATIVES OF THE TEACHER'S UNION TO BLACK SORORITIES ARRIVE FOR A MEETING CALLED AT THE FIRST PENTECOSTAL MOUNT OLIVE CHURCH IN HARLEM.
GLAD YOU COULD MAKE IT, BILL.
GOOD TO SEE YOU AGAIN.
THIS WOULD BE AN 8-PAGE INSERT FOR A SPECIAL SUNDAY EDITION?
THAT'S RIGHT, STEF.
OUR HUMBLE COLORED JANITOR WORKS FOR THE DEFENSE DEPARTMENT.
HE'S DUPED BY THE COMMIES TO TAKE PICTURES OF TOP SECRET PLANS IN AN OFFICE HE CLEANS.
BUT HE HAS SECOND THOUGHTS. DEEP DOWN, HE'S A LOYAL AMERICAN WHO KNOWS WHAT THE REDS HAVE BEEN SPOON FEEDING HIM ABOUT CAPITALISM IS BALONEY.
AND HE ASKS HIS FRIEND FELICITY TO HELP HIM OUT OF A TIGHT SPOT.
THAT'S RIGHT, SHE AND HER NEW BOYFRIEND THE POLICEMAN.
IN A TIME LIKE THIS, THE COLORED COMMUNITY NEEDS THIS KIND OF PATRIOTIC TONIC TO HELP LIGHT THE WAY.

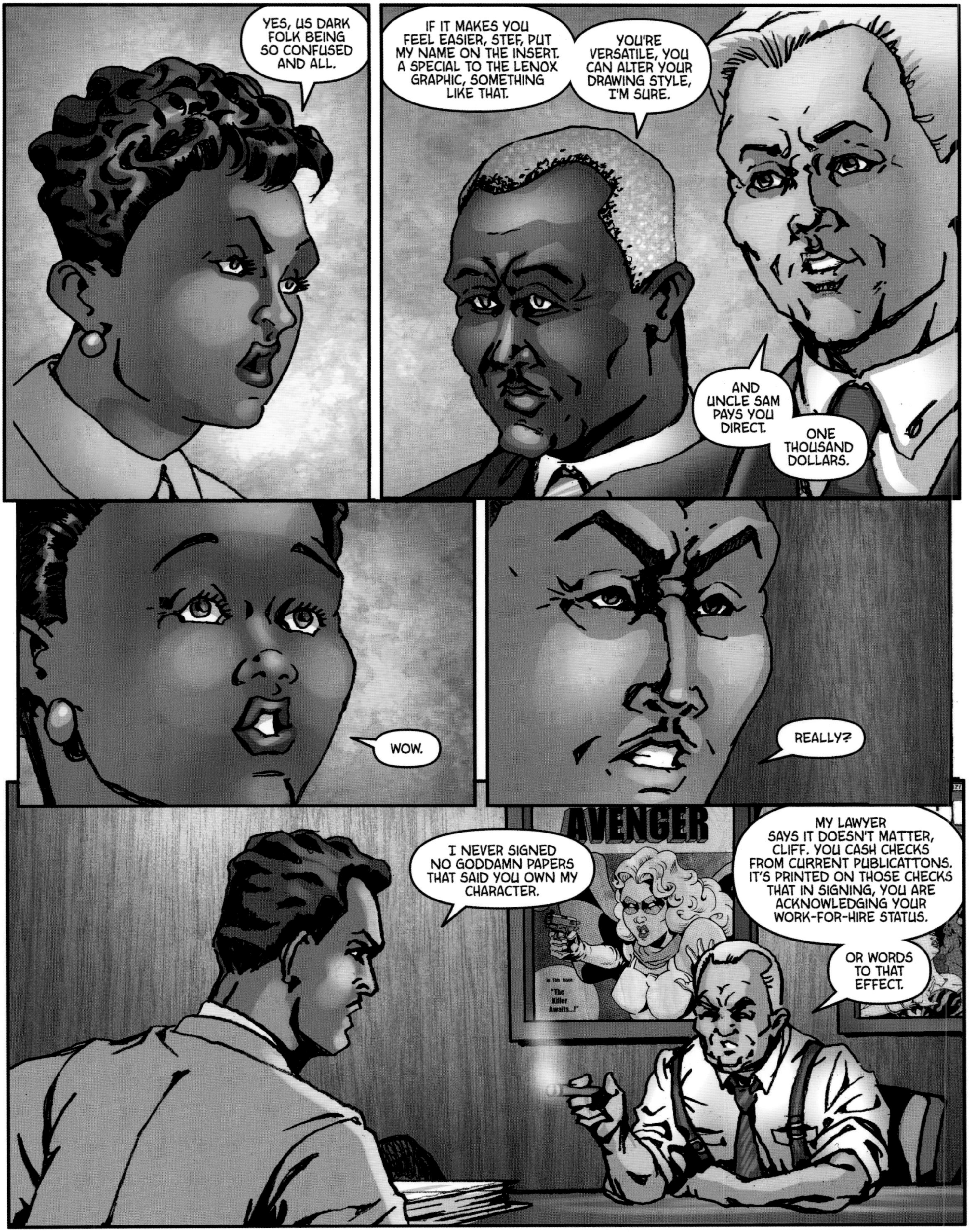
YES, US DARK FOLK BEING SO CONFUSED AND ALL.
IF IT MAKES YOU FEEL EASIER, STEF, PUT MY NAME ON THE INSERT. A SPECIAL TO THE LENOX GRAPHIC, SOMETHING LIKE THAT.
YOU'RE VERSATILE, YOU CAN ALTER YOUR DRAWING STYLE, I'M SURE.
AND UNCLE SAM PAYS YOU DIRECT.
ONE THOUSAND DOLLARS.
WOW.
REALLY?
AVENGER
I NEVER SIGNED NO GODDAMN PAPERS THAT SAID YOU OWN MY CHARACTER.
MY LAWYER SAYS IT DOESN'T MATTER, CLIFF. YOU CASH CHECKS FROM CURRENT PUBLICATTONS. IT'S PRINTED ON THOSE CHECKS THAT IN SIGNING, YOU ARE ACKNOWLEDGING YOUR WORK-FOR-HIRE STATUS.
OR WORDS TO THAT EFFECT.

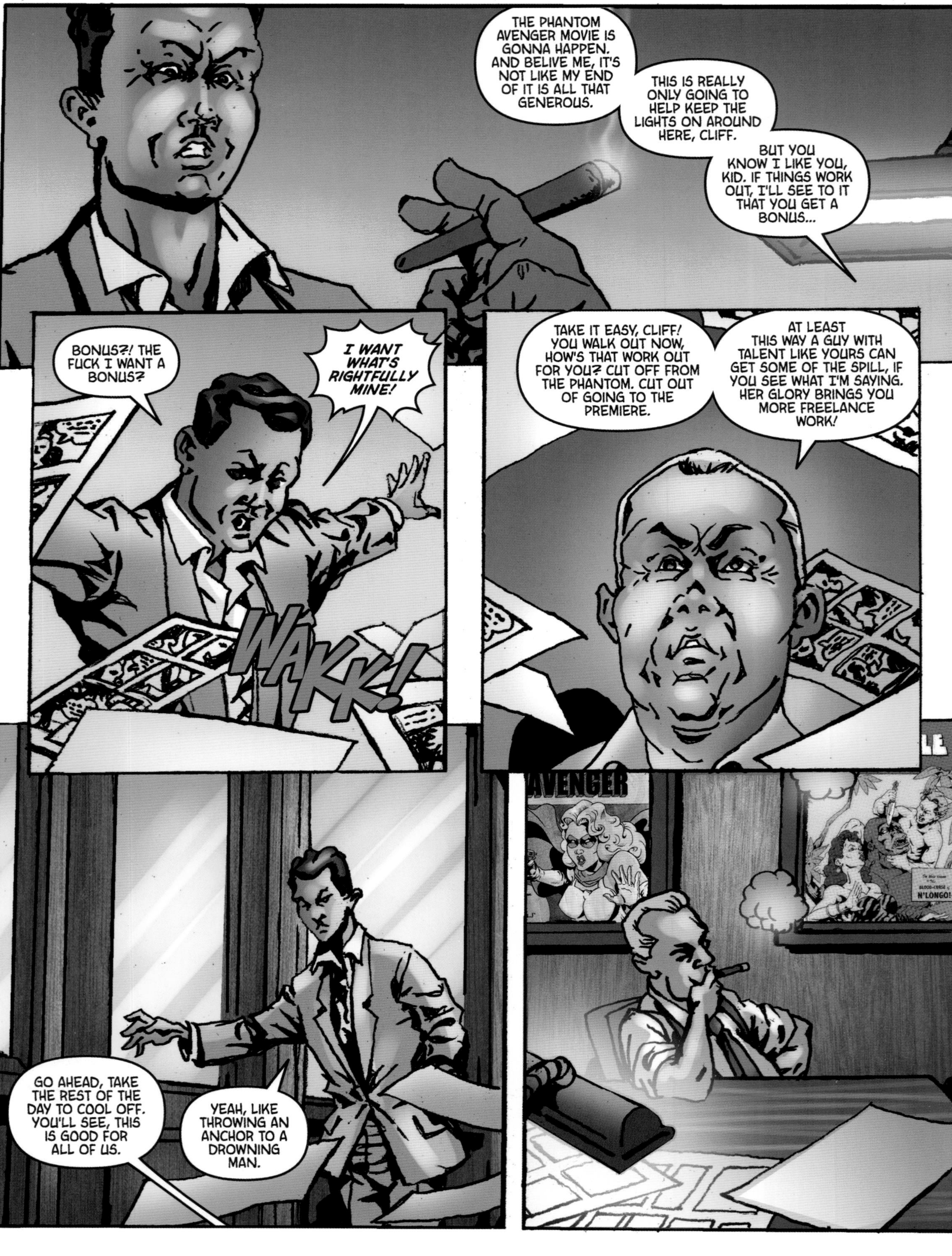
THE PHANTOM AVENGER MOVIE IS GONNA HAPPEN. AND BELIVE ME, IT'S NOT LIKE MY END OF IT IS ALL THAT GENEROUS.
THIS IS REALLY ONLY GOING TO HELP KEEP THE LIGHTS ON AROUND HERE, CLIFF.
BUT YOU KNOW I LIKE YOU, KID. IF THINGS WORK OUT, I'LL SEE TO IT THAT YOU GET A BONUS...
BONUS?! THE FUCK I WANT A BONUS?
I WANT WHAT'S RIGHTFULLY MINE!
WAKK!
TAKE IT EASY, CLIFF! YOU WALK OUT NOW, HOW'S THAT WORK OUT FOR YOU? CUT OFF FROM THE PHANTOM. CUT OUT OF GOING TO THE PREMIERE.
AT LEAST THIS WAY A GUY WITH TALENT LIKE YOURS CAN GET SOME OF THE SPILL, IF YOU SEE WHAT I'M SAYING. HER GLORY BRINGS YOU MORE FREELANCE WORK!
AVENGER
N'LONGO!
GO AHEAD, TAKE THE REST OF THE DAY TO COOL OFF. YOU'LL SEE, THIS IS GOOD FOR ALL OF US.
YEAH, LIKE THROWING AN ANCHOR TO A DROWNING MAN.

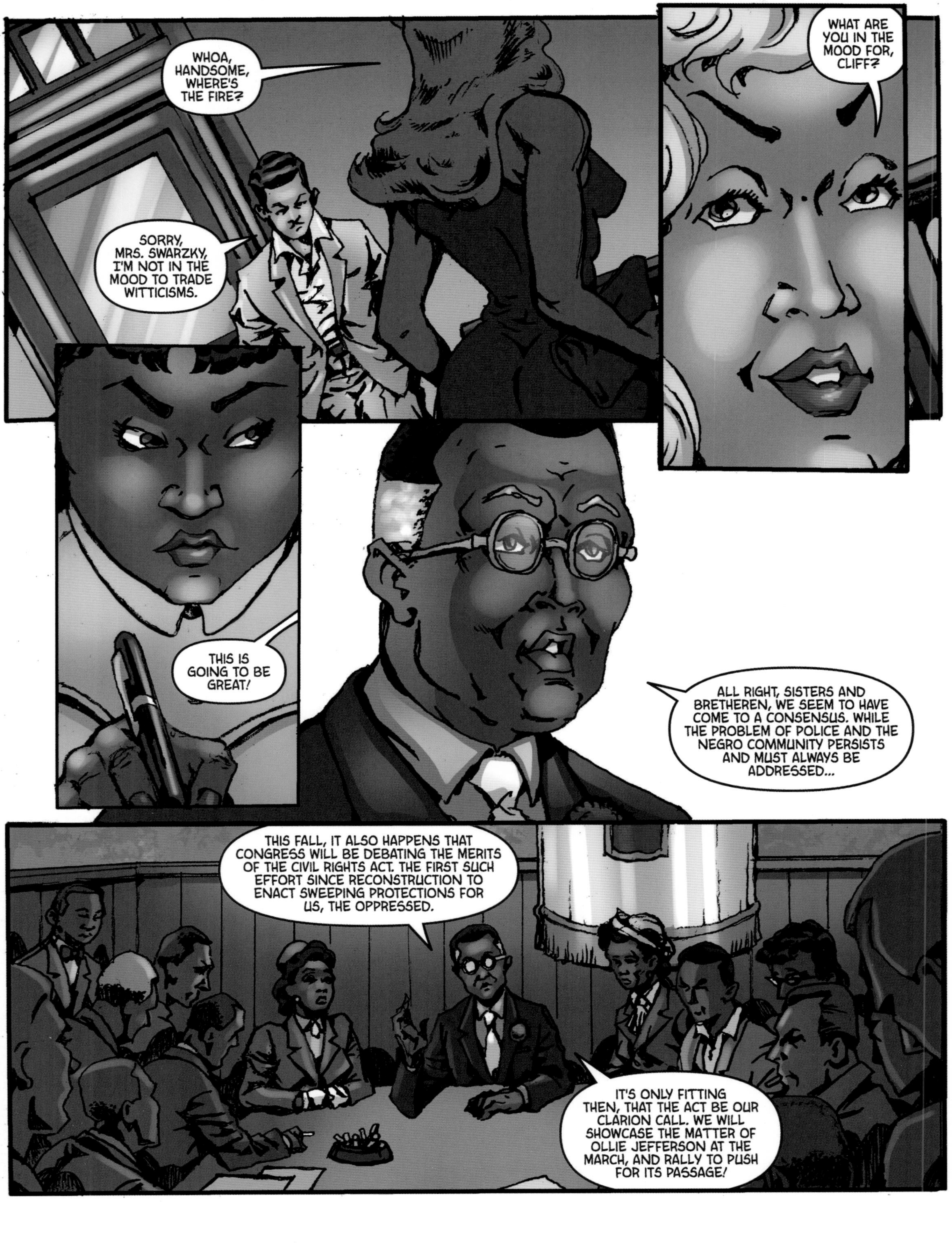
WHOA, HANDSOME, WHERE'S THE FIRE?
SORRY, MRS. SWARZKY, I'M NOT IN THE MOOD TO TRADE WITTICISMS.
WHAT ARE YOU IN THE MOOD FOR, CLIFF?
THIS IS GOING TO BE GREAT!
ALL RIGHT, SISTERS AND BRETHEREN, WE SEEM TO HAVE COME TO A CONSENSUS. WHILE THE PROBLEM OF POLICE AND THE NEGRO COMMUNITY PERSISTS AND MUST ALWAYS BE ADDRESSED...
THIS FALL, IT ALSO HAPPENS THAT CONGRESS WILL BE DEBATING THE MERITS OF THE CIVIL RIGHTS ACT. THE FIRST SUCH EFFORT SINCE RECONSTRUCTION TO ENACT SWEEPING PROTECTIONS FOR US, THE OPPRESSED.
IT'S ONLY FITTING THEN, THAT THE ACT BE OUR CLARION CALL. WE WILL SHOWCASE THE MATTER OF OLLIE JEFFERSON AT THE MARCH, AND RALLY TO PUSH FOR ITS PASSAGE!

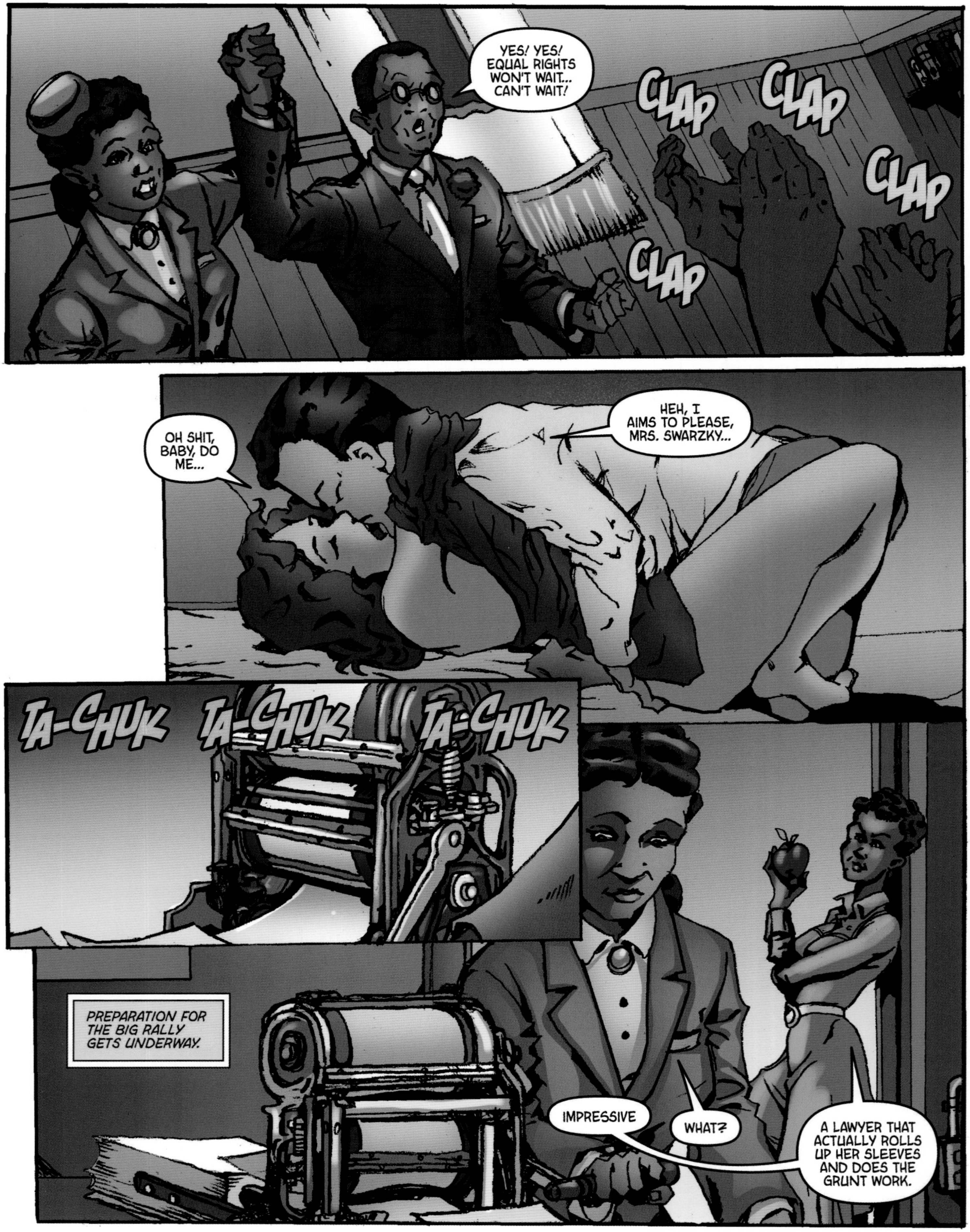
YES! YES! EQUAL RIGHTS WON'T WAIT... CAN'T WAIT!
CLAP
CLAP
CLAP
CLAP
OH SHIT, BABY, DO ME...
HEH, I AIMS TO PLEASE, MRS. SWARZKY...
TA-CHUK TA-CHUK TA-CHUK
PREPARATION FOR THE BIG RALLY GETS UNDERWAY.
IMPRESSIVE
WHAT?
A LAWYER THAT ACTUALLY ROLLS UP HER SLEEVES AND DOES THE GRUNT WORK.

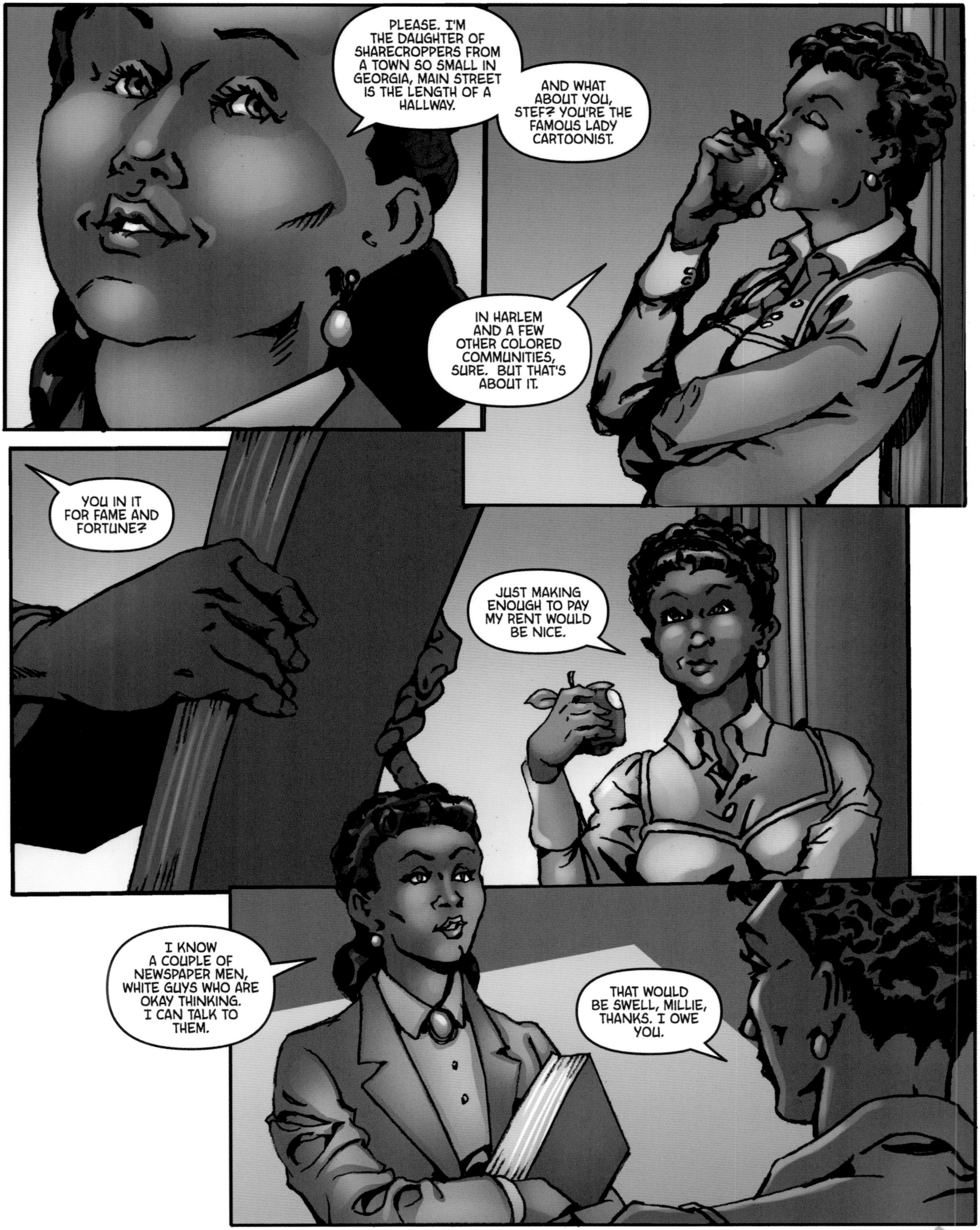
PLEASE. I'M THE DAUGHTER OF SHARECROPPERS FROM A TOWN SO SMALL IN GEORGIA, MAIN STREET IS THE LENGTH OF A HALLWAY.
AND WHAT ABOUT YOU, STEF? YOU'RE THE FAMOUS LADY CARTOONIST.
IN HARLEM AND A FEW OTHER COLORED COMMUNITIES, SURE. BUT THAT'S ABOUT IT.
YOU IN IT FOR FAME AND FORTUNE?
JUST MAKING ENOUGH TO PAY MY RENT WOULD BE NICE.
I KNOW A COUPLE OF NEWSPAPER MEN, WHITE GUYS WHO ARE OKAY THINKING. I CAN TALK TO THEM.
THAT WOULD BE SWELL, MILLIE, THANKS. I OWE YOU.

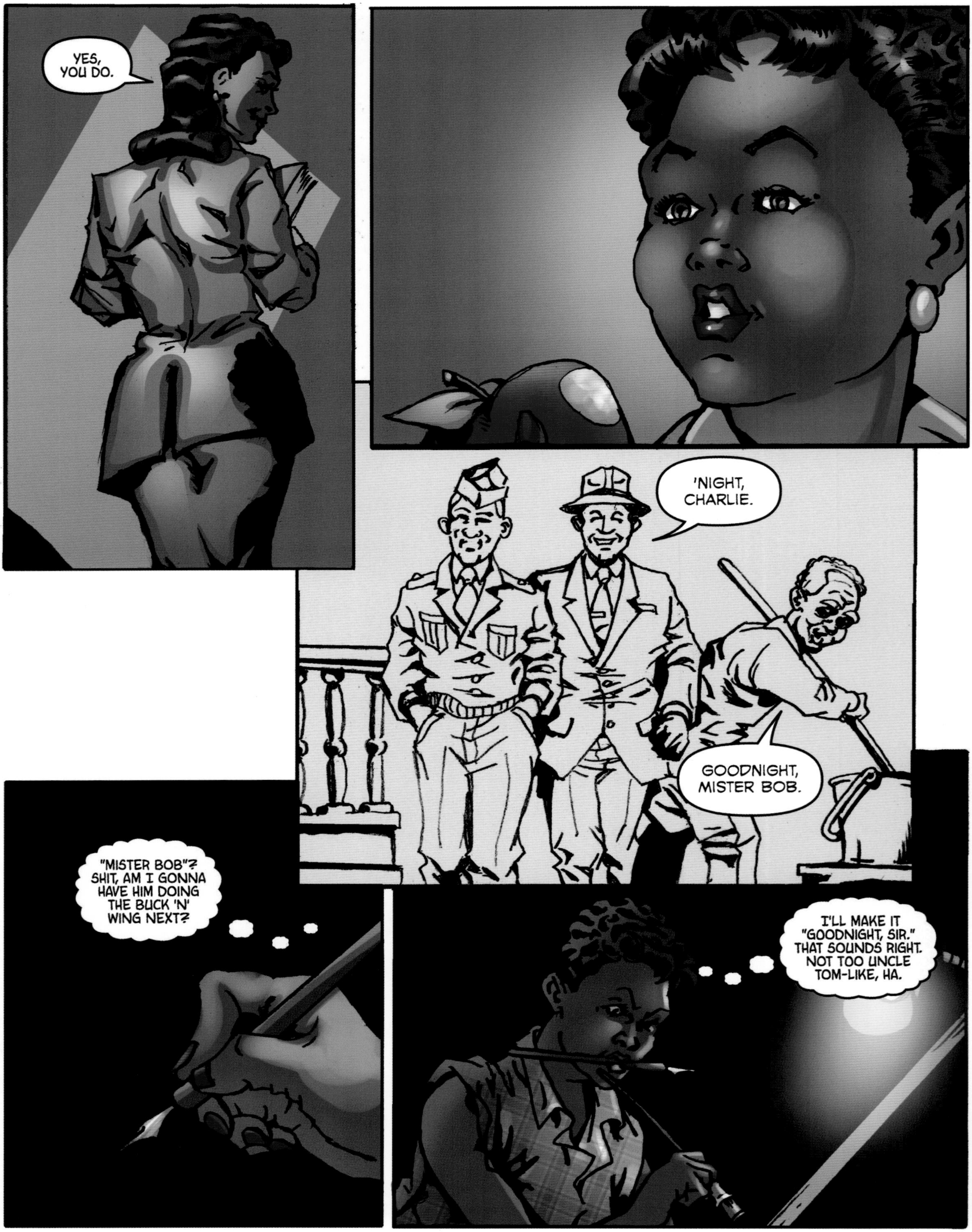
YES, YOU DO.
'NIGHT, CHARLIE.
GOODNIGHT, MISTER BOB.
"MISTER BOB"? SHIT, AM I GONNA HAVE HIM DOING THE BUCK 'N' WING NEXT?
I'LL MAKE IT "GOODNIGHT, SIR." THAT SOUNDS RIGHT. NOT TOO UNCLE TOM-LIKE, HA.

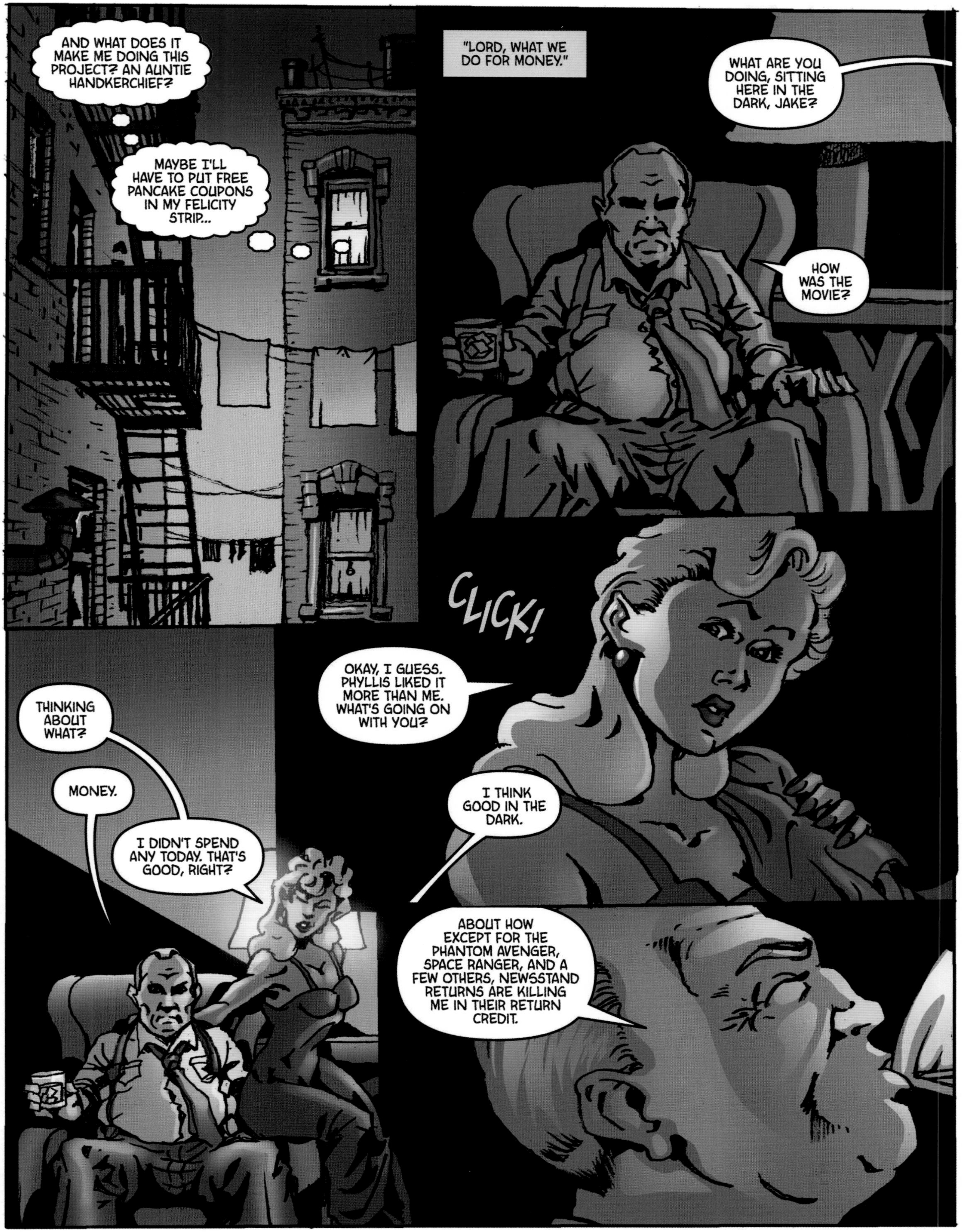
AND WHAT DOES IT MAKE ME DOING THIS PROJECT? AN AUNTIE HANDKERCHIEF?
MAYBE I'LL HAVE TO PUT FREE PANCAKE COUPONS IN MY FELICITY STRIP...
"LORD, WHAT WE DO FOR MONEY."
WHAT ARE YOU DOING, SITTING HERE IN THE DARK, JAKE?
HOW WAS THE MOVIE?
CLICK!
OKAY, I GUESS. PHYLLIS LIKED IT MORE THAN ME. WHAT'S GOING ON WITH YOU?
I THINK GOOD IN THE DARK.
THINKING ABOUT WHAT?
MONEY.
I DIDN'T SPEND ANY TODAY. THAT'S GOOD, RIGHT?
ABOUT HOW EXCEPT FOR THE PHANTOM AVENGER, SPACE RANGER, AND A FEW OTHERS, NEWSSTAND RETURNS ARE KILLING ME IN THEIR RETURN CREDIT.

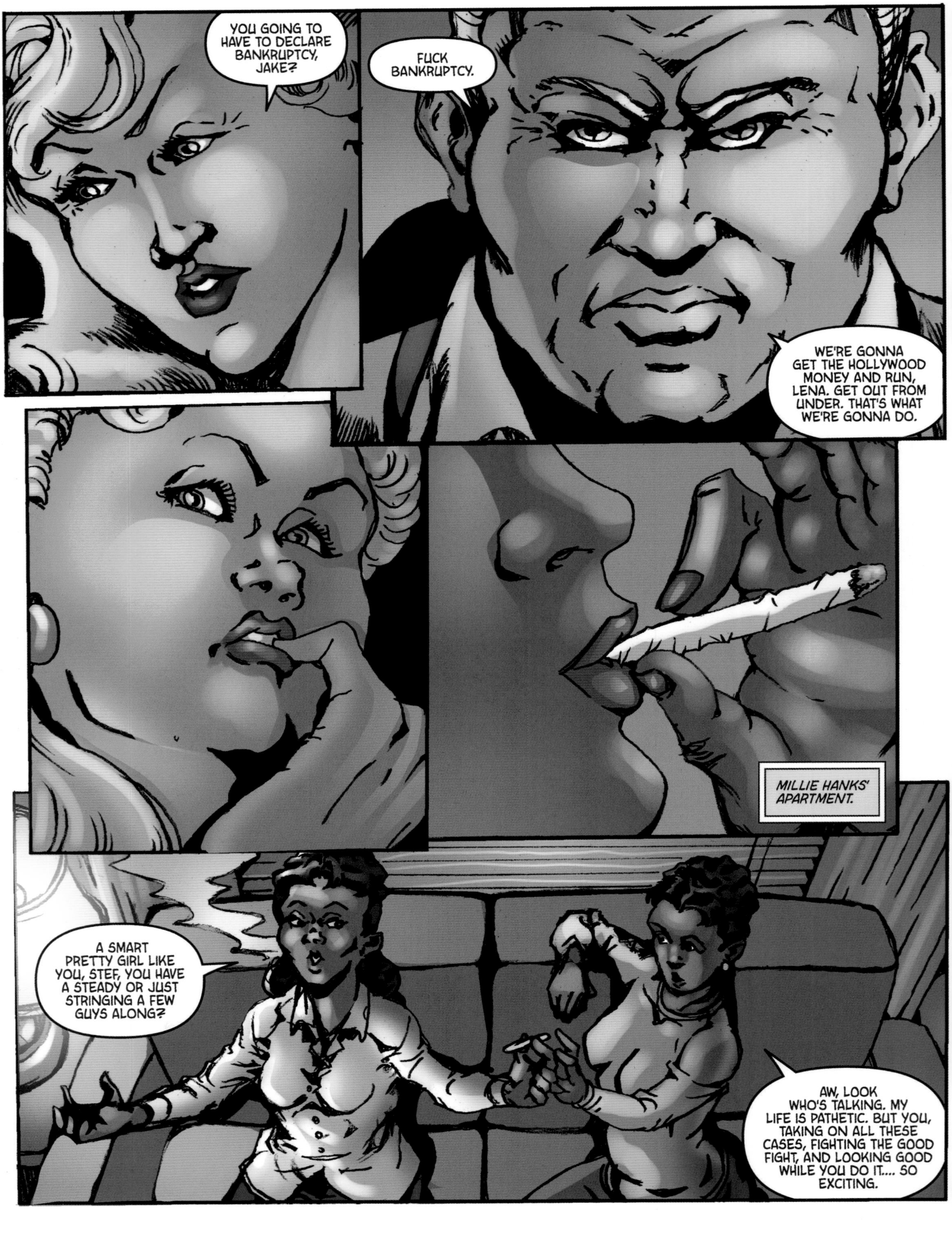
YOU GOING TO HAVE TO DECLARE BANKRUPTCY, JAKE?
FUCK BANKRUPTCY.
WE'RE GONNA GET THE HOLLYWOOD MONEY AND RUN, LENA. GET OUT FROM UNDER. THAT'S WHAT WE'RE GONNA DO.
MILLIE HANKS' APARTMENT.
A SMART PRETTY GIRL LIKE YOU, STEF, YOU HAVE A STEADY OR JUST STRINGING A FEW GUYS ALONG?
AW, LOOK WHO'S TALKING. MY LIFE IS PATHETIC. BUT YOU, TAKING ON ALL THESE CASES, FIGHTING THE GOOD FIGHT, AND LOOKING GOOD WHILE YOU DO IT.... SO EXCITING.

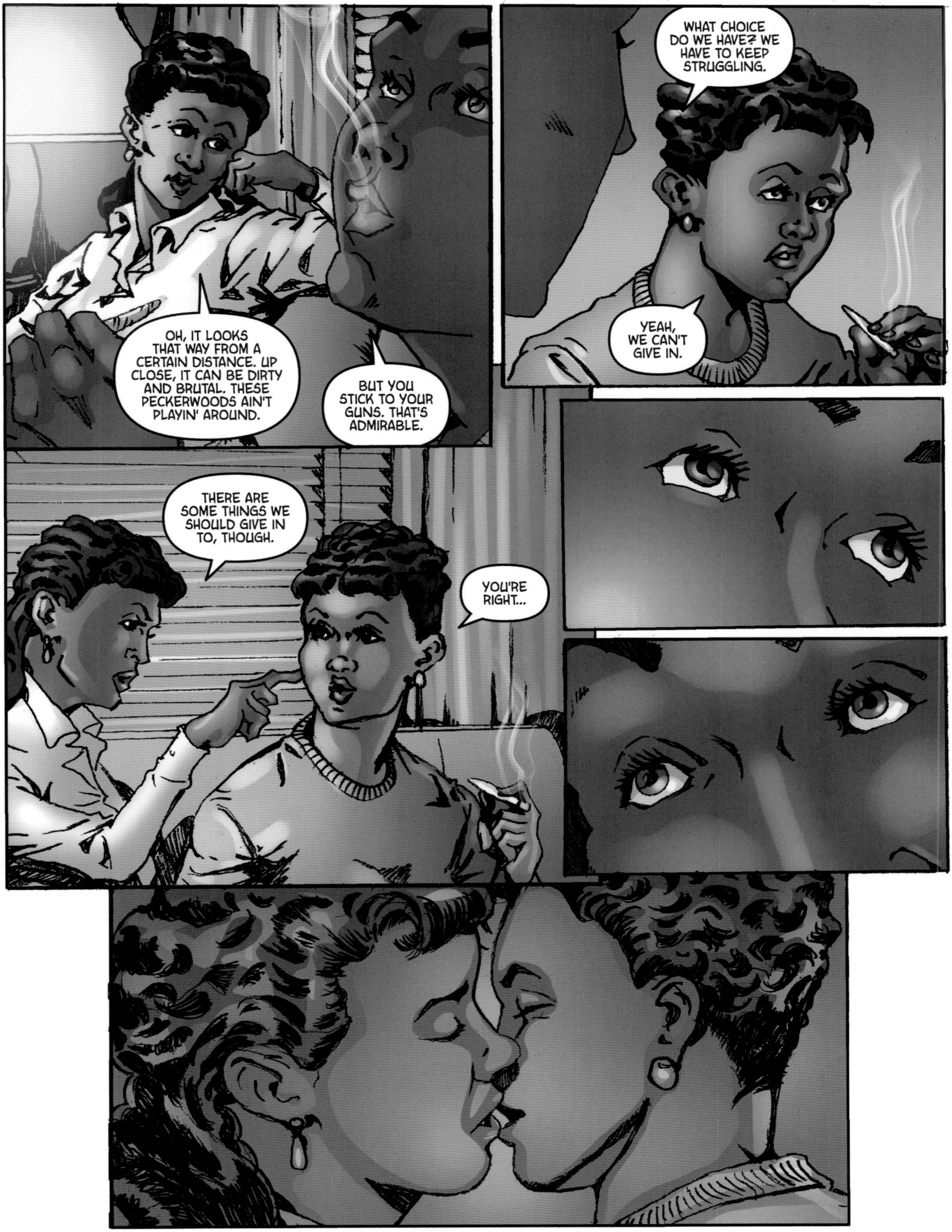
OH, IT LOOKS THAT WAY FROM A CERTAIN DISTANCE. UP CLOSE, IT CAN BE DIRTY AND BRUTAL. THESE PECKERWOODS AIN'T PLAYIN' AROUND.
BUT YOU STICK TO YOUR GUNS. THAT'S ADMIRABLE.
WHAT CHOICE DO WE HAVE? WE HAVE TO KEEP STRUGGLING.
YEAH, WE CAN'T GIVE IN.
THERE ARE SOME THINGS WE SHOULD GIVE IN TO, THOUGH.
YOU'RE RIGHT...

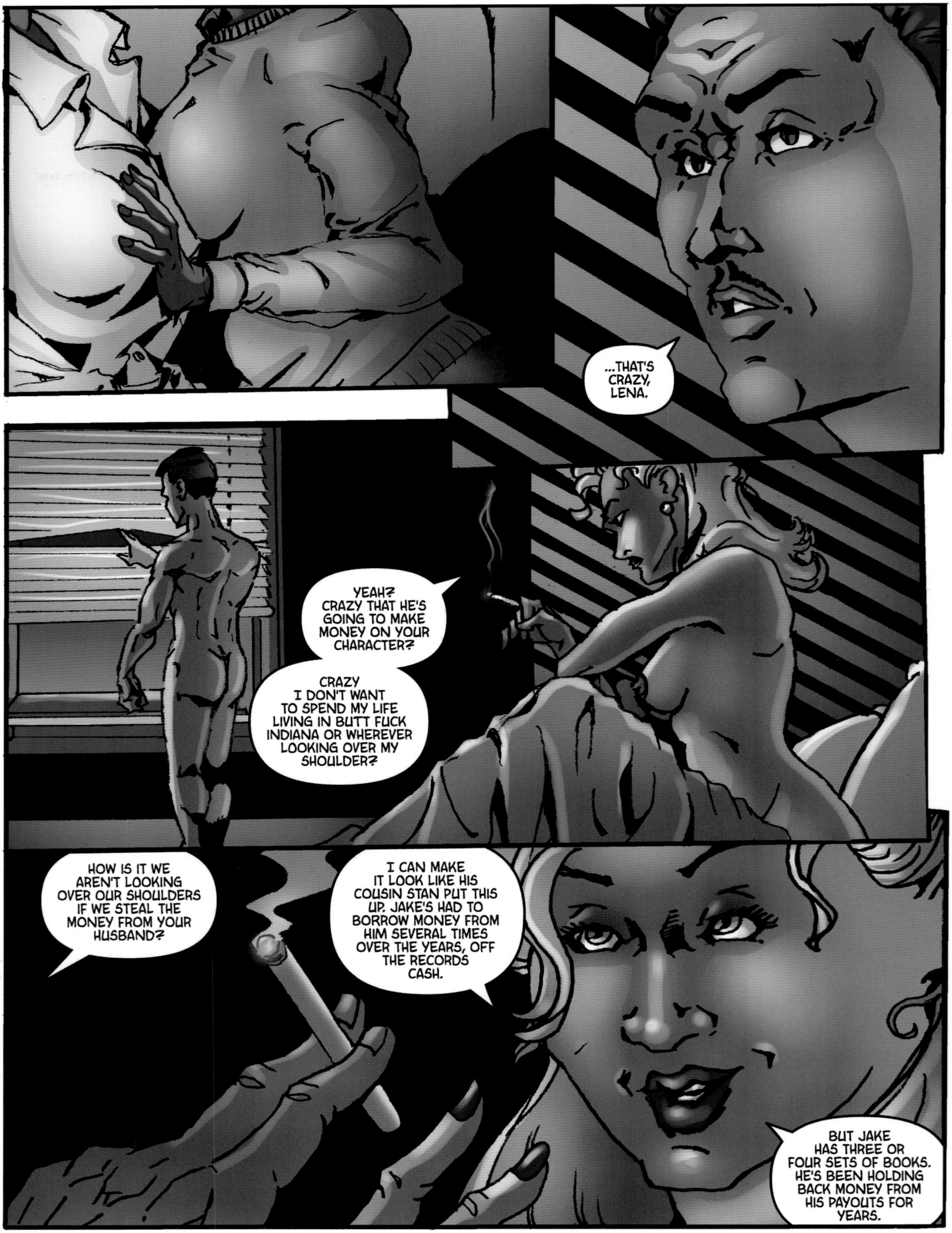
...THAT'S CRAZY, LENA.
YEAH? CRAZY THAT HE'S GOING TO MAKE MONEY ON YOUR CHARACTER?
CRAZY I DON'T WANT TO SPEND MY LIFE LIVING IN BUTT FUCK INDIANA OR WHEREVER LOOKING OVER MY SHOULDER?
HOW IS IT WE AREN'T LOOKING OVER OUR SHOULDERS IF WE STEAL THE MONEY FROM YOUR HUSBAND?
I CAN MAKE IT LOOK LIKE HIS COUSIN STAN PUT THIS UP. JAKE'S HAD TO BORROW MONEY FROM HIM SEVERAL TIMES OVER THE YEARS, OFF THE RECORDS CASH.
BUT JAKE HAS THREE OR FOUR SETS OF BOOKS. HE'S BEEN HOLDING BACK MONEY FROM HIS PAYOUTS FOR YEARS.

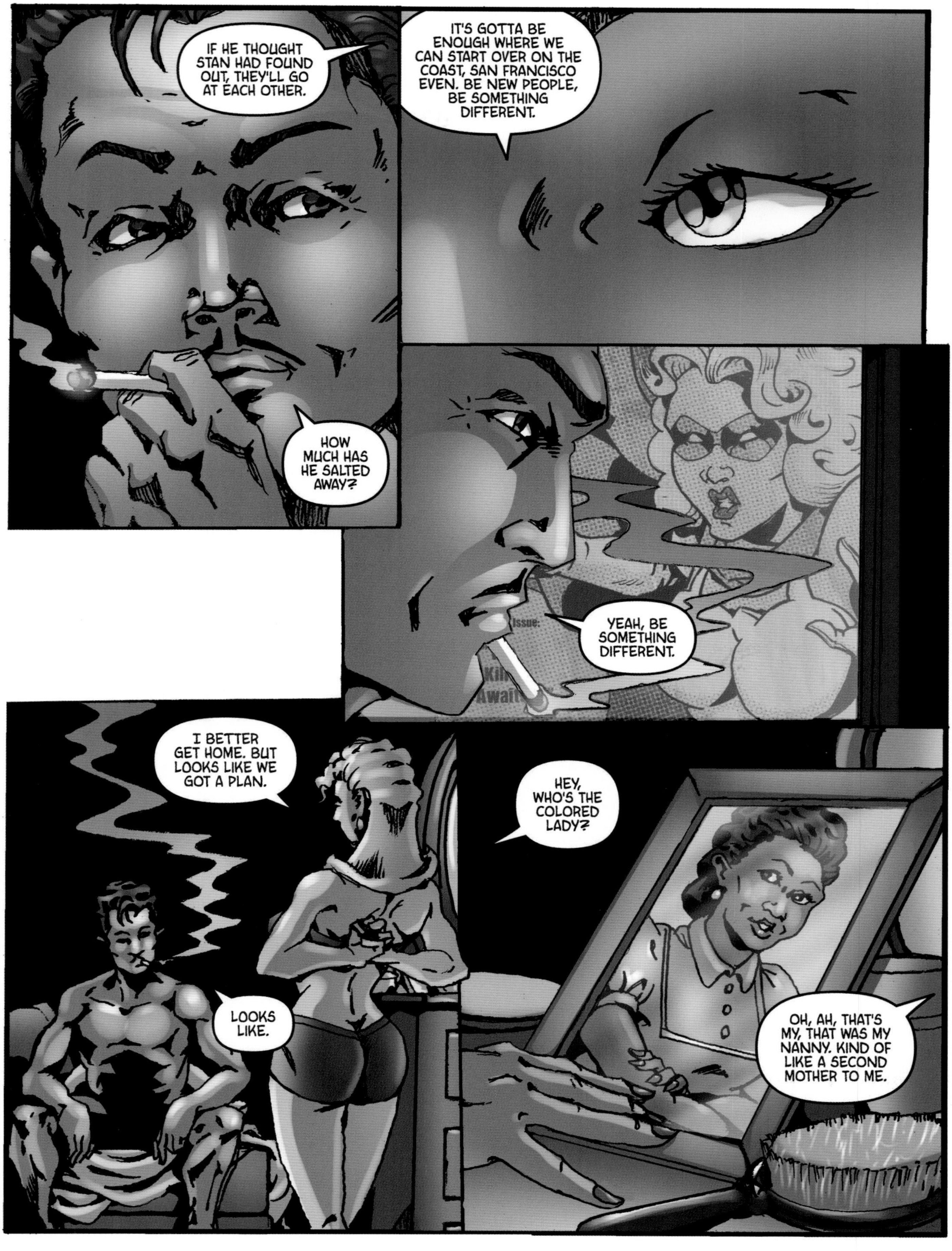
IF HE THOUGHT STAN HAD FOUND OUT, THEY'LL GO AT EACH OTHER.
IT'S GOTTA BE ENOUGH WHERE WE CAN START OVER ON THE COAST, SAN FRANCISCO EVEN. BE NEW PEOPLE, BE SOMETHING DIFFERENT.
HOW MUCH HAS HE SALTED AWAY?
YEAH, BE SOMETHING DIFFERENT.
I BETTER GET HOME. BUT LOOKS LIKE WE GOT A PLAN.
LOOKS LIKE.
HEY, WHO'S THE COLORED LADY?
OH, AH, THAT'S MY, THAT WAS MY NANNY. KIND OF LIKE A SECOND MOTHER TO ME.

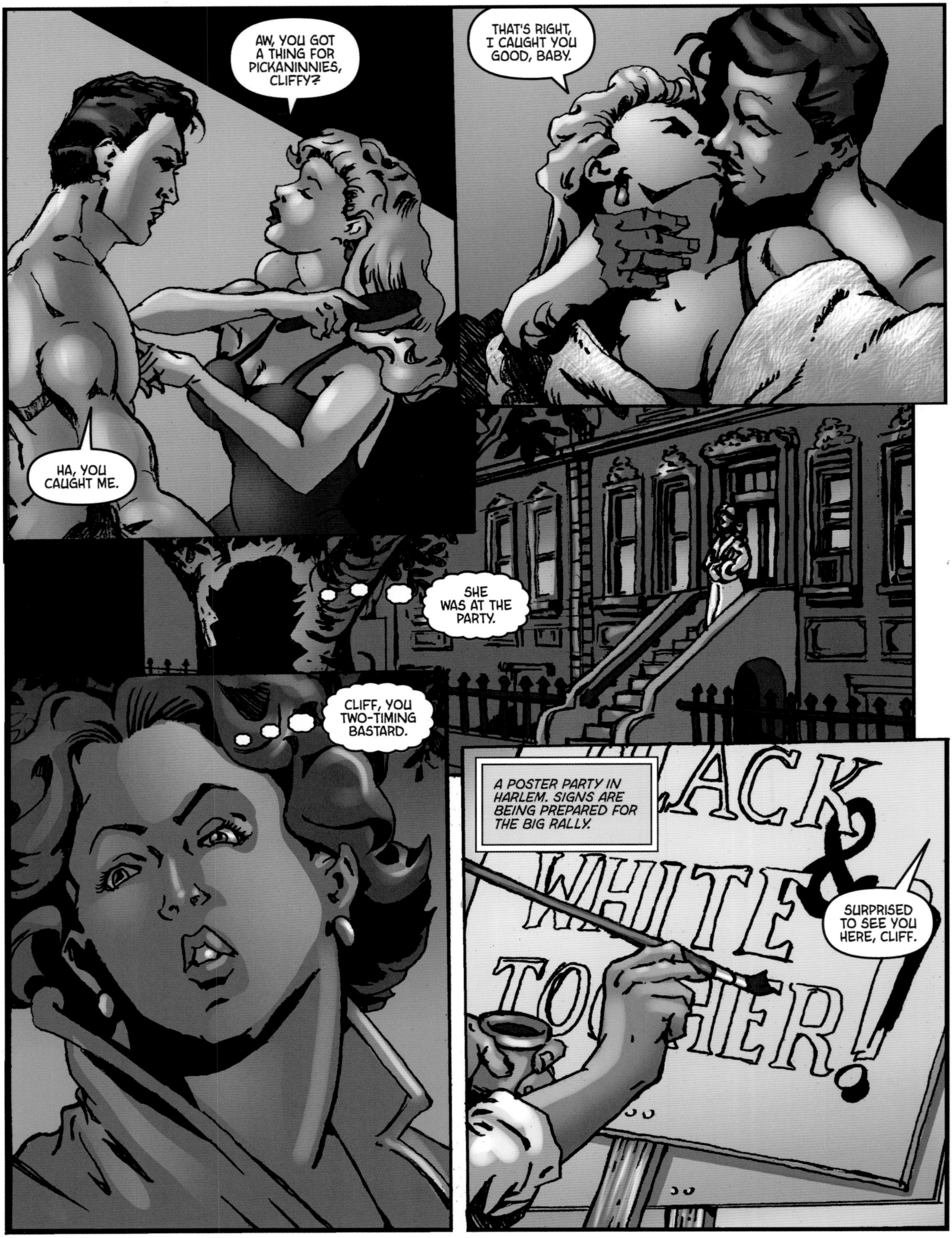
AW, YOU GOT A THING FOR PICKANINNIES, CLIFFY?
HA, YOU CAUGHT ME.
THAT'S RIGHT, I CAUGHT YOU GOOD, BABY.
SHE WAS AT THE PARTY.
CLIFF, YOU TWO-TIMING BASTARD.
A POSTER PARTY IN HARLEM. SIGNS ARE BEING PREPARED FOR THE BIG RALLY.
SURPRISED TO SEE YOU HERE, CLIFF.

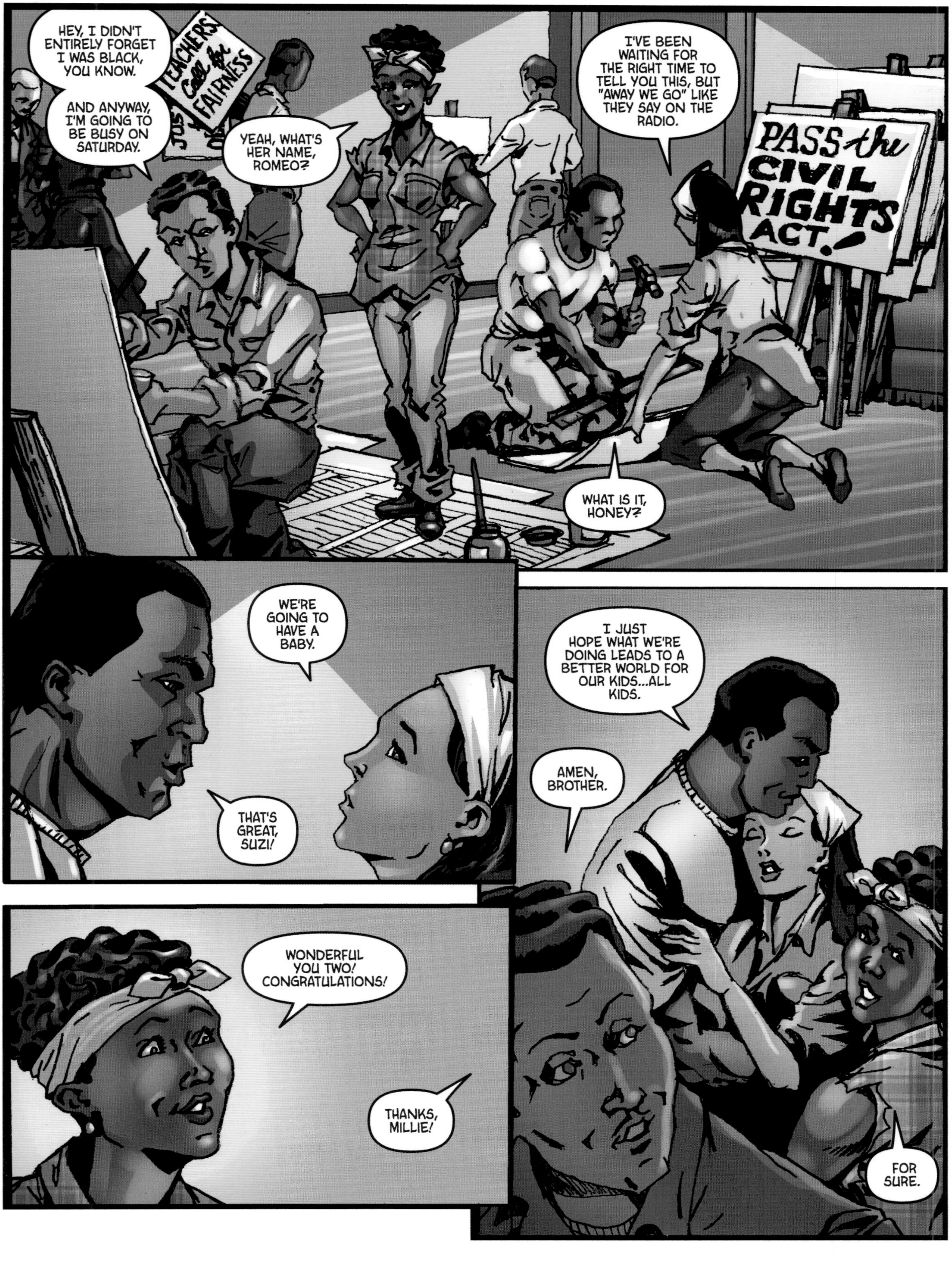
HEY, I DIDN'T ENTIRELY FORGET I WAS BLACK, YOU KNOW.
AND ANYWAY, I'M GOING TO BE BUSY ON SATURDAY.
TEACHERS Call for FAIRNESS
YEAH, WHAT'S HER NAME, ROMEO?
I'VE BEEN WAITING FOR THE RIGHT TIME TO TELL YOU THIS, BUT "AWAY WE GO" LIKE THEY SAY ON THE RADIO.
PASS the CIVIL RIGHTS ACT!
WHAT IS IT, HONEY?
WE'RE GOING TO HAVE A BABY.
THAT'S GREAT, SUZI!
WONDERFUL YOU TWO! CONGRATULATIONS!
THANKS, MILLIE!
I JUST HOPE WHAT WE'RE DOING LEADS TO A BETTER WORLD FOR OUR KIDS...ALL KIDS.
AMEN, BROTHER.
FOR SURE.

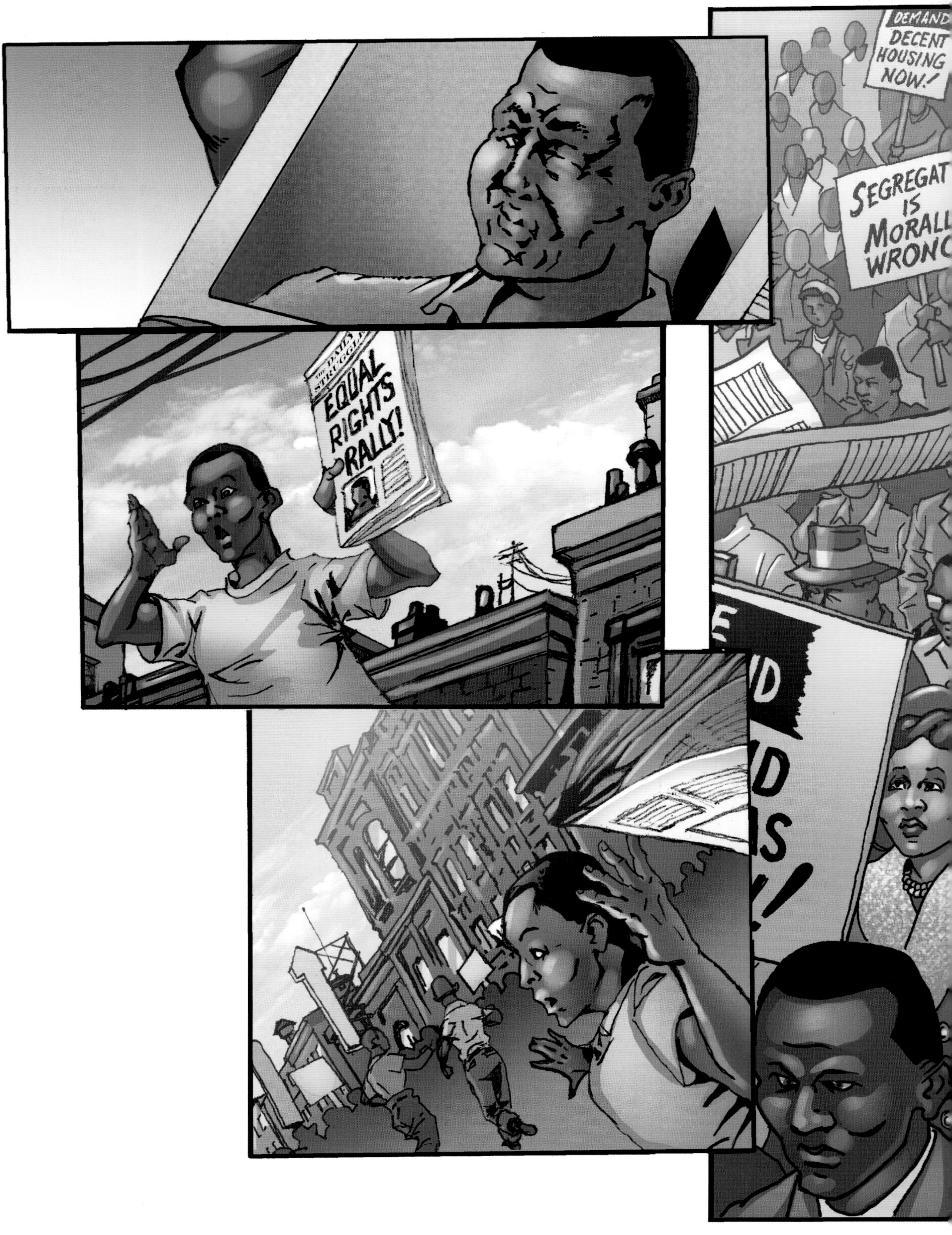
EQUAL RIGHTS RALLY!
DEMAND DECENT HOUSING NOW!
SEGREGAT IS MORALL WRONG

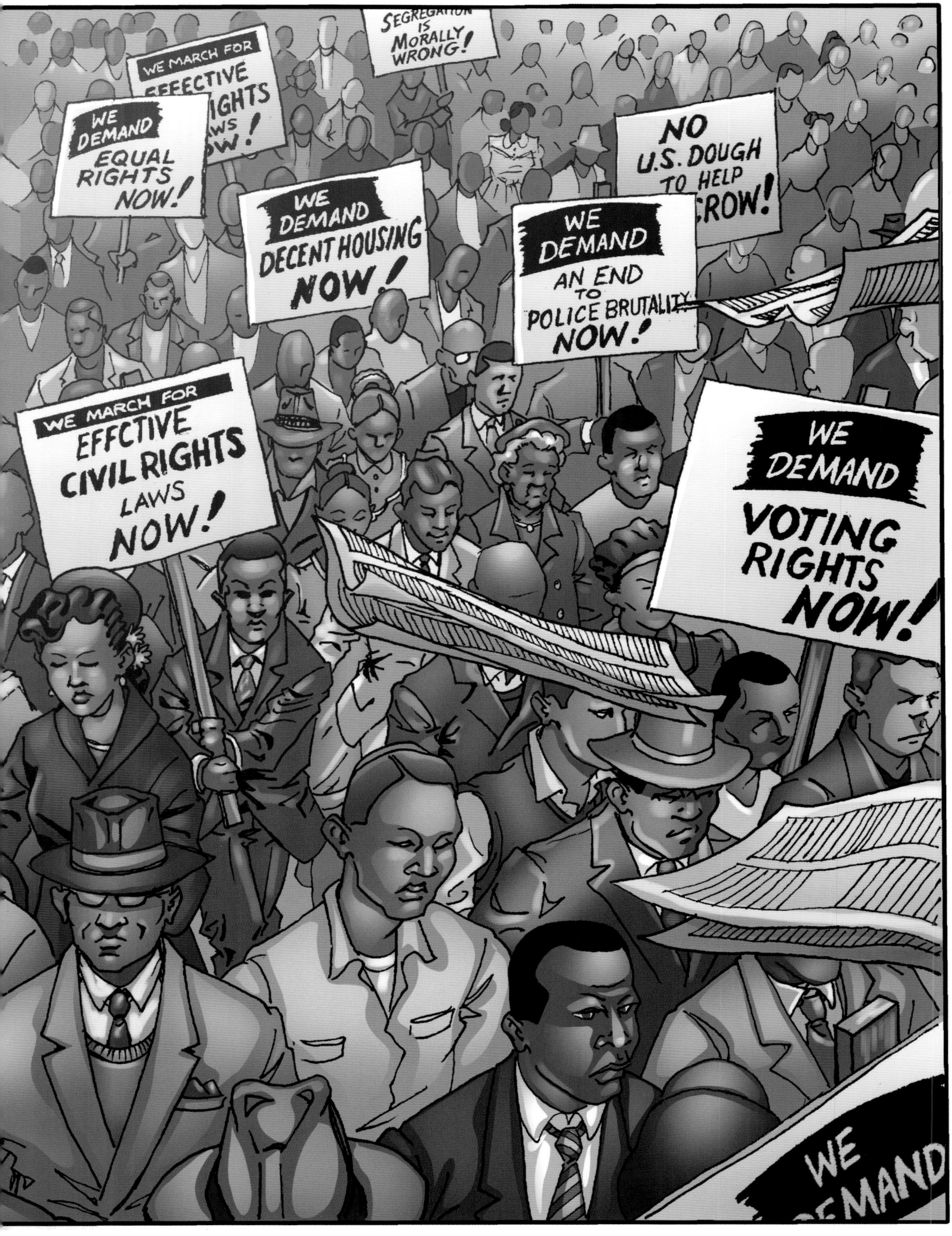
IS
MORALLY
WRONG!
WE MARCH FOR
EFFECTIVE
WE DEMAND
EQUAL RIGHTS NOW!
NO
U.S. DOUGH
TO HELP
WE DEMAND
DECENT HOUSING
NOW!
WE DEMAND
AN END TO POLICE BRUTALITY
NOW!
WE MARCH FOR
EFFCTIVE
CIVIL RIGHTS
LAWS
NOW!
WE DEMAND
VOTING RIGHTS
NOW!
WE

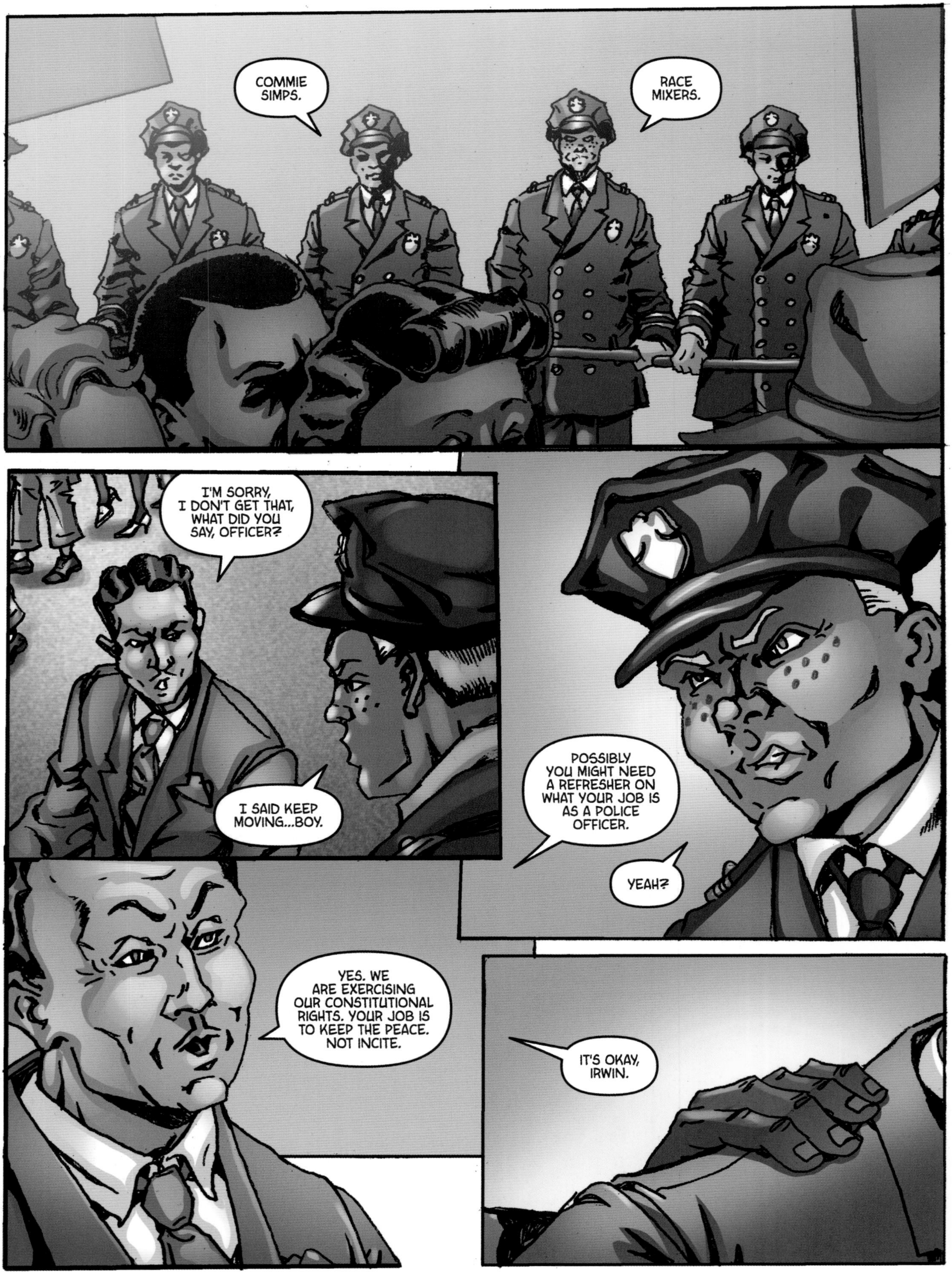
COMMIE SIMPS.
RACE MIXERS.
I'M SORRY, I DON'T GET THAT, WHAT DID YOU SAY, OFFICER?
I SAID KEEP MOVING...BOY.
POSSIBLY YOU MIGHT NEED A REFRESHER ON WHAT YOUR JOB IS AS A POLICE OFFICER.
YEAH?
YES. WE ARE EXERCISING OUR CONSTITUTIONAL RIGHTS. YOUR JOB IS TO KEEP THE PEACE. NOT INCITE.
IT'S OKAY, IRWIN.

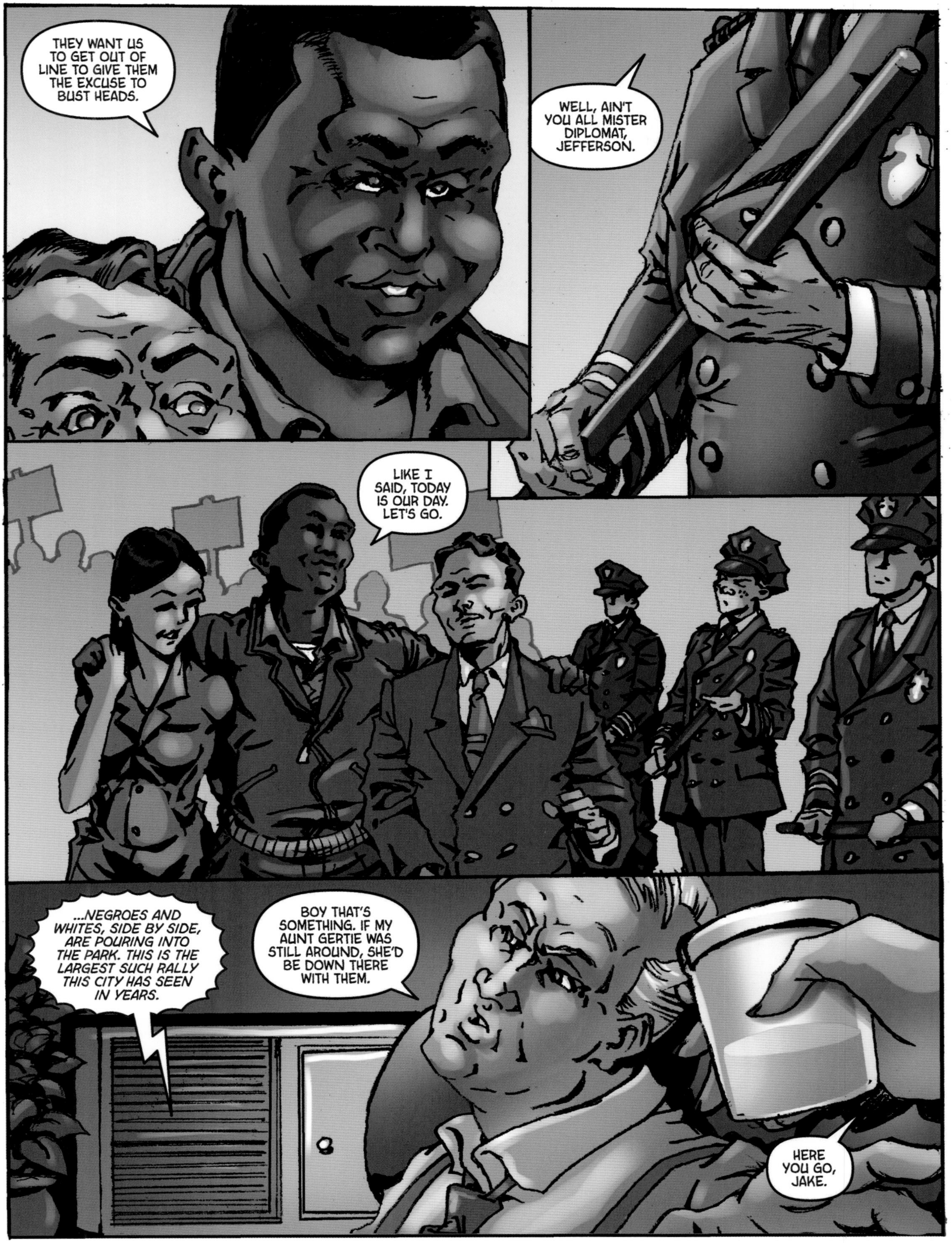
THEY WANT US TO GET OUT OF LINE TO GIVE THEM THE EXCUSE TO BUST HEADS.
WELL, AIN'T YOU ALL MISTER DIPLOMAT, JEFFERSON.
LIKE I SAID, TODAY IS OUR DAY. LET'S GO.
...NEGROES AND WHITES, SIDE BY SIDE, ARE POURING INTO THE PARK. THIS IS THE LARGEST SUCH RALLY THIS CITY HAS SEEN IN YEARS.
BOY THAT'S SOMETHING. IF MY AUNT GERTIE WAS STILL AROUND, SHE'D BE DOWN THERE WITH THEM.
HERE YOU GO, JAKE.

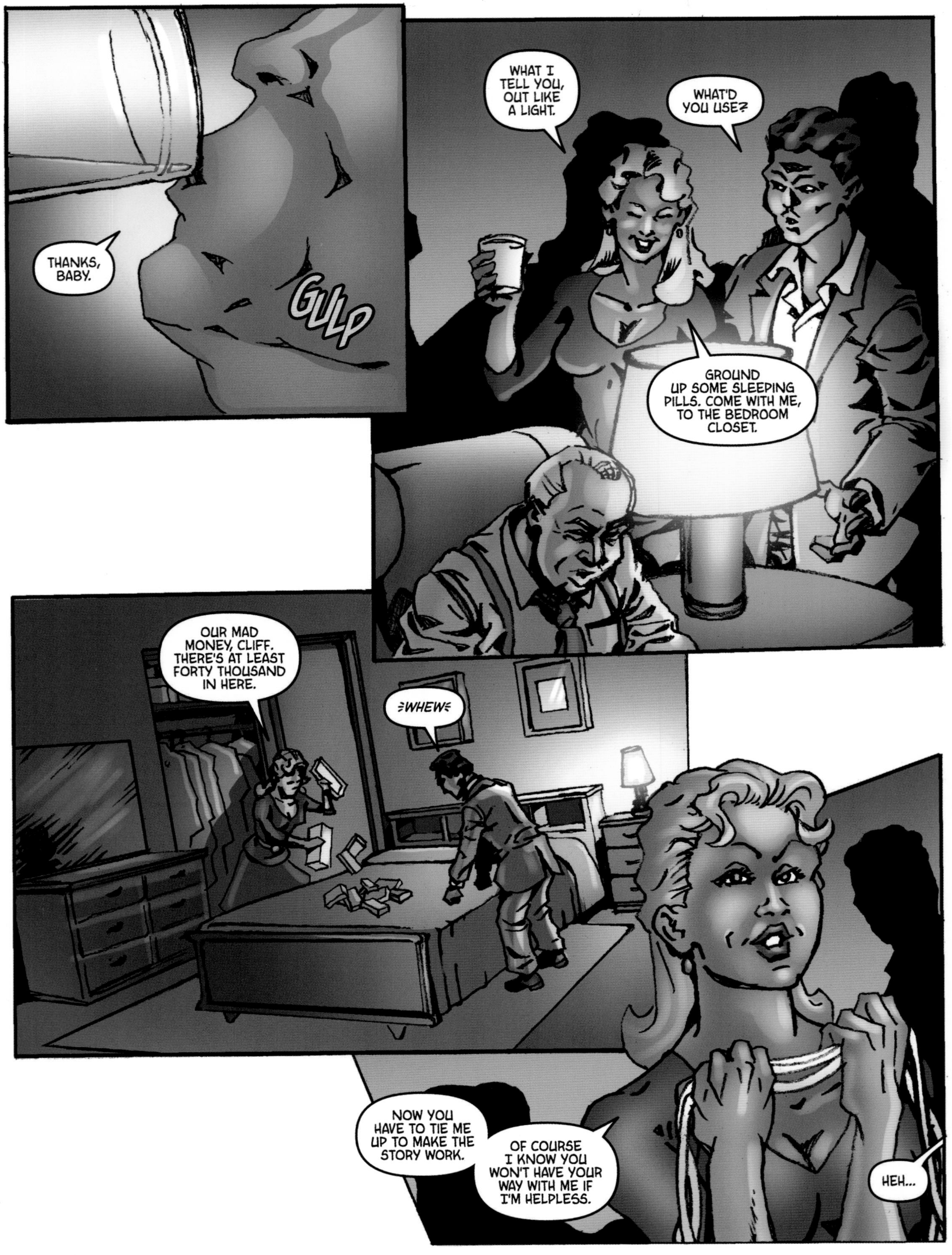
THANKS, BABY.
GULP
WHAT I TELL YOU, OUT LIKE A LIGHT.
WHAT'D YOU USE?
GROUND UP SOME SLEEPING PILLS. COME WITH ME, TO THE BEDROOM CLOSET.
OUR MAD MONEY, CLIFF. THERE'S AT LEAST FORTY THOUSAND IN HERE.
WHEW
NOW YOU HAVE TO TIE ME UP TO MAKE THE STORY WORK.
OF COURSE I KNOW YOU WON'T HAVE YOUR WAY WITH ME IF I'M HELPLESS.
HEH...

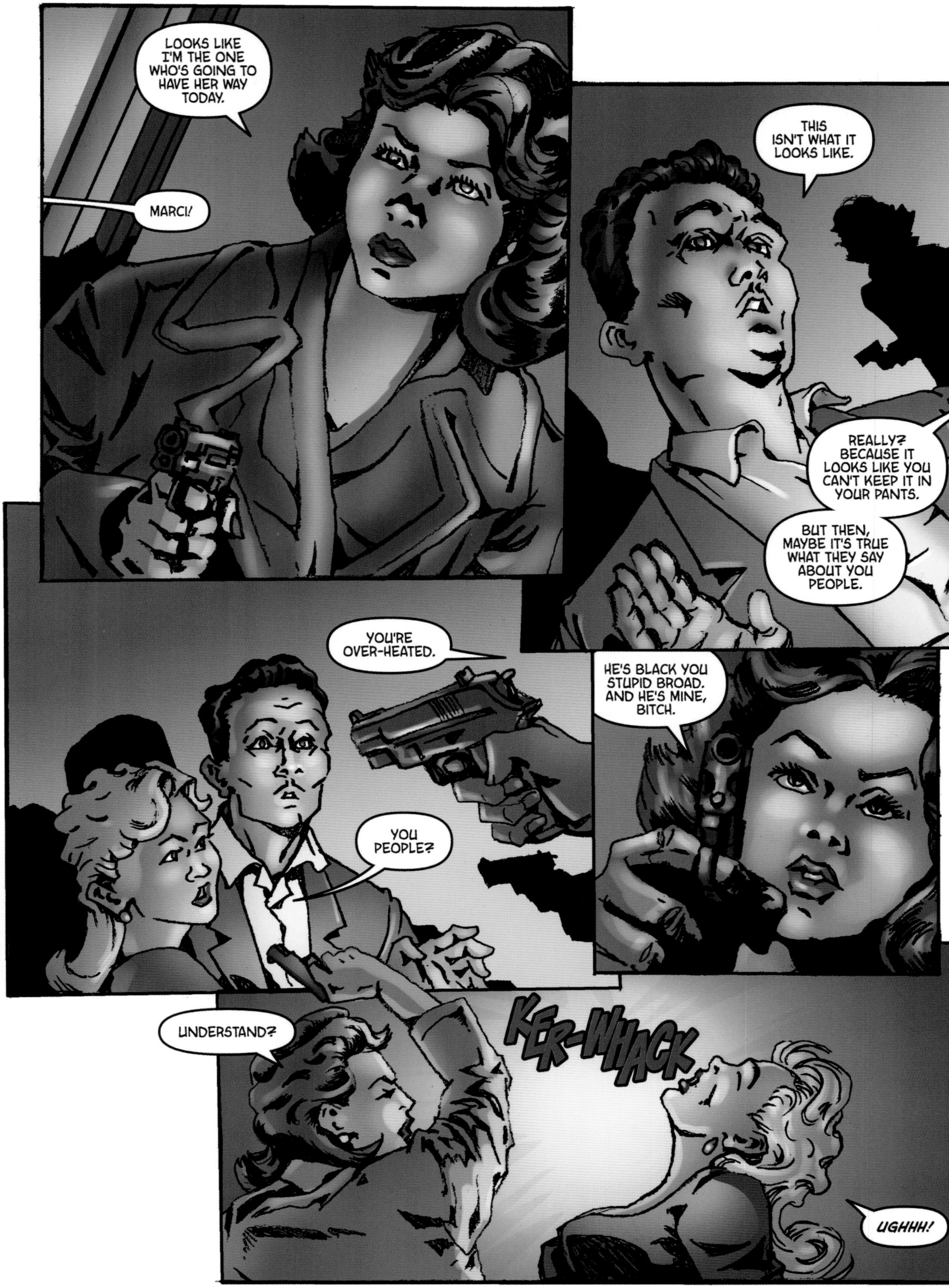
LOOKS LIKE I'M THE ONE WHO'S GOING TO HAVE HER WAY TODAY.
MARCI!
THIS ISN'T WHAT IT LOOKS LIKE.
REALLY? BECAUSE IT LOOKS LIKE YOU CAN'T KEEP IT IN YOUR PANTS.
BUT THEN, MAYBE IT'S TRUE WHAT THEY SAY ABOUT YOU PEOPLE.
YOU'RE OVER-HEATED.
YOU PEOPLE?
HE'S BLACK YOU STUPID BROAD. AND HE'S MINE, BITCH.
UNDERSTAND?
KER-WHACK
UGHHH!

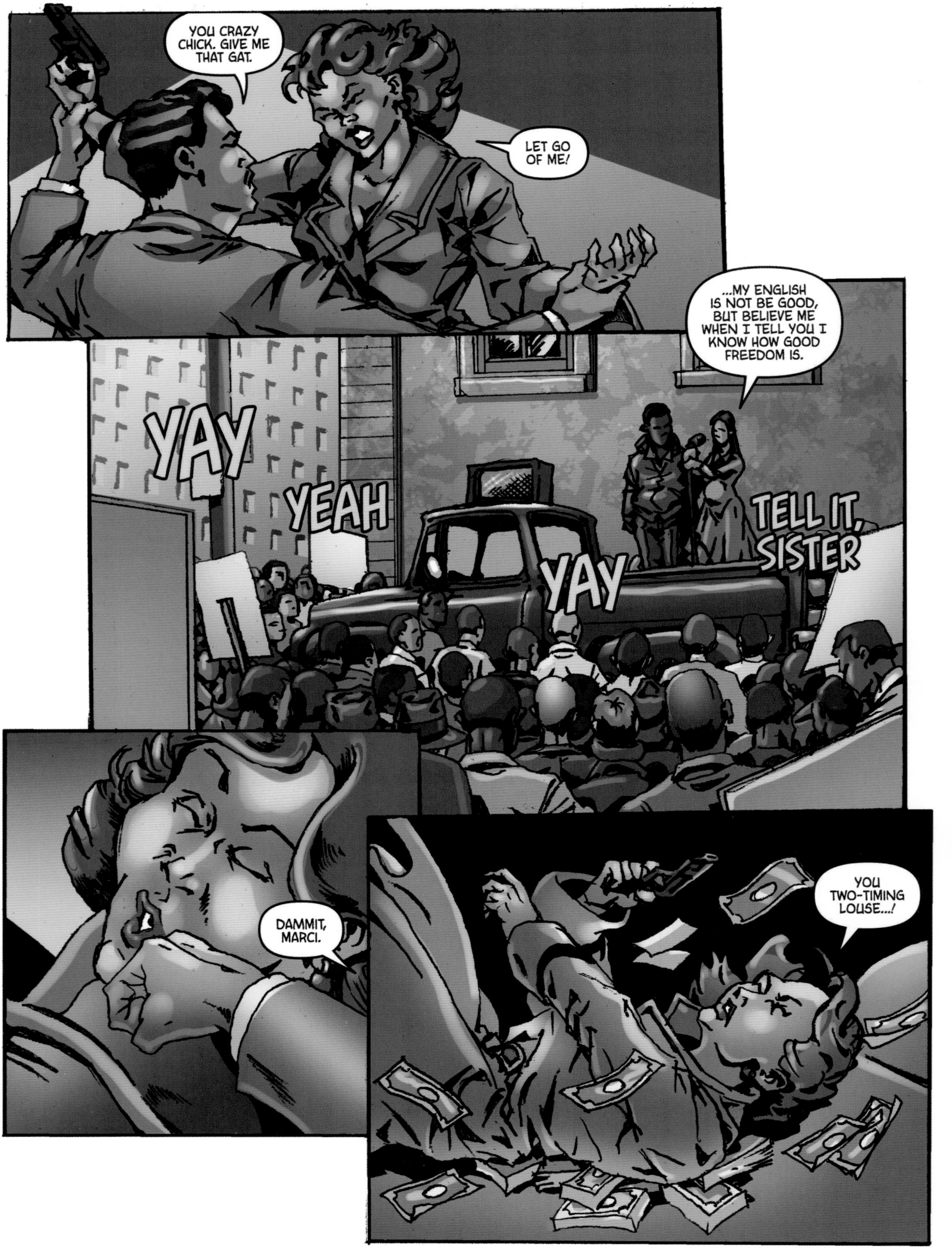
YOU CRAZY CHICK. GIVE ME THAT GAT.
LET GO OF ME!
...MY ENGLISH IS NOT BE GOOD, BUT BELIEVE ME WHEN I TELL YOU I KNOW HOW GOOD FREEDOM IS.
YAY
YEAH
YAY
TELL IT, SISTER
DAMMIT, MARCI.
YOU TWO-TIMING LOUSE...!

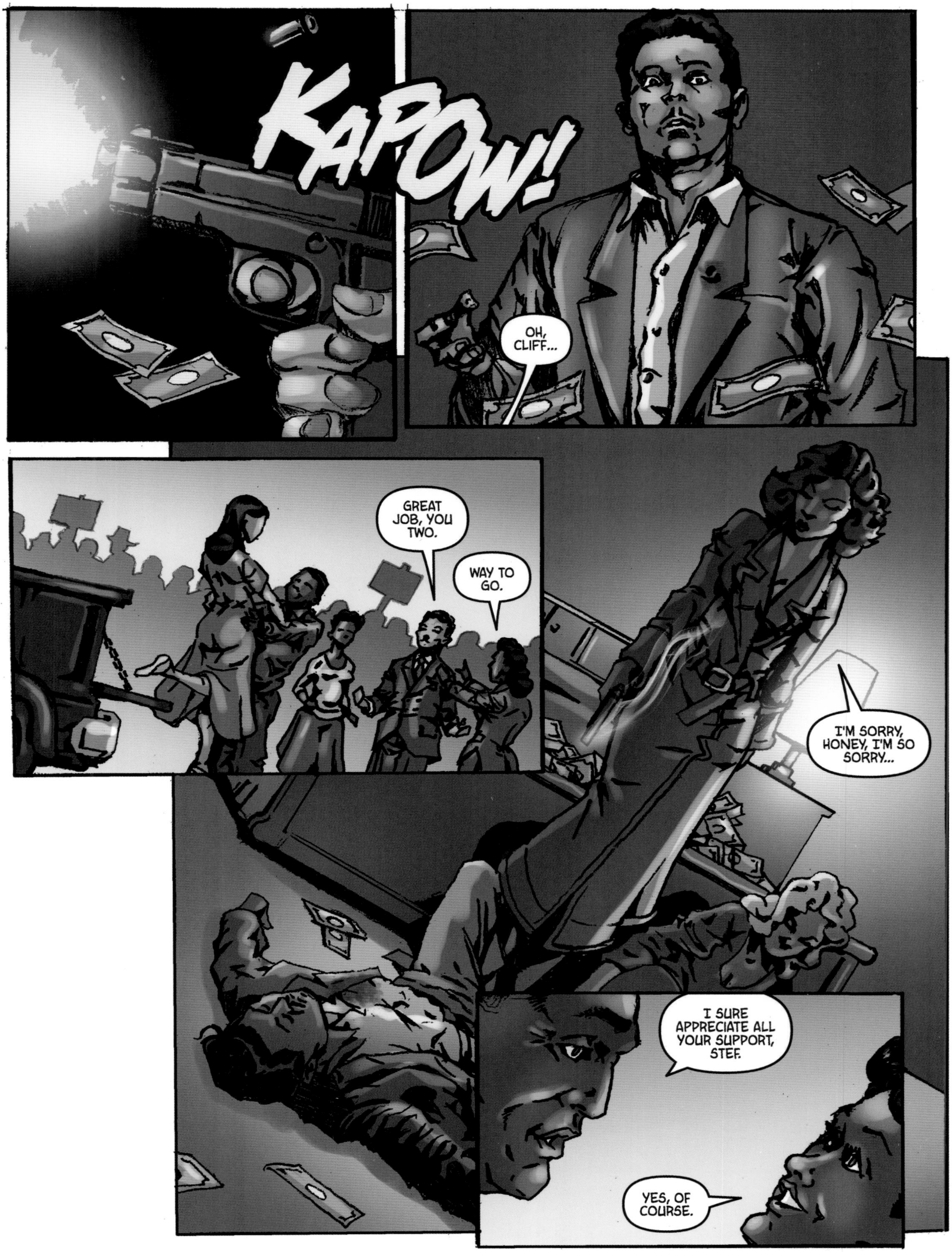
KAPOW!
OH, CLIFF...
GREAT JOB, YOU TWO.
WAY TO GO.
I'M SORRY, HONEY, I'M SO SORRY...
I SURE APPRECIATE ALL YOUR SUPPORT, STEF.
YES, OF COURSE.

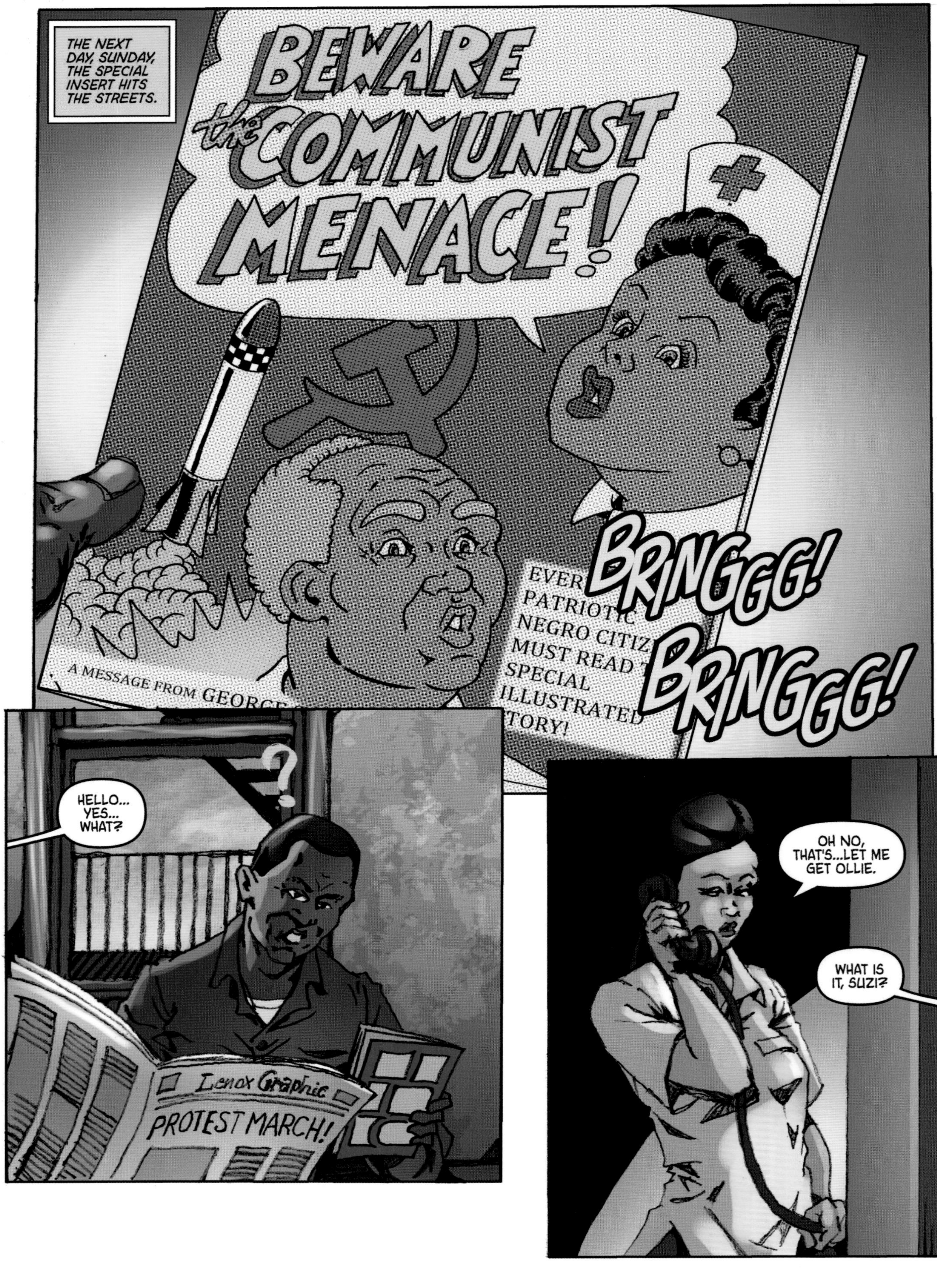
THE NEXT DAY, SUNDAY, THE SPECIAL INSERT HITS THE STREETS.
BEWARE the COMMUNIST MENACE!
EVER
PATRIOTIC
NEGRO CITIZ
MUST READ T
SPECIAL
ILLUSTRATED
TORY!
A MESSAGE FROM GEORGE
BRINGGG!
BRINGGG!
HELLO... YES... WHAT?
?
Lenox Graphic
PROTEST MARCH!
OH NO, THAT'S...LET ME GET OLLIE.
WHAT IS IT, SUZI?

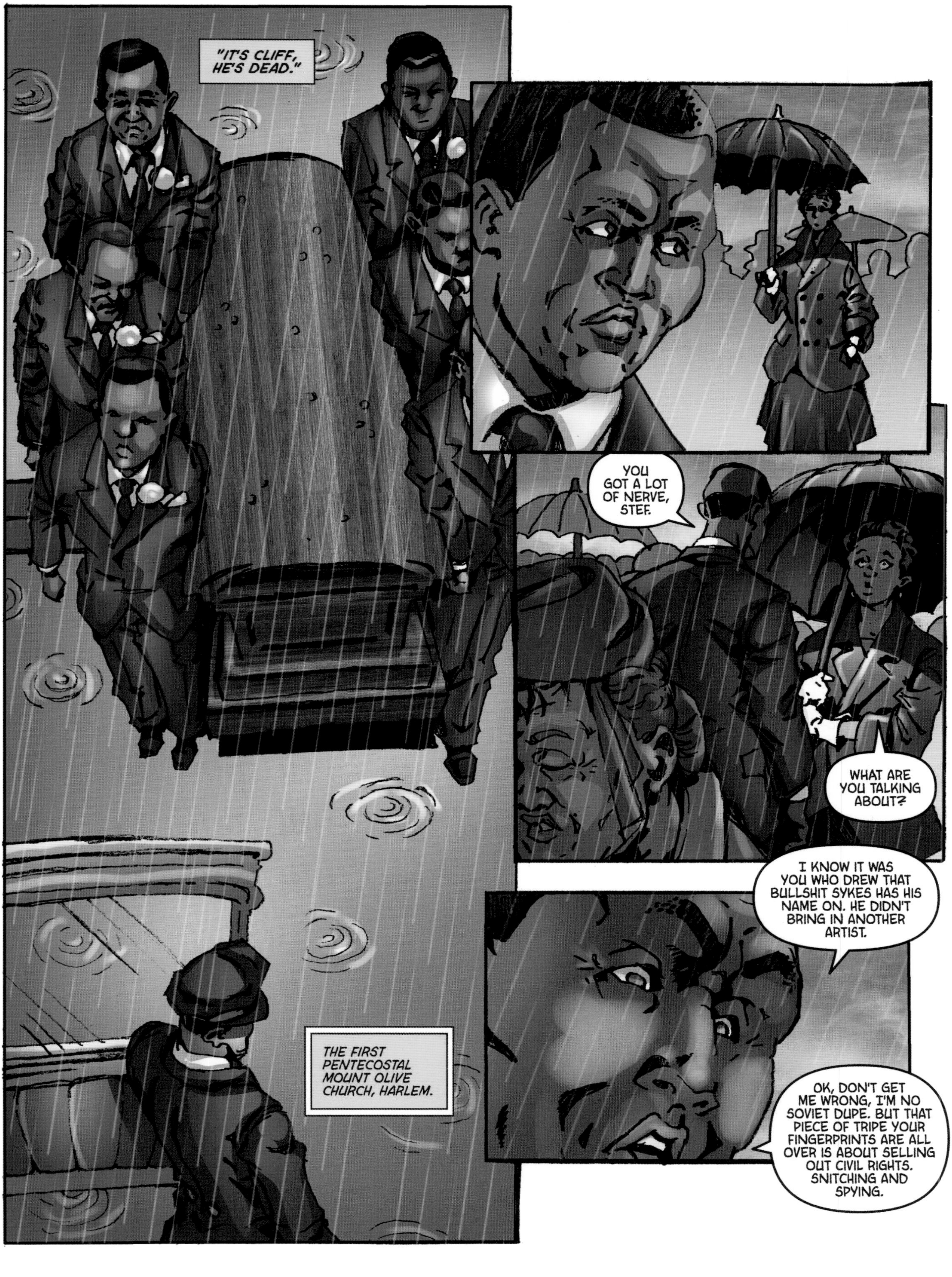
"IT'S CLIFF, HE'S DEAD."
THE FIRST PENTECOSTAL MOUNT OLIVE CHURCH, HARLEM.
YOU GOT A LOT OF NERVE, STEF.
WHAT ARE YOU TALKING ABOUT?
I KNOW IT WAS YOU WHO DREW THAT BULLSHIT SYKES HAS HIS NAME ON. HE DIDN'T BRING IN ANOTHER ARTIST.
OK, DON'T GET ME WRONG, I'M NO SOVIET DUPE. BUT THAT PIECE OF TRIPE YOUR FINGERPRINTS ARE ALL OVER IS ABOUT SELLING OUT CIVIL RIGHTS. SNITCHING AND SPYING.

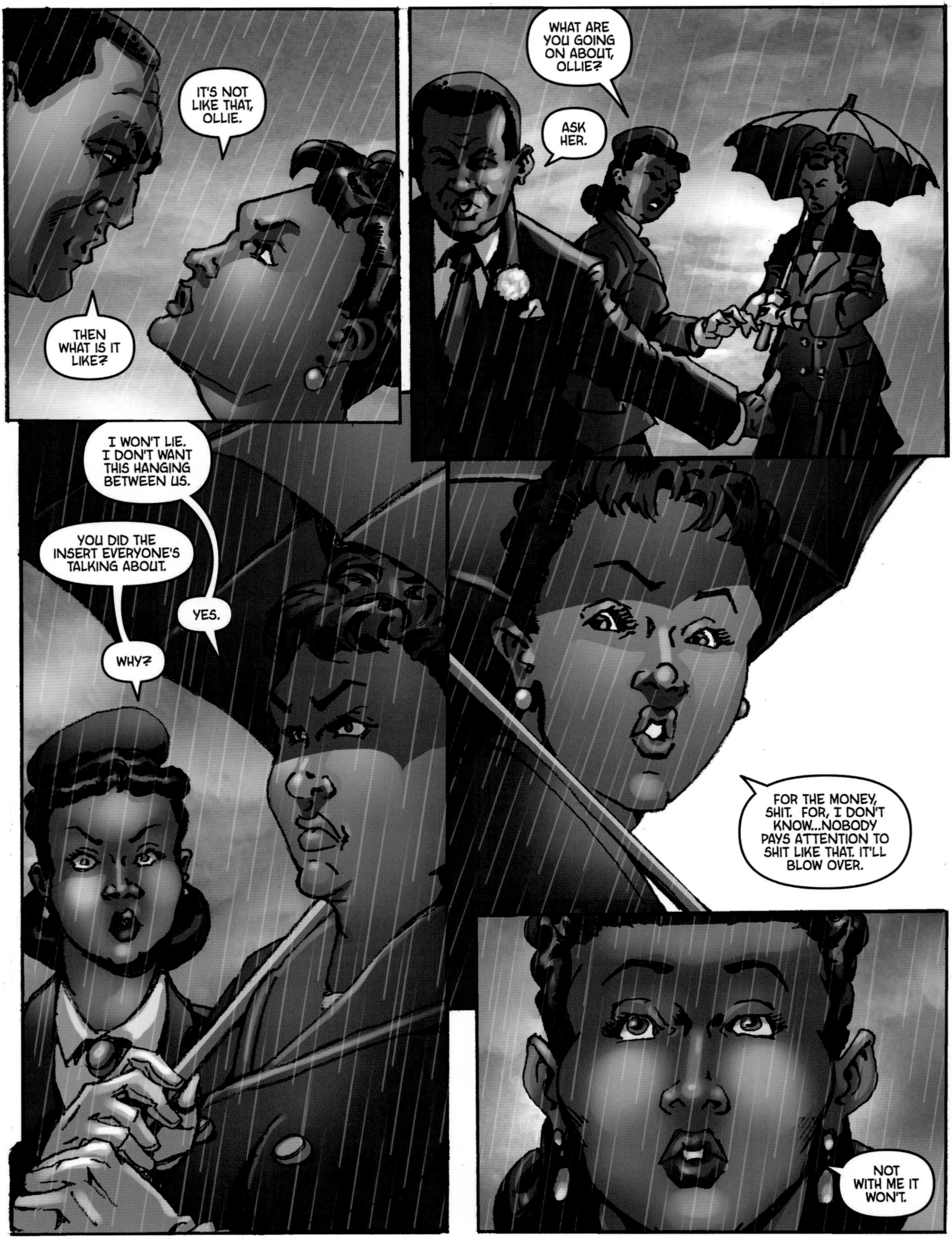
IT'S NOT LIKE THAT, OLLIE.
THEN WHAT IS IT LIKE?
WHAT ARE YOU GOING ON ABOUT, OLLIE?
ASK HER.
I WON'T LIE. I DON'T WANT THIS HANGING BETWEEN US.
YOU DID THE INSERT EVERYONE'S TALKING ABOUT.
YES.
WHY?
FOR THE MONEY, SHIT. FOR, I DON'T KNOW...NOBODY PAYS ATTENTION TO SHIT LIKE THAT. IT'LL BLOW OVER.
NOT WITH ME IT WON'T.

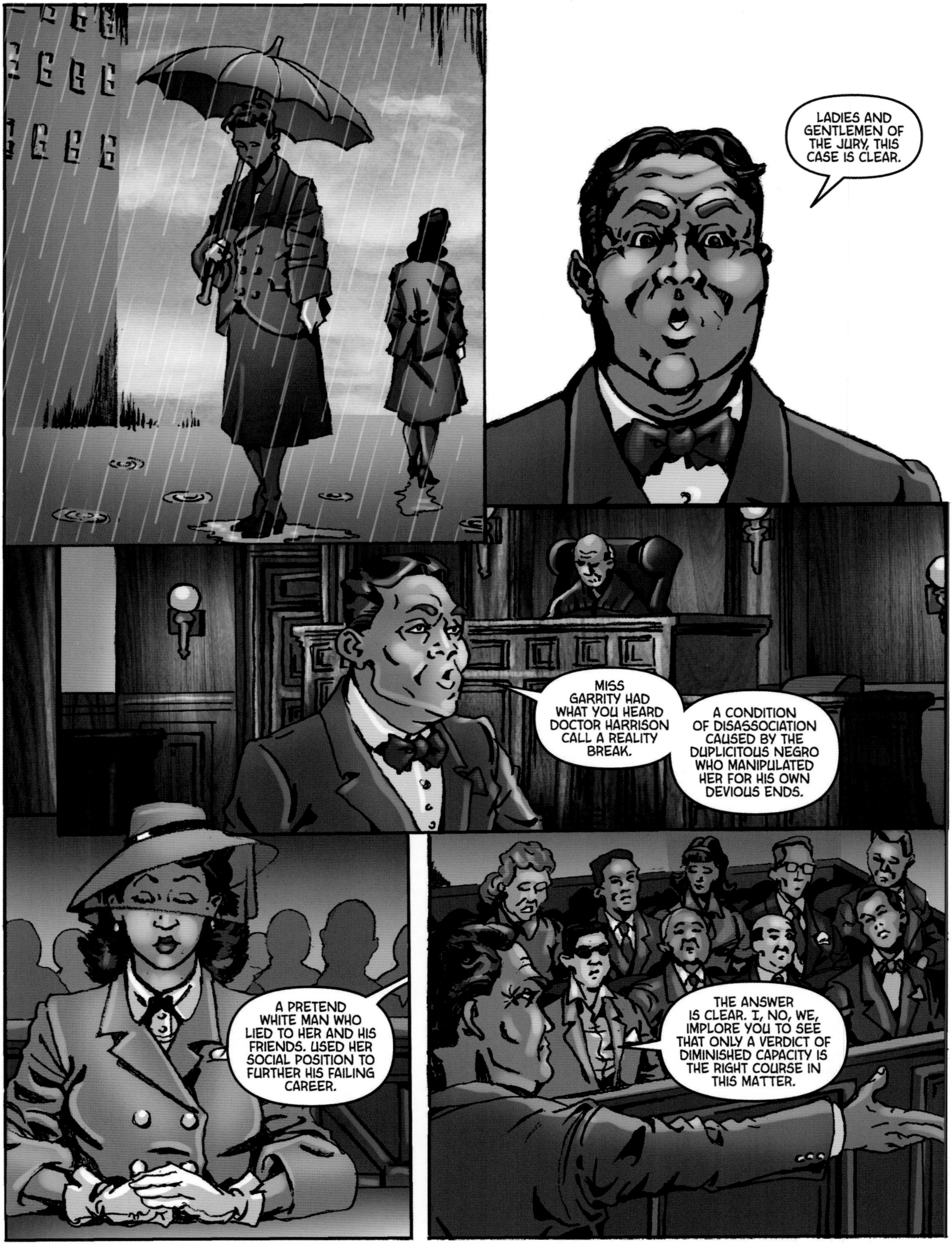
LADIES AND GENTLEMEN OF THE JURY, THIS CASE IS CLEAR.
MISS GARRITY HAD WHAT YOU HEARD DOCTOR HARRISON CALL A REALITY BREAK.
A CONDITION OF DISASSOCIATION CAUSED BY THE DUPLICITOUS NEGRO WHO MANIPULATED HER FOR HIS OWN DEVIOUS ENDS.
A PRETEND WHITE MAN WHO LIED TO HER AND HIS FRIENDS. USED HER SOCIAL POSITION TO FURTHER HIS FAILING CAREER.
THE ANSWER IS CLEAR. I, NO, WE, IMPLORE YOU TO SEE THAT ONLY A VERDICT OF DIMINISHED CAPACITY IS THE RIGHT COURSE IN THIS MATTER.

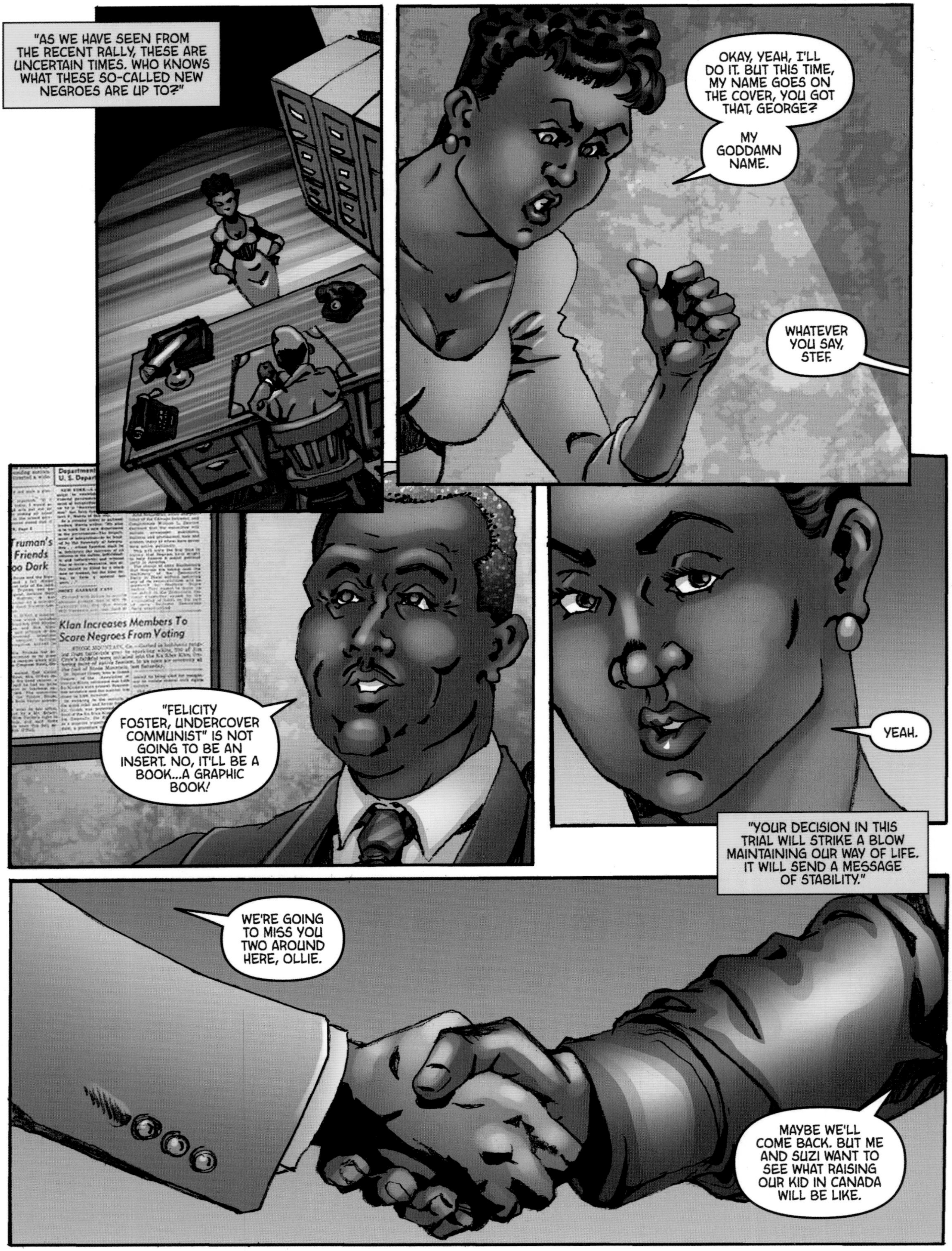
"AS WE HAVE SEEN FROM THE RECENT RALLY, THESE ARE UNCERTAIN TIMES. WHO KNOWS WHAT THESE SO-CALLED NEW NEGROES ARE UP TO?"
OKAY, YEAH, I'LL DO IT. BUT THIS TIME, MY NAME GOES ON THE COVER, YOU GOT THAT, GEORGE?
MY GODDAMN NAME.
WHATEVER YOU SAY, STEF.
Truman's Friends oo Dark
Klan Increases Members To Scare Negroes From Voting
"FELICITY FOSTER, UNDERCOVER COMMUNIST" IS NOT GOING TO BE AN INSERT. NO, IT'LL BE A BOOK...A GRAPHIC BOOK!
YEAH.
"YOUR DECISION IN THIS TRIAL WILL STRIKE A BLOW MAINTAINING OUR WAY OF LIFE. IT WILL SEND A MESSAGE OF STABILITY."
WE'RE GOING TO MISS YOU TWO AROUND HERE, OLLIE.
MAYBE WE'LL COME BACK. BUT ME AND SUZI WANT TO SEE WHAT RAISING OUR KID IN CANADA WILL BE LIKE.

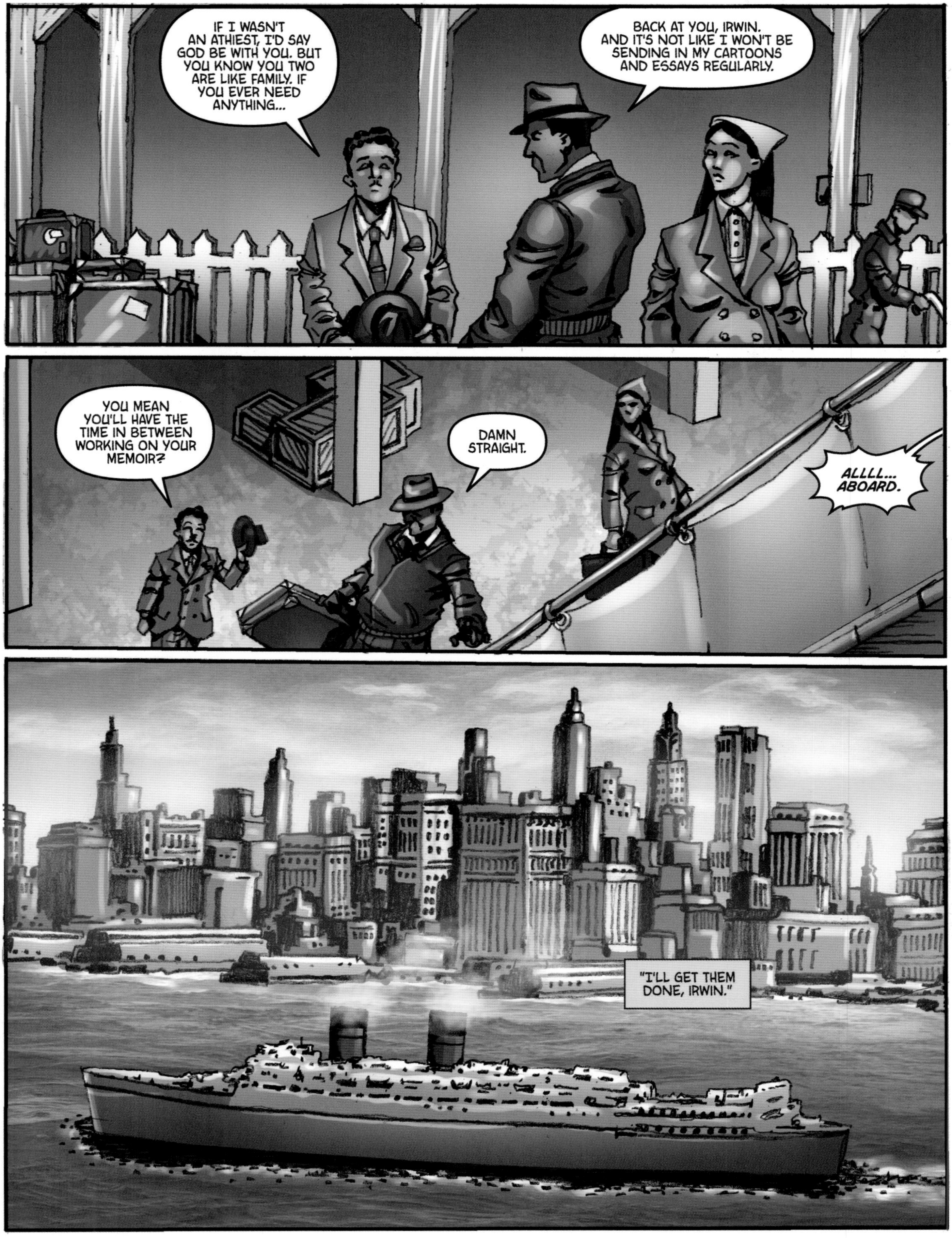
IF I WASN'T AN ATHIEST, I'D SAY GOD BE WITH YOU. BUT YOU KNOW YOU TWO ARE LIKE FAMILY. IF YOU EVER NEED ANYTHING...
BACK AT YOU, IRWIN. AND IT'S NOT LIKE I WON'T BE SENDING IN MY CARTOONS AND ESSAYS REGULARLY.
YOU MEAN YOU'LL HAVE THE TIME IN BETWEEN WORKING ON YOUR MEMOIR?
DAMN STRAIGHT.
ALLLL... ABOARD.
"I'LL GET THEM DONE, IRWIN."

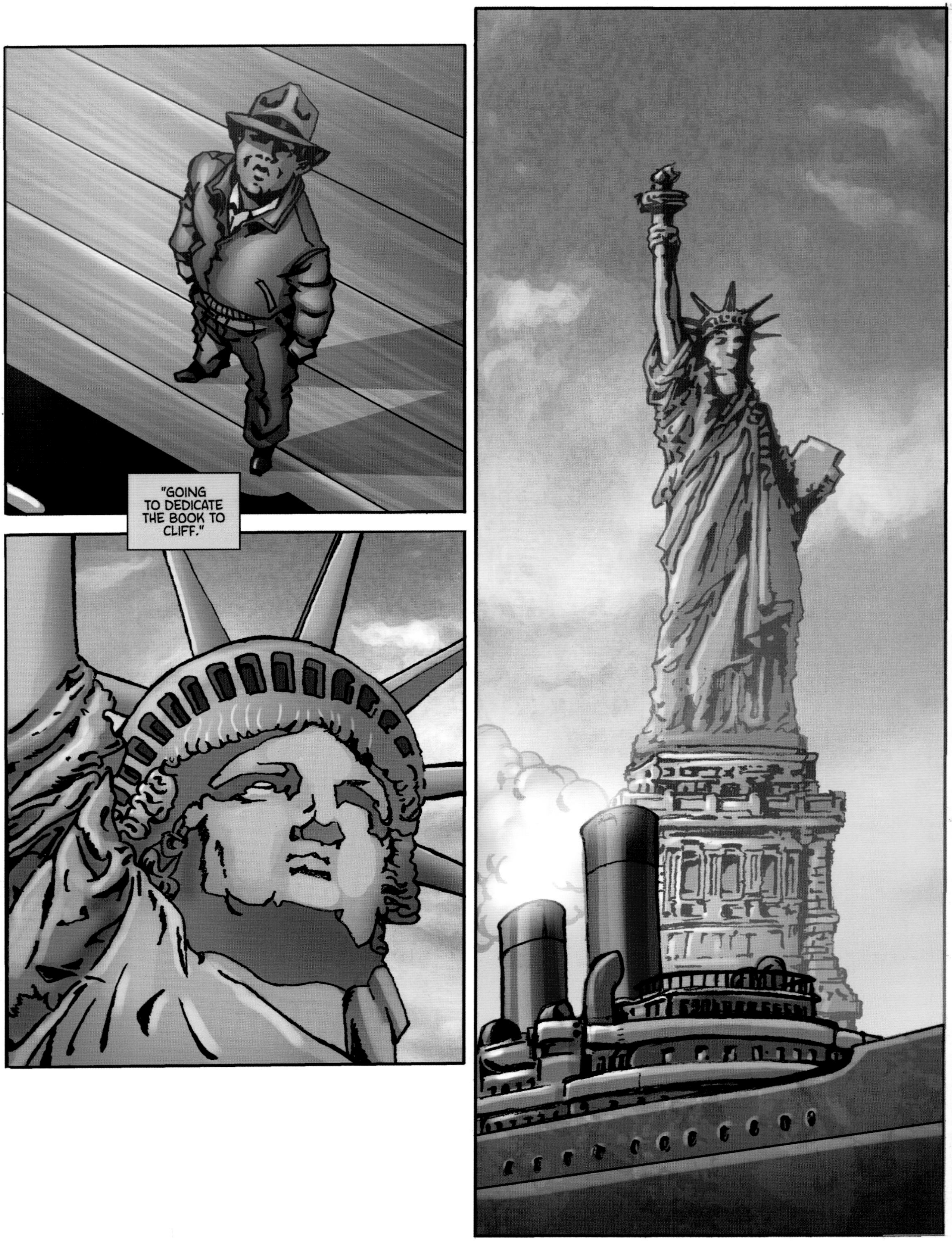
"GOING TO DEDICATE THE BOOK TO CLIFF."

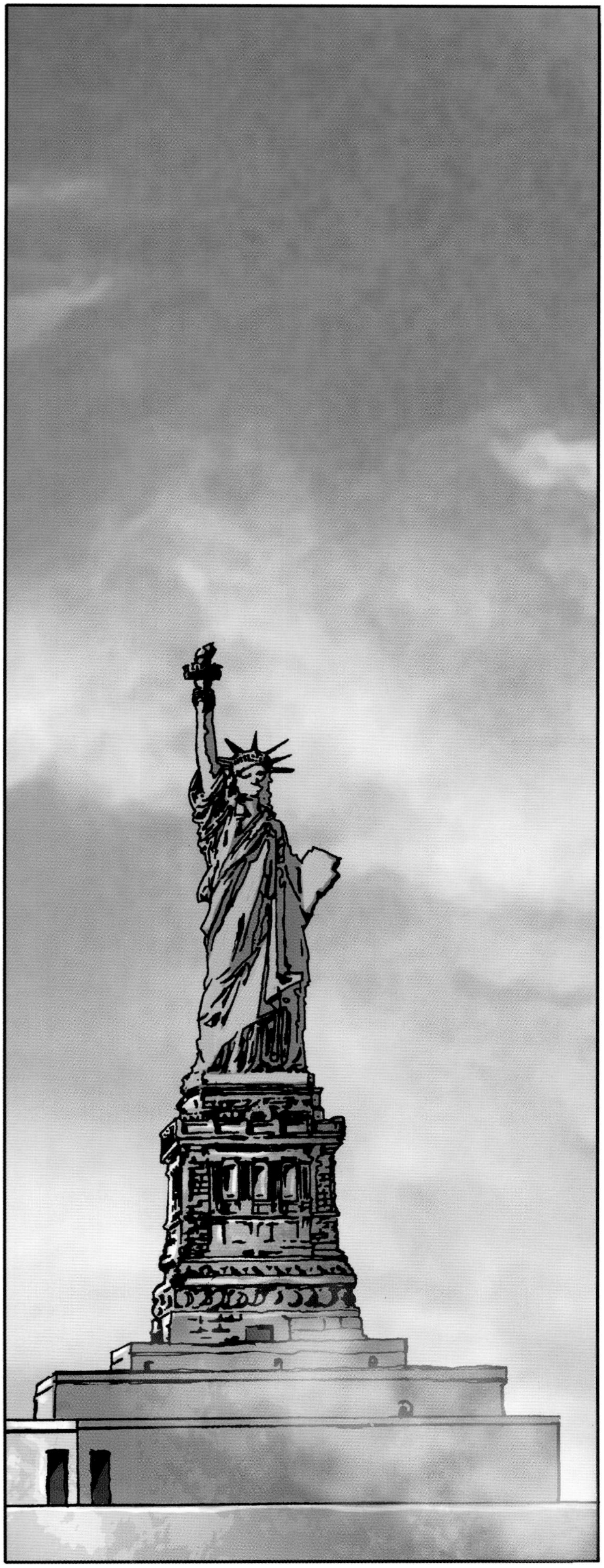

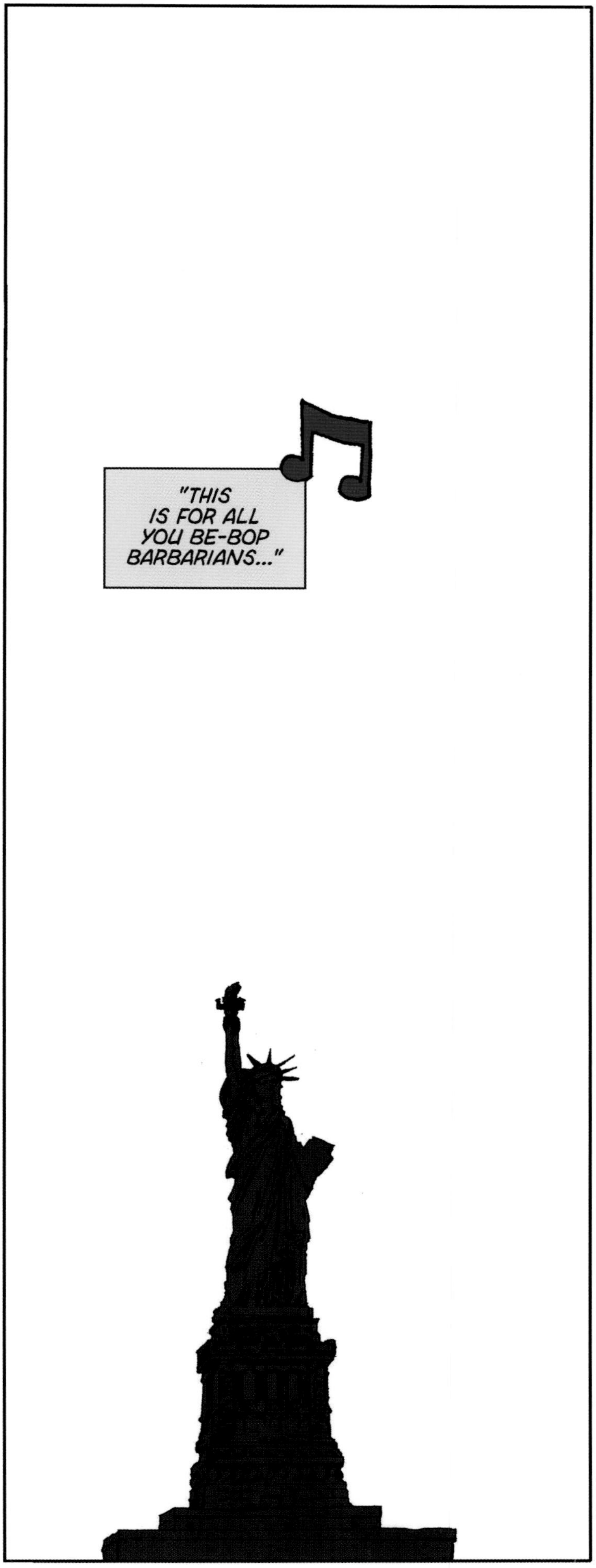
"THIS IS FOR ALL YOU BE-BOP BARBARIANS..."

SKETCHBOOK

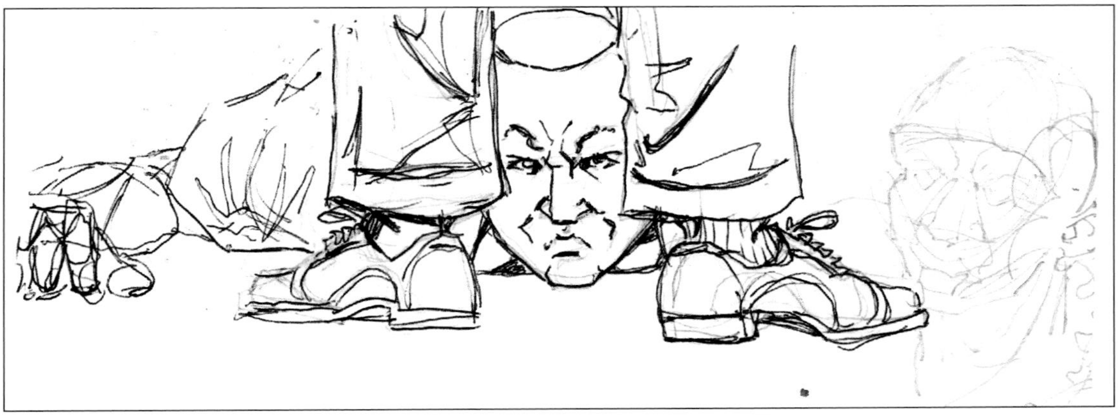

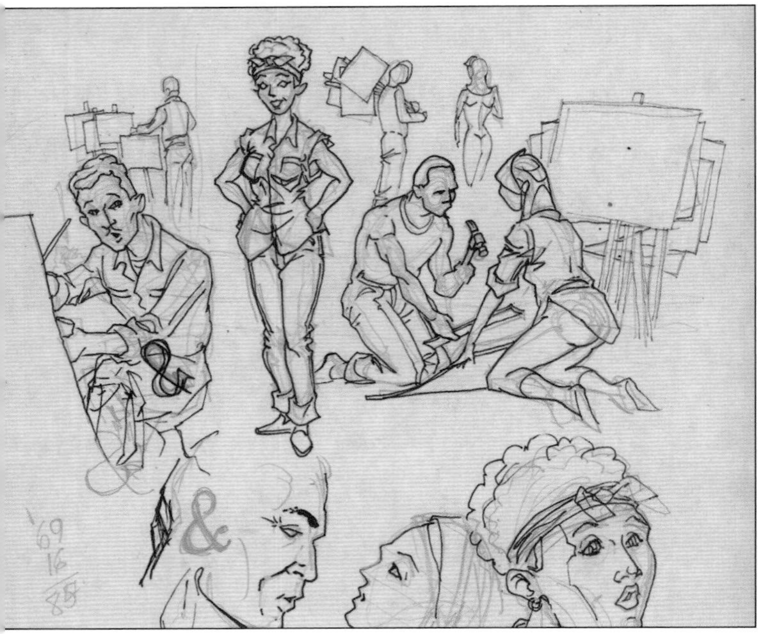

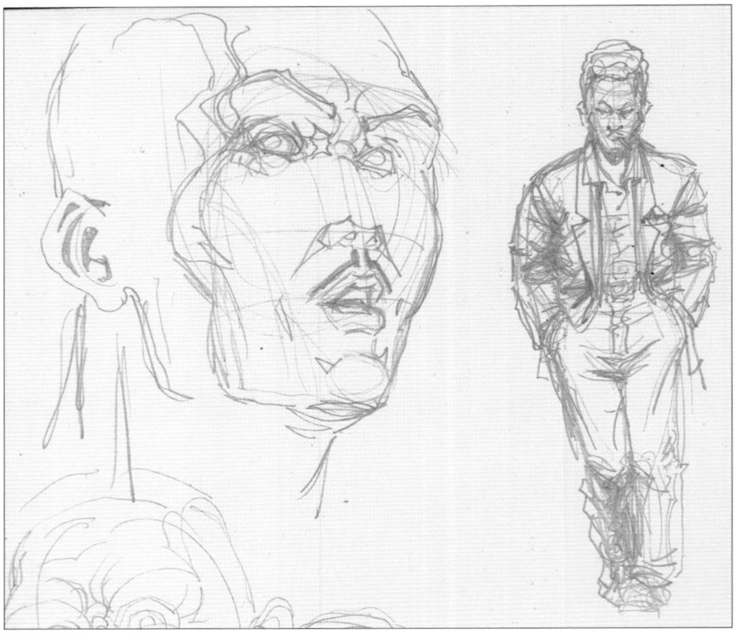

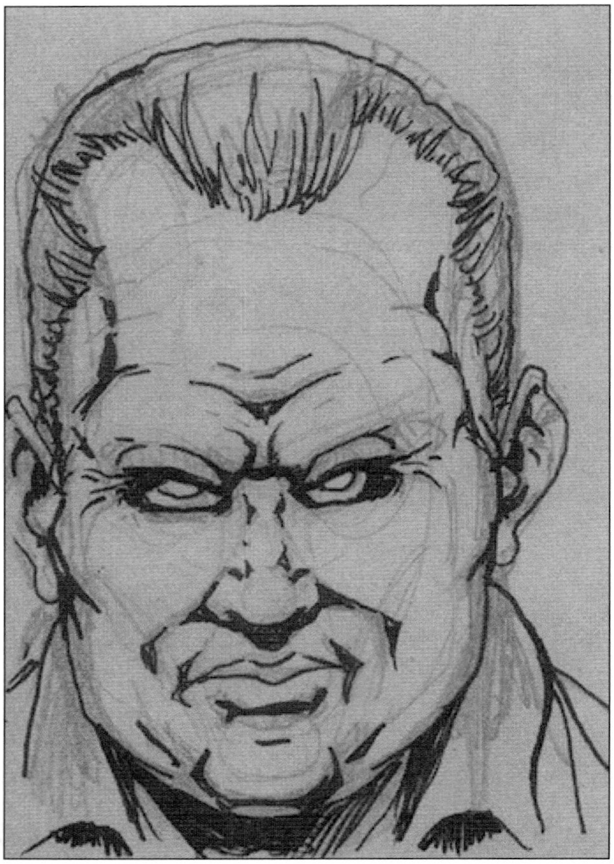

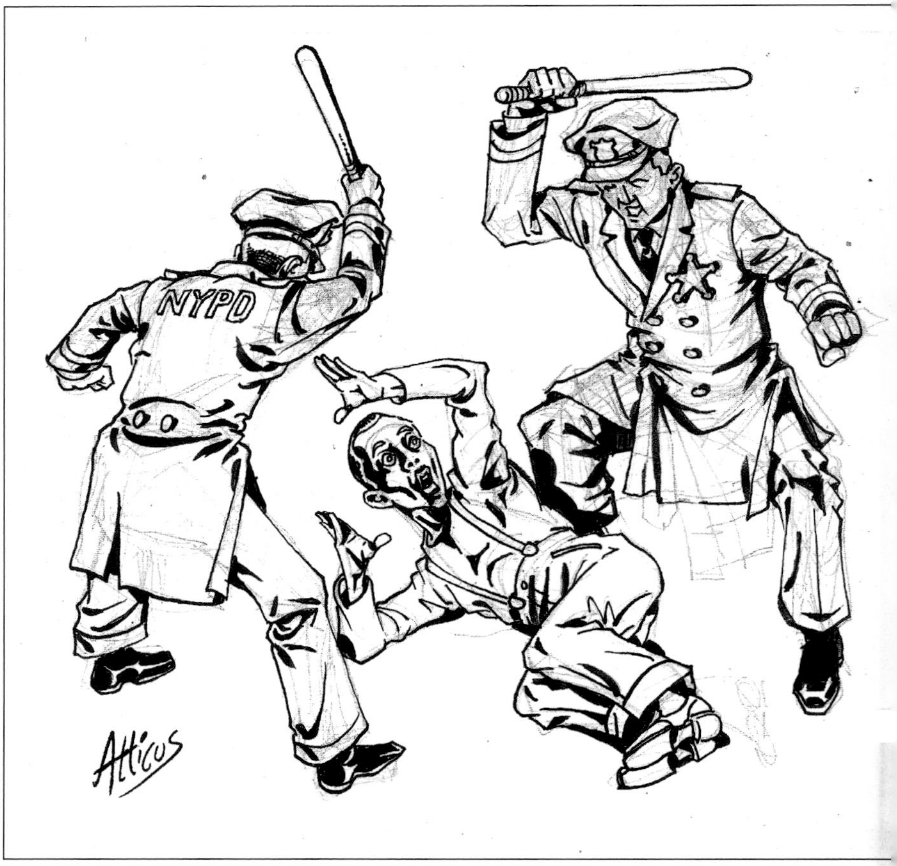
NYPD
Atticus

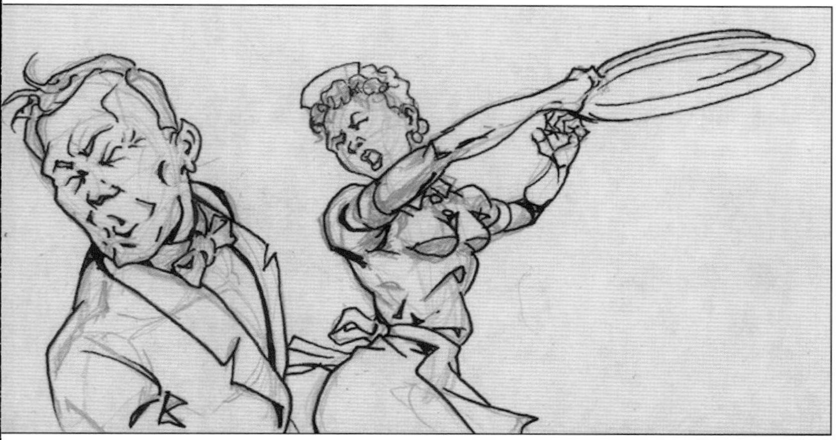

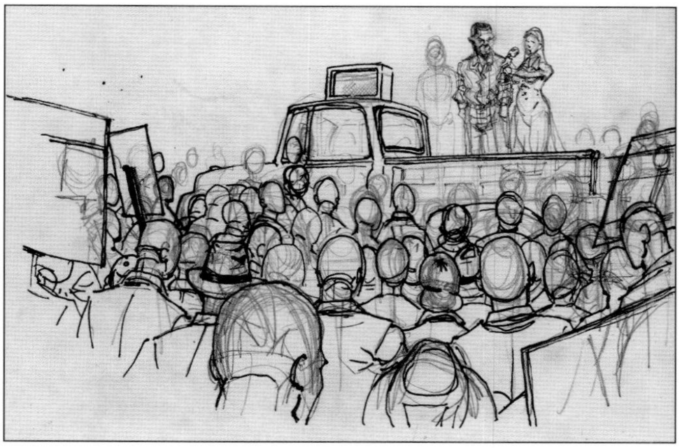

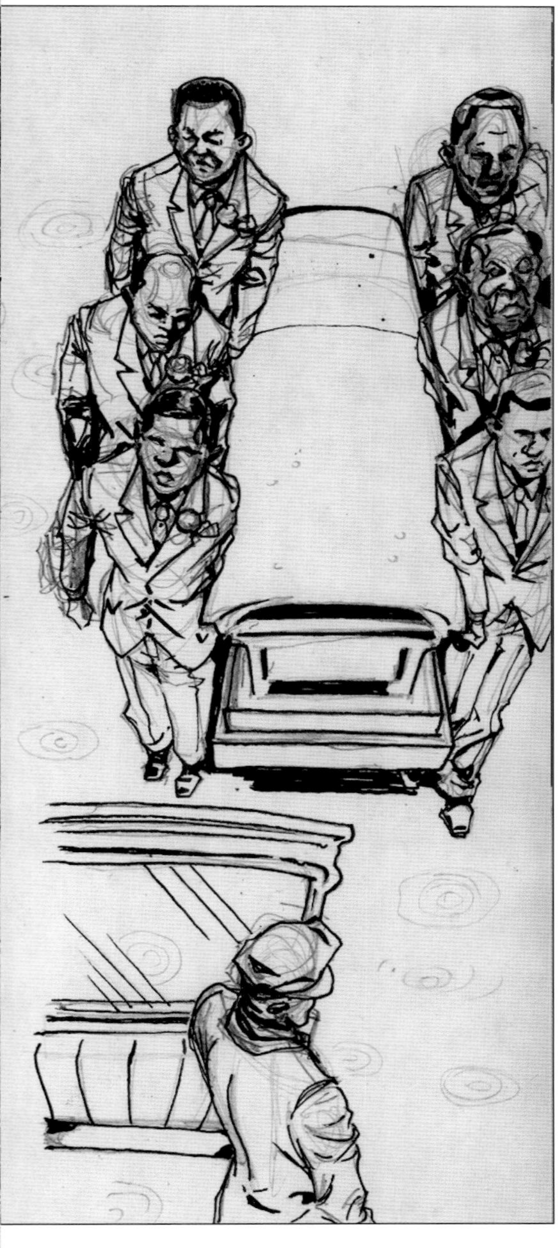

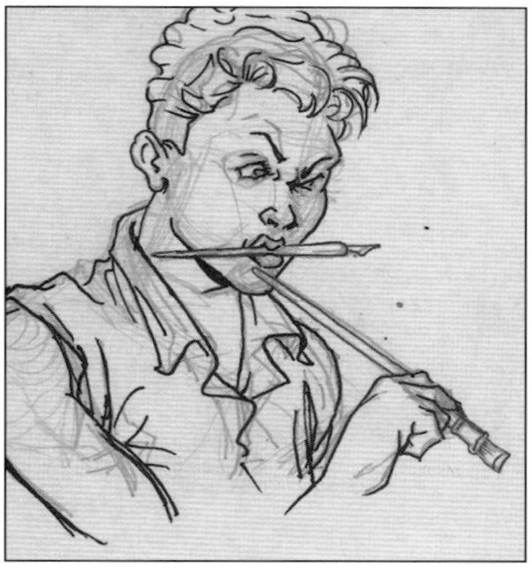

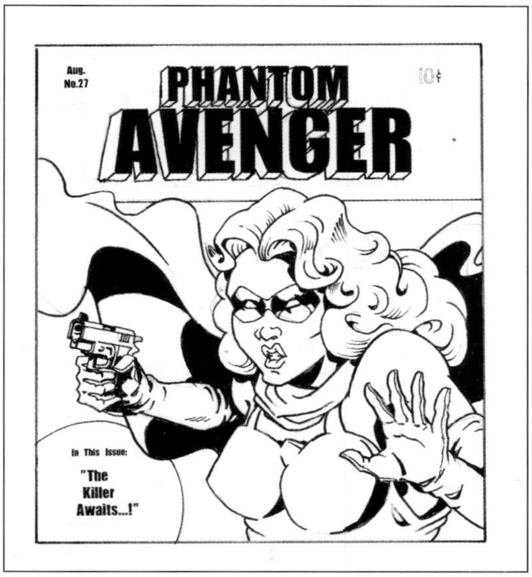
Aug.
No.27
10¢
PHANTOM
AVENGER
In This Issue:
"The
Killer
Awaits...!"

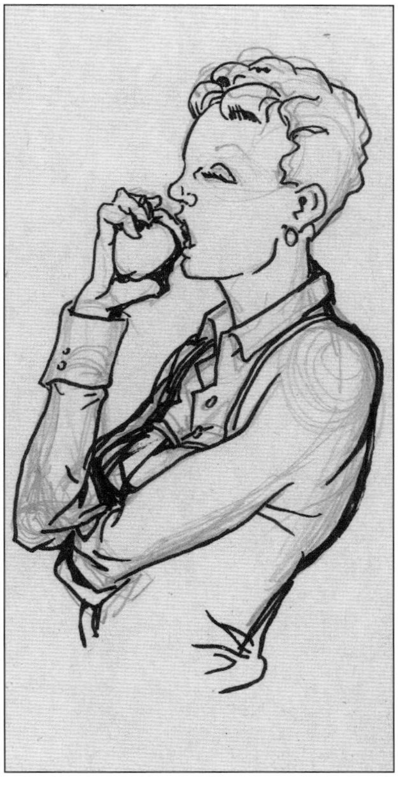

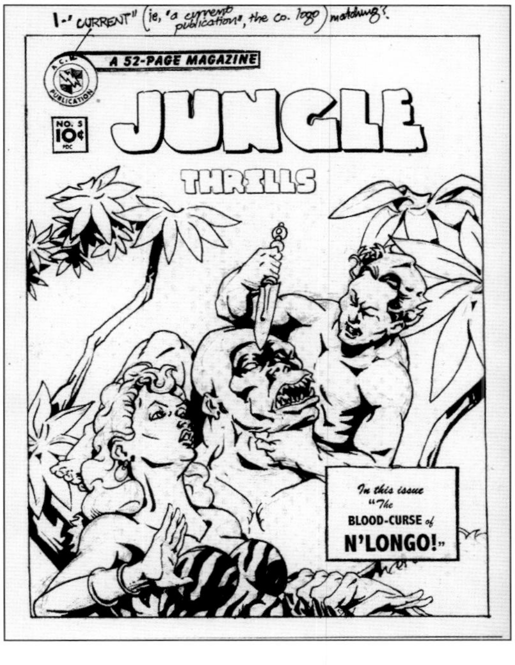
1.-' CURRENT" (ie, "a current publication", the co. logo) matching?
A.C.E.
PUBLICATION
A 52-PAGE MAGAZINE
NO. 5
10¢
PDC
JUNGLE
THRILLS
In this issue
"The
BLOOD-CURSE of
N'LONGO!"

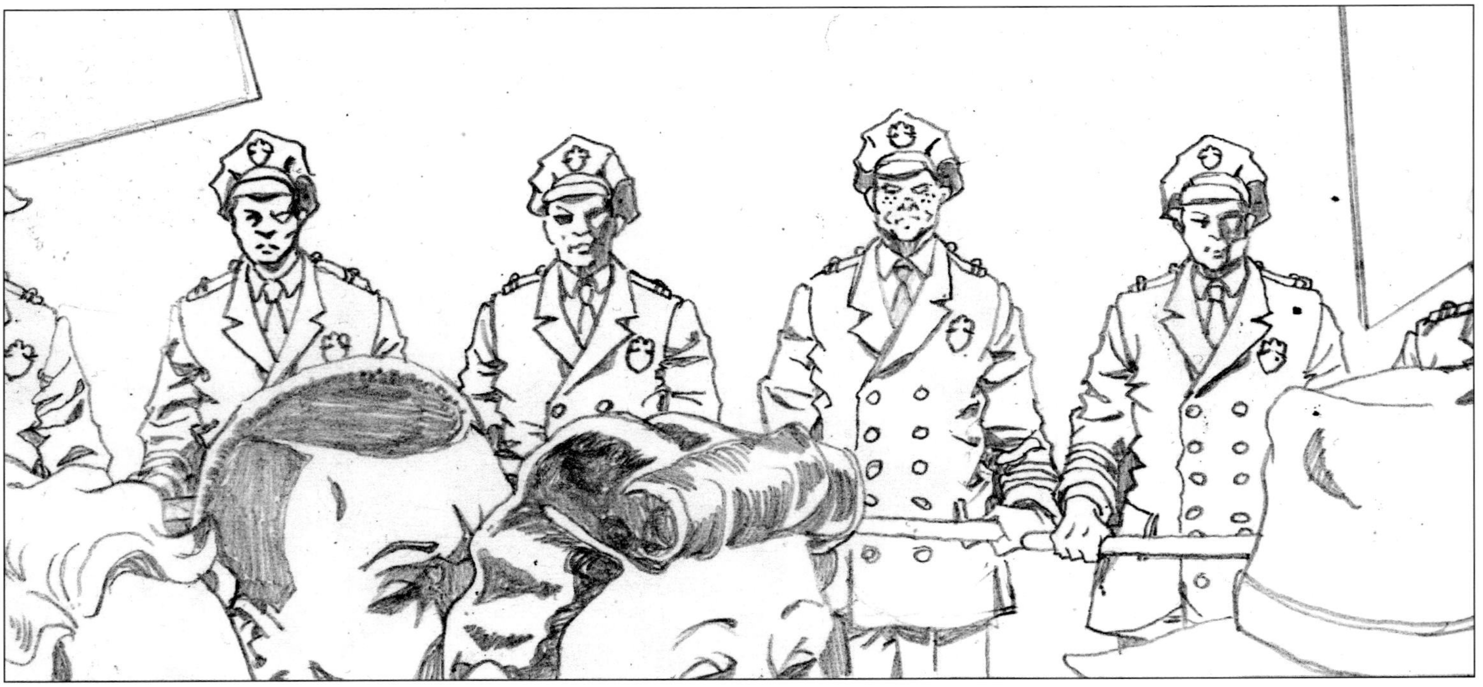

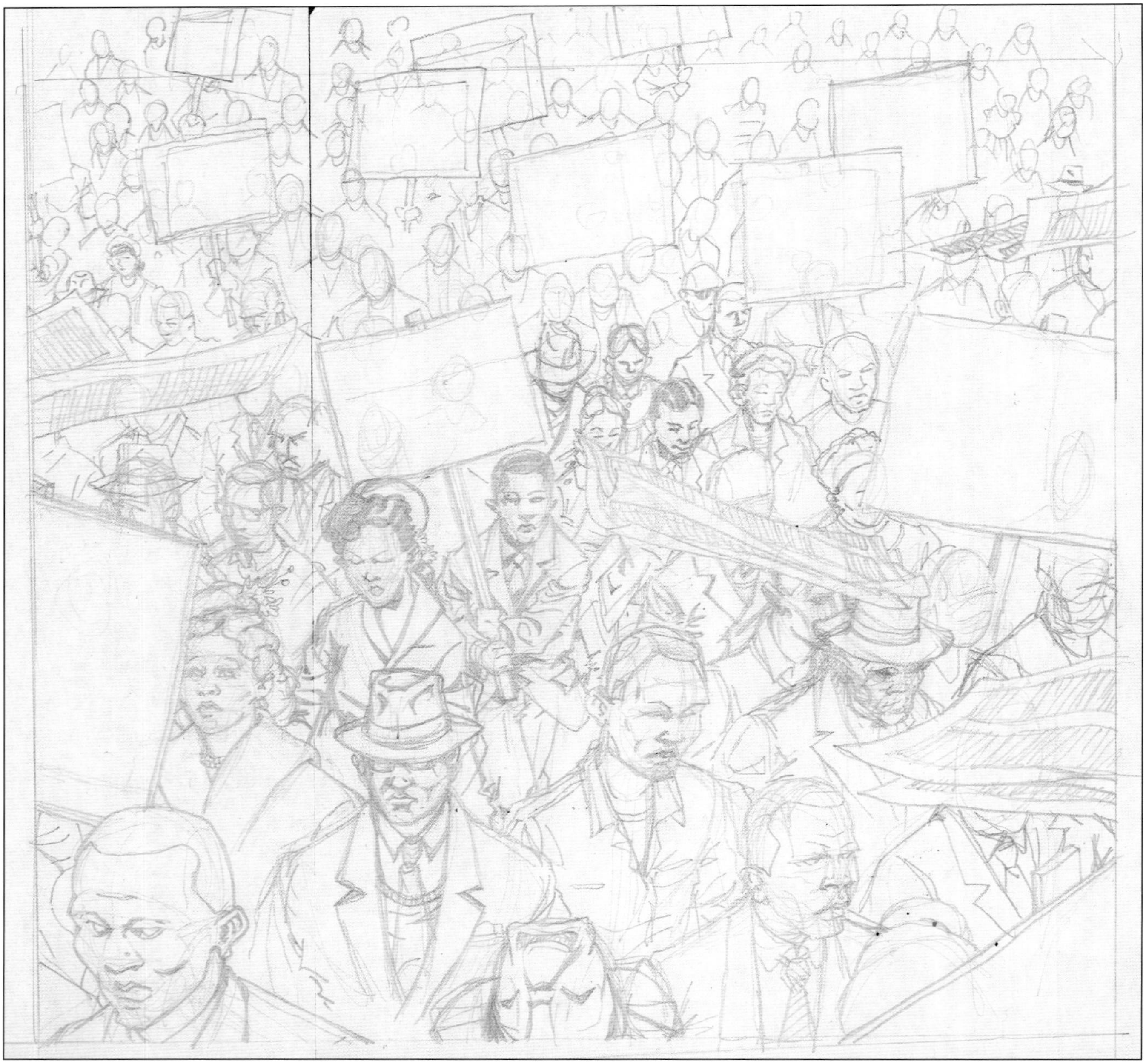

ABOUT THE CREATORS

With roots in the Texas Hill Country and the Mississippi Delta, **GARY PHILLIPS** must keep writing to forestall his appointment at the crossroads. He has among other pursuits delivered dog cages, run a political action committee and edited anthologies including the award-winning *The Obama Inheritance*. He also co-wrote the novelization of the classic Batman vs. Joker graphic novel, *The Killing Joke*. He lives in Los Angeles.

DALE BERRY has created independent comics professionally since 1986. A San Francisco-based writer and illustrator, he is the author of five books in the *Tales of the Moonlight Cutter* graphic novel series. His graphic short stories have appeared in *Alfred Hitchcock's Mystery Magazine* (the first comics creator to do so). His life has included stints as a carnival barker, concert stagehand, rock radio DJ, and fencing instructor, all of which are more related than you'd think.

Visit his website at www.myriadpubs.com.

JUSTIN BIRCH is a Ringo Award-nominated letterer born and raised in the hills of West Virginia. Lettering comics since 2015, he is a member of the lettering studio AndWorld Design and has worked with Action Lab Comics, DMC Comics, IDW, Lion Forge Comics, and numerous indy publishers. Justin still lives in West Virginia, only now it's with his loving wife and their dog, Kirby.

J. BROWN has been coloring comics for twenty-five years. Past clients include Marvel, DC/Milestone, Image, and Dark Horse. In addition to groundbreaking titles such as ICON and HARDWARE for Milestone Media, he has worked on numerous series for Marvel Comics, including *Avengers: Earth's Mightiest Heroes*, *Thunderbolts*, *Secret Invasion*, and *Marvel Adventures*. Specializing in working with independent comics and graphic novel publishers, he has served as Art Director and Editor at Big City Comics Studio, as well as colorist for their titles (*Terminal Alice, Killing Mars, Liar*). He lives outside of Boston, Massachusetts.

Visit his website at www.jbrowncolors.com.